"What do you think you're doing?"

"Kissing you again." He didn't give her a chance to escape.

She resisted at first but then surrendered.

Desire flooded him as her body softened against his. The yearning, the aching need, rose to the top, and he pulled her closer, wrapping his arms around her.

He wanted. Needed. Yearned. His hands clasped her hips and pulled her closer so she couldn't help but feel his desire.

He wanted to lay Keira down in a field of grass with a breeze rippling through it, the wide, blue Wyoming sky arching overhead and the sun warming their skin. He wanted to stroke her skin, to caress her until she cried his name and pulled him close, needing him as he needed her.

But all he could do was kiss her. Endlessly.

Dear Reader,

When I wrote *Reilly's Return* years ago, my editor, Mary-Theresa Hussey, told me that Cody Walker was such a strong secondary character he deserved his own book. So who better to write about when I finally sat down to start writing romance again?

The problem was, part of Cody's appeal was that he was so deeply in love with Mandy Edwards, the heroine of *Reilly's Return*. How could I find a woman to replace Mandy in Cody's heart? I reread *Reilly's Return* until I finally found the clue to the kind of woman Cody needed. Someone very different from Mandy, and yet who in one crucial way was *exactly* like her—a woman who would kill or die to protect the man she loved.

Enter Keira Jones. I hope you'll agree with me that Keira is the *only* woman who could penetrate the shell guarding Cody's tender heart. And I hope you enjoy reading *Cody Walker's Woman* as much as I enjoyed writing it.

I love hearing from my readers. Please email me at AmeliaAutin@aol.com and let me know what you think.

Amelia Autin

CODY WALKER'S WOMAN

Amelia Autin

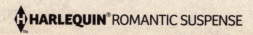
HARLEQUIN® ROMANTIC SUSPENSE

Recycling programs
for this product may
not exist in your area.

ISBN-13: 978-0-373-27892-3

CODY WALKER'S WOMAN

Copyright © 2014 by Amelia Autin Lam

Printed in U.S.A.

www.Harlequin.com

Books by Amelia Autin

Harlequin Romantic Suspense

Cody Walker's Woman #1822

Silhouette Intimate Moments

Gideon's Bride #666
Reilly's Return #820

Other titles by this author available in ebook format.

AMELIA AUTIN

is a voracious reader who can't bear to put a good book down...or part with it. Her bookshelves are crammed with books her husband periodically threatens to donate to a good cause, but he always relents...eventually.

Amelia returned to her first love, romance writing, after a long hiatus, during which she wrote numerous technical manuals and how-to guides, as well as designed and taught classes on a variety of subjects, including technical writing. She is a long-time member of Romance Writers of America (RWA), and served three years as its treasurer.

Amelia currently resides with her Ph.D. engineer husband in quiet Vail, Arizona, where they can see the stars at night and have a "million dollar view" of the Rincon Mountains from their backyard.

For my editor, Mary-Theresa Hussey, who told me years ago that Cody deserved his own book. *Tempus fugit.* And for Vincent...always.

Prologue

"Scream."

Keira Jones pushed the hair out of her eyes with both hands and stared in incomprehension at the man who'd just dragged her kicking and clawing all the way from the other room into this one. His hold had been brutal, crushing her bones as he'd thrown her onto the filthy bed in the corner of this room before moving to shut the door behind them and lock it.

And then nothing. Nothing except that one word uttered in a harsh undertone—*scream.*

"What?" she gasped.

He held one finger to his lips, pressing his ear against the wooden door. He cast a sharp glance around the room, grabbed a rickety chair and propped it under the door handle. Then he moved purposefully toward Keira.

She scrambled off the bed and backed away from him, away from what she thought was coming. If she was going to be raped, she wasn't going to make it easy for him. She looked frantically around the room for something, anything to use as a weapon, but he was on her before she had a chance.

"I said scream, damn it!" His angry voice was pitched to carry no farther than a foot away as he plastered her body against the wall with his muscular frame.

But she couldn't. Her heart was pounding in her chest, and her breath was coming in rapid pants, but no sound emerged from a throat dry with terror she refused to betray.

He made a sound of frustration deep in his throat. He held her squirming body captive with his while his powerful hands gripped the lapels of her cotton blouse and ripped it open from top to bottom. Then she screamed. And screamed again when one hand groped her breast through and beneath the fabric of her bra while the other moved to the juncture of her thighs.

She clawed at his face. He ducked, but she had the savage satisfaction of seeing her fingernails make contact with his skin and leave four red welts before he captured her flailing hands and pinned them both to the wall over her head with one iron hand.

"Damn it, I'm not going to hurt you," he whispered in that same deep undertone.

Blood was oozing from two of the scratches on his face, but he ignored it. And to Keira's shocked amazement he didn't follow up on her physical helplessness. In fact, he turned away from her, listening intently to the sounds emanating from the other room.

Now Keira could hear it, too, over the rasping sound of her own breathing; coarse male laughter and guttural catcalls, as if Keira's screams were entertainment for the men in the other room.

"What—" she began, but he covered her mouth with his free hand.

"Shh." He pressed his lips to her ear, but not in a mockery of a kiss. "We have maybe five minutes to get out of here," he breathed. "Unless you want me to leave you behind to be gang-raped by them," he said, tilting his head in the direction of the other room, "or worse, promise me you'll do *exactly* what I tell you to do, when I tell you to do it. You got that?"

She swallowed as her panicked brain assimilated what he was saying as well as what he was *not* doing. Then she nodded. His hand came off her mouth but hovered close, as if he didn't trust her not to ask questions in a voice that could be heard from the next room. But Keira wasn't stupid. She knew in a flash that instead of trying to rape her he was trying to rescue her.

She didn't know why he was risking his life this way, but she didn't care. Going with him was infinitely preferable to the fate in store for her if she stayed here. And if she was going to die, as she had feared from the moment she'd been kidnapped from beside her car, she'd rather die running, fighting, anything except submitting meekly to being raped and murdered.

"Okay," he whispered. His lean, muscular body was suddenly gone, and Keira sagged for a moment, her own muscles barely able to hold her up. Then she got control of herself and watched him move across the room.

For a big man he moved with incredible stealth. He had seemed to tower over her earlier, but now she saw that, while he was well above six feet, he wasn't a giant of a man; his strength had fooled her into envisioning him as bigger than he actually was.

He was clean shaven, and while his angular features weren't pretty-boy handsome, they were attractive in a masculine way. His sun-streaked blond hair was close-cropped, though not in military fashion. And the snug jeans he wore left no doubt that he was in perfect physical shape. The kind of man, in fact, she thought with hysterical abstraction, most women would give a second—and third—glance at if they passed him on the street.

He was trying to open the single window in the room,

but it resisted his efforts, and Keira could tell he wasn't using his full strength because he was trying to get it open without anyone in the next room hearing, and if he pushed too hard the glass might shatter.

She started toward him to help, but before she got there he reached down into his boot and came up with a wicked-looking six-inch steel-blade knife. He grimaced, as if he hated to sacrifice his knife in this way, then inserted the blade between the window and the frame and exerted downward pressure.

With a slight creak of warped wood, a crack opened up, then widened enough for him to get his fingers underneath. Then Keira was there, and together they got the window open far enough for them to climb through.

"Tie up your shirt," he breathed next to her ear, and all at once Keira realized it was gaping open, all the buttons gone from when he had tried to make her scream. And her bra was awry, too, from when he'd mauled her. She quickly adjusted her bra and pulled the ends of her blouse together, knotting them beneath her breasts. It wasn't neat, but at least she was decently covered.

"You go first," he said in a whisper. "I'll let you down nice and easy. Try not to make any noise when you move away from the window."

She nodded, not trusting her voice. He put his hands on her waist and lifted her effortlessly, high enough for her to slide her feet through the window embrasure. He balanced her on the window sill for a moment while she ducked her head under the window, then his hands slid beneath her armpits and he lowered her to the ground.

Keira carefully backed away to allow him room to clamber out, trying not to brush up against anything that would rustle. Then he took her hand in his and looked down at her. There was barely enough moonlight to see a few feet in any direction, but there was enough light to see his determined expression as he whispered urgently, "Trust me."

"I will," she said. She knew it was crazy; they were still in imminent danger. At any minute someone might try to enter the room they'd just left and discover they were gone, and a murderous chase would be on. And she knew absolutely nothing about this man other than the fact he hadn't raped her when he'd had the chance. But that one fact was enough, and she knew instinctively she could trust him with her life.

"Good," he said, an unexpected smile slashing across his face. "Let's get the hell out of here."

Chapter 1

Cody Walker sat at his government-issued desk in his office in the agency's sprawling complex on the northern outskirts of Denver Thursday morning, ostensibly rereading the revised report he'd just printed out to check it for errors before submitting it to his superiors. But instead of reading, he was thinking about the things he *hadn't* put into the report.

Like the way Keira had looked at him in the moonlight, her face paper-white beneath a dusting of freckles, so scared and yet so brave, with that mop of red-gold curls no comb could tame. Like the way her brown eyes had met his when he'd told her to trust him and she'd said without hesitation, *I will.* Like the way her breast had felt beneath his hand when—

With a muttered oath, he cut off the memory. *You've got no business remembering that,* he told himself firmly. The fingers of his right hand brushed over the four barely visible welts on his left check where she'd branded him; the scratches were still there, but after nearly a week they were almost healed. *Guess you deserved this after all.*

He didn't hold it against her. Sure, he'd been trying to rescue her, but she couldn't have known it at the time. She'd fought him like a wildcat, and he respected her for it. Although they looked nothing alike, Keira somehow reminded him of his feisty best friend growing up. *Mandy would have done exactly the same thing under the circumstances,* he thought with a mixture of admiration and amusement.

Without realizing it, his hand went to the scar on his left shoulder. Beneath his shirt he could feel the raised edges of the healed bullet wound where Mandy had shot him six years ago because she'd thought he was about to kill the man she loved. Mandy hadn't known the truth then any more than Keira had the other night.

Keira. He'd blown his assignment to hell and gone for her, but he couldn't have done anything differently. Not and still call himself a man. He couldn't have left an innocent woman there in that isolated shack in the mountains west of Denver with the incipient terrorist gang members he was meeting with in his undercover persona as an illegal arms dealer. They would have raped her at the very least, and probably would have killed her afterward—they wouldn't want to leave a witness behind.

He remembered his first sight of her last Friday night when the three men had half dragged, half carried her into the shack where he'd been negotiating with two other gang members. She'd been fighting her captors every step of the way, refusing to surrender to them despite the terror any woman would have felt in that situation, struggling against ravaging hands and lewd suggestions, unwilling to give them the satisfaction of seeing her cry or beg for mercy she had to have known was nonexistent.

His desperate plan had been born in an instant. He'd had leverage because they wanted something from him— Stinger man-portable surface-to-air missiles, Kalashnikov AK-47 assault rifles and magazines, and other sundry weapons of destruction. And he'd used that leverage to claim "first rights" to Keira, using the coarse language they'd expected in that situation. Then he'd triumphantly claimed his "prize" and dragged her into the other room, and...

Well, that part was in his report anyway.

He threw the papers on his desk, momentarily disgusted, and swiveled around to stare at the picture on his wall—a large, blown-up reproduction of his rustic cabin and the surrounding woods in the Big Horn Mountains of Wyoming. He wondered why he'd ever left it and the relatively easy job as sheriff back then.

He sighed. He knew why he'd left. Just as he knew why he'd taken this job. But sometimes it didn't seem worth it.

He'd been unofficially reprimanded for compromising his assignment—no way would they have dared to make it an official reprimand under the circumstances, special rule seven notwithstanding—although what his immediate supervisor and his partner thought he could have done other than what he *had* done was a mystery to him.

He'd managed to electronically send the "abort mission" signal to his partner, waiting with a backup team a mile away, without Keira seeing him. He hadn't wanted her to know she'd interrupted a covert operation, hadn't wanted her to have any suspicions of what he was or why he was there. But he'd had a lot of explaining to do later that night about why the op had to be aborted.

He was just thankful he'd been at the right place at the right time. Thankful they'd both escaped and he'd seen her safely back to her car and on the road home. Thankful he hadn't had to kill anyone in the process—the red tape on that would have included a mandatory desk assignment while the incident was thoroughly investigated. Not that he had any doubts he would have been cleared.

But it would have been a time-consuming hassle, and he hated being chained to a desk.

Besides, he'd only ever taken one life, and he wasn't in any hurry to repeat that experience unless he had no other option. Now if only he could get the feel of Keira's taut, unyielding body beneath his out of his mind...

The phone on his desk shrilled. He swiveled around and picked it up automatically. "Walker," he said crisply. He relaxed back in his chair. "Hey, Callahan," he said, "I was just thinking about you." He listened to the voice on the other end of the line for a second, then added, "Well, not you, exactly. I was thinking about the time your wife shot me."

"No more than you deserved," Ryan Callahan responded promptly. "At least from her perspective."

"Yeah, yeah, yeah," Cody replied. "Tell that to the marines."

That was something he and Callahan had in common—they'd both served in the U.S. Marine Corps, but at different times, since Callahan was quite a bit older. Cody thought for a second. If he was thirty-seven, that meant Callahan had to be forty-five now, close to forty-six. *We're none of us getting any younger.*

They'd also both worked the same undercover operation six years ago, bringing down the New World Militia together when Cody had been the sheriff of Black Rock, Wyoming, a position Callahan now held.

They had something else in common, too—they'd both been in love with Mandy Edwards. Mandy Edwards *Callahan,* Cody corrected himself with a wry smile. He wasn't in love with Mandy anymore. Well, not much anyway. There would always be a small corner of his heart devoted to her, but once Callahan had come back into her life, Cody had known there was no chance for him. He'd left Black Rock and had joined the Drug Enforcement Administration after he recovered from the gunshot that had almost killed him.

But his work in the DEA hadn't satisfied him somehow. He'd been restless and had needed something more, so he'd been ripe for change when he'd been approached by Nick D'Arcy to join a newly created ultrasecret agency not quite two years later. His new job was more demanding, both mentally and physically, and more rewarding, too. And it had allowed him to forget about losing Mandy to Ryan Callahan.

"So what's up?" he asked.

There was just the slightest hesitation on the other end. "Something we both thought was dead and buried is raising its ugly head again."

"What?" Cody sat up straight in his chair and gripped the phone a little tighter. He knew instantly what Callahan was referring to. "The New World Militia?"

"Got it in one."

"Don't B.S. me," he said roughly, doing a rapid mental review of the facts as he knew them. "Pennington's dead," he said, referring to David Pennington, the founder of the New World Militia. Silently he added, *We both killed him,* though it wasn't something he wanted to brag about or mention over the phone. "And the militia's other high-ranking officers are all serving long prison terms. How—"

Callahan cut him off. "Don't ask me how I know, not over an unsecured phone line." He let that sink in before adding, "Just trust me on this, okay?"

Cody thought about it for all of half a minute. Callahan had once trusted him with his life six years ago, even though he'd known how Cody felt about Mandy, had known other things, too. Despite that, Callahan had saved Cody's life after Mandy shot him—wasting precious seconds to apply a makeshift pressure bandage to the wound, even though both men had known Mandy was out there somewhere, in danger from Pennington. If he hadn't done that, Cody wouldn't be alive today.

"Okay," Cody said, but he knew that one word was enough—Callahan got the message. "We need to talk."

"Not over the phone."

"Where, then?"

"Can you come to Black Rock? I'd come to Denver, but…"

He didn't have to finish. Cody knew Callahan would never leave Mandy and their three children, not if danger threatened them. And if the New World Militia really had been resurrected, Callahan, and anyone close to him, could be in grave danger.

You, too, he thought for a second, before brushing it aside as immaterial. He'd been undercover himself for four years in the New World Militia before he and Callahan had killed Pennington and smashed the anarchist paramilitary organization that had also had its fingers in gunrunning and drug trafficking, as well as other illegal activities. If Callahan was in danger, so was he.

"I'll have to tell my supervisor, not to mention my partner."

There was a long, pregnant pause while Callahan considered this. "Isn't Nick D'Arcy still the head of the Denver branch of the agency?"

"Yeah."

"How about telling him first? This octopus could have tentacles everywhere," he said, referring obliquely to the New World Militia. "I trust you and D'Arcy, and maybe one other person, but…"

Cody's first reaction was to hotly defend his colleagues, especially his partner, but then he remembered how insidious the militia had once been. If Callahan was right, if new life had been breathed into the organization, there was no telling where the infection had spread.

"Okay," he said. "I'll try to get in to see him as soon as I get off the phone. I'll let you know what he says."

"Don't call my office," Callahan warned, referring to the Black Rock sheriff's office. "And don't call the house. I haven't told Mandy yet, and if you call there, she'll suspect something. She'll kill me when she finds out I've kept her in the dark this long, but…"

Cody knew the other man well enough to know he was shrugging his shoulders. Neither of them had ever wanted to put Mandy in danger, so they'd both kept secrets from her. That hadn't always been a good idea, and Cody had the scar to prove it.

"And don't call my cell phone, either," Callahan added.

"Then how am I—"

"Call this number," Callahan said, rattling off ten digits, and Cody jotted them down on a scratch pad. "That's a throwaway cell. I probably don't need to tell you this, but it would be a good idea to call me from a pay phone or another throwaway cell."

"You're right," Cody responded drily. "You don't need to tell me that."

He hung up when Callahan did, then sat for a moment staring at the cell-phone number he'd just written down, memorizing it. "Damn it!" he cursed under his breath.

He ripped the paper into tiny shreds, got up and strode toward the elevator, dropping the scraps of paper into the slot of the locked "burn barrel" nearest the door. He rang for the elevator, waiting impatiently until it arrived, his mind taken up with what Callahan had just told him… and what he hadn't.

"Damn," he said again, but it didn't relieve his feelings one bit.

Cody walked into the outer office and addressed the executive assistant who guarded Nick D'Arcy from unimportant interruptions like a dragon. "I need to see Baker Street," he told her, using the nickname everyone in the agency used when talking about D'Arcy, and sometimes even when thinking about him. He was omniscient—so much so it was scary at times—and every agent who worked for him had experienced that omniscience at least once. So it wasn't surprising he was known by the sobriquet of "Baker Street," a tip of the hat to Sherlock Holmes.

The executive assistant assessed Cody, noting the determined, set expression on his face. She picked up the phone and pushed a button. "Cody Walker to see you, sir." She listened for a couple of seconds, then said, "No, he didn't tell me what it's about and I didn't ask." She hung up the phone. "You can go in," she told him.

"Come in, Walker," Nick D'Arcy said when Cody entered and closed the door behind him. He indicated a chair in front of his desk and said, "Have a seat." He sat down himself, and after Cody was sitting, he said, "Is this about what happened last Friday?"

"No, it's—" Cody broke off. "How do you know about that already?"

"It's my business to know everything, didn't you know?" D'Arcy chuckled, his dark-skinned face breaking into a broad smile. "But seriously, you did the right thing. Oh, yes," he said, holding up one hand, palm outward. "I know there are those who are upset your cover was blown and that we'll have to start all over from scratch with that investigation, but...I'd have done the same thing under the circumstances."

"Thank you, sir. It's good to know not everyone thinks I blew it."

D'Arcy smiled as if he knew something Cody didn't. "So if this isn't about last week, then what is it?"

"The New World Militia."

That wiped the smile from the other man's face. "How'd you hear about that?" he asked sharply.

"Ryan Callahan. He called me a few minutes ago."

"Damn." The word held no heat, but Cody could tell D'Arcy was not pleased. "I was hoping I was wrong, but if Callahan is involved…" He bent a narrow-eyed gaze on Cody. "What did he tell you?"

"He wouldn't tell me much over the phone," Cody said, then repeated the conversation nearly verbatim, including Callahan's statement about who he trusted… and who he didn't.

D'Arcy didn't say anything after Cody finished, just sat there contemplating the pencil he picked up off his desk. He seemed to reach a decision, because he looked at Cody and said, "I've heard rumblings of this before today. I've already got a team working on it." He leaned over and pressed a switch. "Can you see if you can locate McKinnon and Jones for me? If they're in the building, I need to see them right away."

"McKinnon?" Cody asked after D'Arcy cut off the connection. "That wouldn't be Trace McKinnon, would it?"

"Yeah. You remember him from six years ago, don't you? I've got a feeling he's the third man Callahan was referring to, the other man he trusts."

"I remember him, but I thought he was still a federal marshal. I didn't know he worked for the agency."

D'Arcy let out a bark of laughter. "Compartmental-ization. I guess it does work sometimes." He looked at

Cody from under his brows. "McKinnon was the first person I recruited after *I* was recruited. He'd worked for me for years before I came here—I'd trust him with my life. I knew he'd be perfect for this agency, just like I knew you would be, too."

The corner of Cody's mouth curved up in a rueful smile. "Not so perfect—on my part, that is. Last week—"

D'Arcy waved his hand. "I already told you to forget last week, didn't I?" He hesitated. "I wasn't going to tell you until all the paperwork was processed, but there will be a commendation in your personnel jacket if I have anything to say about it."

That means it's a done deal, Cody thought, knowing how highly respected Nick D'Arcy was by the head of their agency in Washington, D.C. "Thank you. I appreciate it." He thought for a second, then confessed, "I couldn't have done anything else, but…I'm glad it won't be a mark against me."

"Not to worry."

Then Cody remembered the other thing D'Arcy had said, and he asked, "Rumblings? You said you've heard rumblings about the New World Militia?"

D'Arcy grimaced. "The FBI has been keeping a watchful eye on certain individuals for years," he said. "But even after all this time since 9/11, we still don't have the interagency cooperation we should have. They don't tell us everything they know, and we're not much better."

"But if they aren't telling you what they know…"

"I have my own sources within the FBI…and a few other places" was all D'Arcy would say.

The phone buzzed, and D'Arcy pressed the intercom button. "Yes?"

"McKinnon and Jones are here, sir."

"Send them in."

Cody stood up as the door opened and Trace McKinnon walked in. Cody recognized him immediately, even though it had been almost five years since he'd last seen him. Along with Callahan, Cody owed his life to this man, who'd given him first aid before the medevac chopper had airlifted him to the hospital in Sheridan. He had thanked McKinnon afterward, but except for seeing him at the trials that followed the arrests of the upper echelons of the New World Militia, their paths hadn't crossed until now.

Cody started forward, his hand outstretched. "Good to see you, McKinnon," he said. Then he stopped as abruptly as if he'd been shot. Following McKinnon into the room was the woman with the mop of red-gold curls no comb could tame. The woman he'd blown his assignment to rescue. The woman he couldn't get out of his mind.

Keira.

Chapter 2

"Special Agent Keira Jones," Nick D'Arcy was saying. "I think you know Special Agent Cody Walker, don't you?"

Keira held out her hand to Cody. "Good to see you again" was all she said as she shook his hand.

"Same here," Cody told her.

Cody threw a sideways questioning glance at D'Arcy, which Keira caught, but he didn't say anything. Out of the corner of her eye she saw her partner stiffen and his eyes narrow, and she knew she'd made a mistake admitting she knew Cody. She wondered if Trace was making the connection.

She'd told him the bare bones about her kidnapping and near-miraculous escape, but hadn't given any specifics. And she hadn't told him the name of her rescuer for a very good reason—she'd recognized Cody's name as soon as he said it, had known he worked for the same agency as she did, and had hoped and prayed the story wouldn't make the rounds of the office.

It was hard enough even now for a woman to make a career in a job that had traditionally been a man's world, especially within the agency; she didn't want to become the butt of office laughter over allowing herself to be kidnapped in that fashion and needing to be rescued by a fellow agent. A *male* agent.

She hadn't recognized him that night. She and Cody had never met before; they didn't work in the same division and their case loads hadn't overlapped. But she'd heard the name Cody Walker when he'd received an agency commendation the year before, and Cody was an unusual name. When they'd made it to his car, breathless and panting after running through the night, he'd introduced himself almost as an afterthought.

She'd known then who he was, but she'd only told him her name was Keira. The Jones part would probably have been safe enough, but…she didn't want to risk it.

They'd driven in silence for a few minutes before she'd even thought to say thanks. That was when he'd apologized for manhandling her, and she'd apologized for scratching him. But when he'd tried to take her to the hospital, she'd adamantly refused. The same for going to the police.

She'd asked him to drop her at her car instead, and he'd reluctantly agreed. When they'd reached her car, he'd insisted on finishing changing the tire for her and then had followed her all the way to I-70 to make sure she got back safely on the road to Denver.

She'd reported the incident, of course. Even though she hadn't been working when she'd been kidnapped, once she'd made the connection between her rescuer and a fellow agent, she'd realized he had probably been on an undercover operation himself. If so, his cover had been blown, and she owed it to him to make sure he didn't suffer any disagreeable consequences as a result.

But she hadn't reported it up the chain of command. She couldn't bring herself to do that; it would have been too humiliating. Instead, she'd made an appointment to see Baker Street himself—Nick D'Arcy—first thing Monday morning and had confessed everything. While McKinnon and Walker exchanged a few words, her thoughts winged back to that stark interview.

D'Arcy listened in silence until she was done, then asked a few questions. She tried to keep emotion out of her responses, as if she were merely an agent reporting to a superior officer regarding an assignment.

"You weren't raped? You can tell me the truth."

She flinched but answered him honestly. "No, sir. But I would have been, probably killed, too, if not for Walker."

"You didn't lose your service weapon?"

"No, sir. I wasn't carrying it. I was on mandatory use-it-or-lose-it vacation."

"What were you doing out there?"

"My family has a cabin near Dillon Reservoir, closer to Keystone than to Silverthorne. My partner called me Friday afternoon, asked me to come back early from vacation because he had a hot lead on one of the cases we're working and wanted my assistance following up on it. He knows me, knows I'd want to be involved if… Well, anyway, he wanted us to get together early Saturday. I was driving home to Denver Friday evening when I had a flat tire on Loveland Pass Road. I was in the middle of changing the flat when a car pulled up behind me. The driver got out and asked if I needed help. I told him no, thanks, but then…the other two men got out of the car."

She hesitated, knowing she could never tell D'Arcy the fear that had gripped her in that instant…and the despair. Fear and despair she'd refused to give in to, but which she would remember forever. "I do have a carry permit for a personal weapon, sir, but the gun was locked in my glove compartment. Maybe I should have had it handy, but it's not as if Loveland Pass is deserted—cars pass there all the time. I didn't think...just changing a tire... And it wasn't even dark yet at that point..."

"They didn't get your gun?"

"No, sir. They didn't touch my car. Not even to get my wallet. Just me."

"How did you recover your car?"

"Walker dropped me there. He didn't want to, but I insisted. He followed me all the way to the highway to make sure I was okay."

D'Arcy sat in silence for a few minutes, digesting her answers. "Thank you for telling me this," he said finally.

In a small voice, Keira said, "I realize it doesn't reflect well on the agency, sir, or on me. If you think I should resign, I will."

He frowned. "I don't think that's necessary. We all make mistakes. And you weren't even on duty at the time."

"No, but—"

"No," he said. "It's not a mistake you'll repeat. And the fact that you've reported it to me is a plus. It says a lot about you."

"I just didn't want Walker to get into trouble," she said. "It wouldn't be right—not after he saved my life." She glanced down at her hands, saw the bruises around her wrists that her long-sleeved blouse didn't cover and surreptitiously pulled down her cuffs.

But she wasn't fast enough, and D'Arcy said, "Have you seen a doctor?"

She nodded. "Walker wanted to take me to the hospital Friday night, but I wouldn't let him. And I wouldn't let him take me to file a police report, either. I figured his cover had been blown, but I didn't know what else his operation had entailed. I didn't want to draw police attention to that area, just in case there was something else going down. But I did see my own doctor first thing Saturday morning, before I met my partner." Her lips tightened, then she added as if she couldn't help herself, "Trace and I closed that case yesterday, sir." It wasn't much compared to how she felt about botching Walker's operation, but it was something positive at least.

D'Arcy rubbed his chin with his long fingers, then said, "Okay, then." He smiled encouragingly at her. "You've done the right thing by telling me, but that's as far as it goes. Don't be afraid it will get out—I'm not even going to put a notation in your jacket," he said. "You're an excellent agent and you've done some outstanding work for this agency. I don't want to lose you. And don't brood about it. Take a lesson from it and move on."

Now, in Nick D'Arcy's office for the second time in a week, Keira remembered the sense of relief that had flooded her when he'd refused her resignation. She loved her job, loved the challenge, the excitement of solving cases no one else could solve. But most of all she loved making a difference, making the world a safer place—the same reason she'd joined the Marine Corps right out of high school. She'd felt honor bound to tender her resignation to D'Arcy but was grateful it hadn't come to that.

At D'Arcy's invitation, Keira sat down between her partner and Cody Walker. Then D'Arcy said four words, "The New World Militia." Trace started to speak, glanced at Cody over Keira's head and kept mum. "I'm bringing Walker in on this investigation," D'Arcy explained. "Ryan Callahan called him."

"Callahan?" McKinnon said. "Damn. That means the rumors *are* true."

"Who's Ryan Callahan?" Keira asked, looking from one face to the other and settling on her partner.

Before Trace could respond, Cody said, "Former cop. Undercover for five years with the New World Militia at the instigation of the FBI. Practically single-handedly brought down the organization six years ago."

"I think you had something to do with that yourself," D'Arcy said drily.

Cody made a dismissive gesture. "Maybe. But without him there wouldn't have been much of a case to prosecute in the first place." He looked at Keira. "He called me this afternoon, said that he *knows* the organization has been resurrected. He wouldn't tell me how he knew, over what he said was an unsecured phone line, but I'll tell you this—if he says he knows, I damn well believe him."

A long silence followed his harsh statement. Then D'Arcy looked at Keira and Trace. "I know you haven't been working this case very long, but what have you got?"

Keira glanced at Trace, who made a gesture signaling for her to go ahead. "We took the information you gave us," she told D'Arcy, "and we checked it out. There's no tangible proof yet, nothing we can take to a grand jury regarding the New World Militia. But there *is* a common thread connecting everyone on your list. They are part of a political action committee—a super PAC, actually—called NOANC. It can't be a coincidence."

D'Arcy leaned back in his chair, rubbed his hand over his face and sighed. "I was hoping I was wrong." He looked at Cody and said softly, "Five senators, more than two dozen congressmen and I don't know who all else."

"What?" Cody sat up in his chair. "That's not possible. The organization was *destroyed* six years ago. How—"

"That's what you're going to find out," D'Arcy said.

"You're relieved of the rest of your case load as of right now, Walker. I'll clear it down the line. And since Callahan prefers not to have your partner in on this…" He shrugged. "That's the way it will have to be for now."

He looked at Keira and Trace. "Because of his extensive background with the New World Militia and his connection with Callahan, I'm putting Walker in charge—you'll report directly to him. Turn over any other cases you've got running to your supervisor. I'll make sure he understands, but brief him thoroughly."

His expression was deadly serious as he faced the three agents in front of him. "I'm sending you to Black Rock to talk with Callahan, find out what he's got. Bring him in on the investigation, if that's what it takes. No one knows better than him that this organization is a cancer, and if we don't excise it—fast!—it might be too late."

Cody glanced at Keira, then back at D'Arcy. "Callahan won't like it," he said. He looked at Keira again, an apology in his eyes. "Callahan doesn't know you and he doesn't trust you. I don't think he'll talk if you're there."

D'Arcy nodded, acknowledging the truth of Cody's statement as far as it went. "He might not like it, but there's one thing he knows as well as I do—the New World Militia doesn't recruit women. There's not a chance in hell Special Agent Jones is a member." He looked at the two men. "I can't say that about either of you."

Cody and Trace looked at each other. Glancing from one man to the other, Keira saw the sudden suspicion in both sets of eyes. "Stop it," she said, "both of you. I *know* Trace," she told Cody. "He's been my partner for three years, ever since I joined the agency. I know him like I know myself." She looked at Trace. "I don't know

Cody the way I know you, but I trust him with my life, the same way I trust you."

Trace's eyes narrowed again, and he looked as if he were going to demand further elucidation of her statement, but Nick D'Arcy preempted him. "That's enough," he said. "I just wanted to make a point. That's why I'm sending Special Agent Jones as well as the two of you. Even though Callahan might not trust her, I do. End of discussion."

It was a dismissal, and all three agents rose and filed out. Cody walked toward the elevator and punched the button, Keira and Trace right behind him.

"Wait up," Keira said. "We need to talk about next steps."

Cody glanced down at her and gave her an assessing look. "I've got to talk to Callahan, see what he says."

"Shouldn't we talk about it first, the three of us?"

"Look," he said, "don't take this the wrong way. But O'Neill is a tad, shall we say, old-school?"

"O'Neill?" She knew her face reflected her puzzlement. "I thought his name was Callahan."

Cody rubbed the bridge of his nose, his lips pursing at his mistake. "It is. But when I first knew him, he was going by the name of Reilly O'Neill. Sometimes I still call him that out of habit."

"Oh, I see." She thought a moment. "What do you mean he's a tad old-school?"

The elevator arrived, and they all crowded in. "What floor?" Cody asked.

"Twelve," Trace volunteered.

Cody pushed the button for the twelfth floor as well as the fifth-floor button for his own office.

Keira reiterated her question. "What do you mean he's a tad old-school?"

Cody looked at Trace. "You know him, too, Mc-Kinnon. Wouldn't you say he's a throwback?"

Trace laughed. "That's an understatement."

Cody grimaced. "There's no easy way to tell you, but…Callahan won't like it that a woman is involved in the investigation."

"You're kidding, right?" She glanced from Cody to her partner, then back again. Both faces had that expression men hid behind when they didn't know what to say to a woman because no matter what they said, it was suicide one way or the other. "That's not just old-school—he must be a dinosaur."

Cody laughed but said, "I have to talk to him about this, get his okay before we plan anything. I don't care what Baker Street says—if Callahan says no, it's no."

Keira opened her mouth, then closed it again. She made a sound of disbelief, but she didn't know what to say. She turned accusatory eyes on her partner. "Is that how you feel, too?"

Trace had that "deer in the headlights" look, but all he said was "It's not my call," then added in an undertone, "thank God."

"I don't believe this," Keira said to him, hurt battling anger for dominance as she confronted him. "We've been partners for three years. I thought you trusted me."

"I do," Trace reassured her. "But I'm not Callahan. I can't speak for him."

"Look," Cody began. "It's nothing against you personally.…"

The elevator door opened on the twelfth floor and Trace made his escape, but Keira stayed right where she was. She put her arm across the elevator door, preventing it from closing again, and when she did, her sleeve pulled up, exposing an ugly green-and-yellow bruise that encircled her wrist.

"God," Cody said, suddenly distressed. "Did I do that to you?" He reached out and touched her wrist with two fingers, brushing the bruise so lightly it didn't hurt. He raised a troubled face to hers.

"I don't know," she answered honestly. "It might have been you. Or it might have been one of the animals who jumped me."

He moved closer and held the elevator door open with his shoulder while he fit his fingers around her wrist. They matched the bruise exactly. "I am so sorry," he said. She saw him swallow hard. "I didn't realize…" He reached for her other wrist and pushed the sleeve back before she could stop him, exposing an even uglier bruise. His face contracted as if the sight hurt him.

"It's okay," she assured him. "I bruise easily. You did what you had to do to save me. I don't blame you. I…" He was brushing his fingers lightly over the bruise, back and forth, as if he could erase it that way, and the touch of his fingers was somehow erotic. She drew her hand away and pulled down the sleeve. "I'd far rather have the bruises than what else might have happened to me." Her chin tilted up.

There was just a second when she saw something in his eyes—a look of admiration tinged with frank, male appreciation—but it was gone so quickly she thought she must have imagined it.

"Besides," she added, pointing to the faint scratch marks on his left cheek. "I hurt you, too."

His hand rose involuntarily, as if he'd forgotten all about the marks she'd left on him. But then she could see him remembering what he'd done to her to make her scratch him so violently, and remorse filled his face.

"Don't think about that," Keira said swiftly, and repeated, "You did what you had to do, and—" she made each of her next words a separate sentence for emphasis "—I. Don't. Blame. You."

"I didn't mean to be so…brutal."

"What you did was nothing compared to what they had in mind," she reminded him.

"Yeah, but…"

"But nothing," she said firmly. "Forget about it. I have," she lied.

He didn't say anything, just looked at her in a way that reminded her of the moment when he'd told her to tie up her shirt that first night, and she felt her cheeks grow warm. That was the worst thing about having the pale skin that accompanied her red hair; any change in coloration was noticeable.

Two people approached the elevator, glancing curiously at Cody and Keira talking so intently. Keira brushed past the other two agents, and Cody followed her out. The elevator doors slid closed behind them.

"Wait," he said. "We're not quite finished."

She turned around, darting a quick look around to see if anyone was watching them, then asked, "What is it?"

"I started to say it's nothing against you personally why O'Ne—I mean Callahan probably won't want to include you." He punched the elevator button again. "It's a long story, and maybe I'll tell you sometime, but I've got a bullet hole in me because Callahan didn't even trust the woman he eventually married with the truth."

Keira shook her head in puzzlement. "I don't get it. If he didn't trust her, why did he marry her?"

Cody chuckled. "Good question. Seriously, though, by the time he married her, he *did* trust her. But it wasn't easy for him." The elevator doors swooshed open, and he stepped inside, holding the door for a minute while he finished. "Callahan doesn't trust many people, and I'd say Mandy's probably the only woman he does trust."

The elevator doors closed, and Keira stood there for a moment, staring blankly at the brushed metal, her sixth sense humming. There was something in the way Cody had said Mandy's name. Most people probably wouldn't have noticed. But then most people didn't work for the agency, either. It was just the slightest softening when he spoke her name. A certain inflection. And Keira knew beyond a shadow of a doubt that Mandy, whoever she was, had once meant something special to Cody. Maybe still did.

She turned and walked down the hall toward her office. Without realizing it, her right hand touched her left wrist and felt the bruise there. She looked down at both wrists, thinking absently about the other bruises on her body hidden beneath her clothes that no one but she—and her doctor—had seen. Including the imprint of four fingers and a thumb on one still-tender breast.

Keira walked into her office and sat at her desk. She knew she should be upset that she might be unfairly excluded from this investigation because Callahan was a throwback to the bad old days and didn't think women were up to the job. She knew she could prove him wrong—if she got the chance. She'd been fighting her whole life to be taken seriously, and she wasn't ready to give up; not by a long shot.

But she wasn't thinking about that at this moment. She wasn't thinking about proving herself to Callahan. It made absolutely no sense to her because she'd never allowed her personal feelings to infringe on her work before, but all she could think about in that instant were the marks Cody had left on her body—and the way he'd said Mandy's name.

Chapter 3

Cody stood at a pay phone ten blocks from the agency's complex, dropping quarters into the slot. It was a good thing he had enough change on him—who carried much cash anymore in this day of plastic?

It also hadn't been easy even finding a pay phone—almost everyone had a cell phone these days, so a lot of the pay phones had been removed because they no longer generated enough income to make them worthwhile—and he'd almost given up before he found one that was still functional...ten blocks away.

He'd noted the location without drawing attention to it, then had walked several more blocks in a random pattern, "checking six" every so often to make sure he wasn't being tailed. When he'd been sure he was clear, he'd doubled back to the pay phone and dialed the number he'd memorized earlier.

"Yeah?" Callahan's gritty voice sounded in his ear.

"It's me." Cody knew he didn't have to identify himself. "D'Arcy gave me the green light, but there's one small problem."

"What's that?"

Cody watched the passersby carefully without letting on he was doing it, making sure no one was evincing interest in his conversation or got close enough to hear him. "He's sending three of us to Black Rock."

"No."

"Just wait," Cody said. "Don't say no until you know who."

"Okay," Callahan said. "Tell me who, so I can tell you no."

Cody laughed and shook his head. "Damn, you haven't changed."

"I'm alive." Callahan seemed to think that was explanation enough.

"Besides me, D'Arcy wants to send Trace McKinnon."

A short pause was followed by a reluctant "I guess I'm okay with that. McKinnon can probably be trusted, especially if D'Arcy says so." His voice sharpened. "That's two. Who's the third?"

"Keira Jones, McKinnon's partner. You don't know her, but—"

"No."

"Just hear me out," Cody said. "D'Arcy already had them working on this investigation weeks before you called, so they're two steps ahead of me. I told D'Arcy you wouldn't like having a woman involved—"

"Damn straight."

"But he said," Cody continued as if he hadn't been interrupted, "there's one thing you know as well as he does—the organization doesn't recruit women."

There was a long pause. "He's got a point," Callahan finally acknowledged grudgingly. "But I don't know her. Do you?"

Cody rapidly reviewed his meager options. He could stretch the truth—lie, in essence, which he really didn't want to do to Callahan—or he could come clean and play the odds. "I've known her less than a week," he admitted, deciding only the truth would serve. "Before you say no," he rushed to add, "let me tell you how I met her."

He related the whole story in a few brief sentences, knowing he didn't have to paint the entire picture for Callahan to get the point. "Physically she's no match for a man," he concluded, "but she's got guts and brains. And she'll fight to the death, if that's what it takes. You can't ask for much more than that."

Cody heard Callahan breathe deeply on the other end of the line and knew the decision was hanging in the balance. He played his trump card. "She reminds me a lot of Mandy—she'd shoot me if she had to."

Callahan laughed, and Cody knew he'd won this round. "Okay," said the voice on the other end. "How soon can you get here?"

"I'm not sure. There aren't a lot of flights to either Sheridan or Buffalo. It might be easier, and maybe even faster, if we drove, especially since we'll need reliable transportation while we're there. We can drive up in six hours, but I don't know how soon we can leave."

"Let me know. We'll need to set up a place to meet." *Where we can't be seen,* he didn't have to add.

"What about my cabin near Granite Pass?" Cody offered as the idea occurred to him. "I haven't been up there in six weeks, but I assume it's still standing. I figure you'd have said something before now if it wasn't."

"That's not a bad idea," Callahan said slowly.

"The three of us could stay there, too. Then no one would know we were even near Black Rock," Cody said. "If things are as dicey as you intimated earlier..."

Callahan chuckled, but there was little humor in it. "You know, Walker, for an amateur you're not half-bad."

"Thanks," Cody said drily. "I'll take that as a compliment." Both men hung up, and Cody laughed softly to himself. "Amateur," he said and laughed again.

He walked back to the office listing in his mind all the things they needed to do before they left for Black Rock. *D'Arcy and Callahan are right,* he thought. *We need to move on this fast.* But he wasn't so lost in thought he didn't take every opportunity to check to see if he was being followed. And when he turned a corner two blocks before the outer gate of the agency's complex, he let his gaze swing wide in the direction from which he'd just come, out of habit more than anything else. That was when he spotted him.

The man looked no different from anyone else on the street. He blended in—almost too well. There wasn't a single thing that made him stand out from the crowd. Cody couldn't have said what it was about him, but there was *something*…and he knew he was being tailed.

He didn't let on he'd marked the tail, just kept heading toward the agency's front gate. While he walked, he reviewed the scene at the pay phone in his mind, and his first spurt of adrenaline subsided. This man had not been there; Cody was sure of it. Or if he had, he hadn't been close enough to hear Cody's side of the conversation.

But Cody knew he wouldn't risk using a public pay phone again. *Throwaway cell phones and encryption software,* he added to his mental list, which was growing longer by the minute.

Cody managed another glimpse of the man when he reached the front gate, and he imprinted the face, rough height and weight, and other general characteristics in his mind. That was when a cold, sinking feeling hit him.

He'd seen the guy before.

Two days ago when Cody was filling his truck with gas on the way to work, this man had been in the next bay over doing the same thing to a little blue subcompact. He hadn't picked up on it at the time. But now that Cody realized he was being followed, the memory returned to him. *How long?* he wondered. *How long has someone been following me? I should have picked up on it earlier—I'm getting too damn lazy. Is it related to Callahan somehow? Or a different case?*

Either way, he didn't like it. It meant he was slipping, and that was a bad sign for a special agent.

Cody flashed his ID badge to the guard at the gate, then badged into the building using the electronic stripe on his ID card, without which no one entered the agency's building. No one. Early on in his career with the agency, Cody had forgotten his badge one morning and had been forced to return home to retrieve it.

But he still had to run the human gauntlet. Two agency security guards stood watch at the front desk, armed and alert. Even if someone stole an electronic ID card, they still had to match the photo on the badge, and both guards perused Cody's badge carefully before allowing him to enter the elevator. In the morning there were always two sets of guards on duty to make the line move faster, but it was never quick. But that made the building ultra secure. And there were things that went on in the agency they didn't want the general public to know.

Going up in the elevator, Cody clipped his ID badge to the lapel of his jacket, remembering what D'Arcy had said about interagency cooperation—or lack of it. The CIA and the FBI both knew about the existence of the agency—they just didn't like it. Maybe that was why they grudgingly shared information, and only when they had to.

The agency was a hybrid, created in secret long after 9/11 to do what neither the CIA nor the FBI had managed to do alone before that catastrophe. The agency was the "suspenders" portion of a "belt and suspenders" defense. *Or you could call it a "better safe than sorry" organization,* Cody thought with a touch of wry humor, even though part of him was still turning over in his mind what it meant that he was being followed.

Either way you looked at it, the agency could legally do things the "alphabet soup" agencies—the CIA, FBI, NSA, DEA, ATF and DHS—couldn't.

That didn't mean the agency was above the law. Cody couldn't have worked there if it was—he still retained a strict moral code about that, a holdover from the way he'd been raised and the small-town sheriff he'd once been. The agency's goal was still to obtain prosecutable evidence of crimes and turn that evidence over to federal prosecutors. But…they had latitude.

It wouldn't work if the agency didn't have people like D'Arcy running it, Cody acknowledged to himself. He still believed in the old adage that power corrupts and absolute power corrupts absolutely. But there *were* a few absolutely incorruptible people, and Nick D'Arcy was one of them.

Cody started to get off at the fifth floor, then realized he had something else he had to do first. He punched the button for the top floor, riding the elevator all the way up impatiently. He walked into D'Arcy's outer office and told his executive assistant, "I need five minutes of his time."

She assessed him as she had earlier in the day, then picked up the phone and pushed a button. "Cody Walker is back. He needs five minutes." She hung up the phone. "You can go in." She glanced at her watch, and Cody knew she'd be timing him.

He didn't waste any seconds on small talk. As soon

as he closed the door, he said, "I talked to Callahan. He's fine with McKinnon. I also convinced him we need Jones in on this, but it wasn't easy."

D'Arcy flashed his teeth in a smile. "I figured you'd manage somehow. How'd you swing it?"

"I reminded him of what you said—that she couldn't possibly be in the organization." He hesitated, then added, "And I told him how I met her. That I—"

D'Arcy frowned and interrupted him. "Was that absolutely necessary?"

Cody made a face of regret, but nodded. "He needed to understand the kind of woman she is." He stopped short as he realized the other man *knew* how he'd met Keira. Then he remembered D'Arcy's curious comment earlier, that Keira already knew Cody. "How do you know how I met her? I never said..."

"It's my business to know everything," D'Arcy said with a faint smile. Then he stated unequivocally, "I told her the story wouldn't get out."

"She told you what happened?" Cody was surprised.

"She came to me Monday morning. Said she felt she owed it to you to see that you didn't get into trouble over blowing your cover. She even offered me her resignation, which I obviously didn't accept."

"I don't follow you." Cody's brows knit in puzzlement. "How did she know I was a fellow agent?"

"She recognized your name when you introduced yourself afterward. Said she knew then who you were, that you had to be undercover. Said she wouldn't let you take her to the hospital or to the police because she didn't want to compromise whatever operation was in play any more than she already had."

"Damn," Cody said. "I wish I'd known." He drew a quick breath. "But even if I had, I would still have needed leverage to convince Callahan." He chuckled ruefully. "I told him Keira reminded me of his wife, that she would shoot me if necessary."

D'Arcy was forced to laugh. He'd been there in the aftermath of what had gone down six years ago, when Mandy had shot Cody through a tragic misunderstanding. And he also knew there was no surer way to Callahan's trust than to compare someone to the wife who would have killed her childhood friend to protect him.

Cody added, "I don't need to tell you Callahan won't reveal a word of this to anyone. Keira doesn't have to worry about the story getting around."

The phone buzzed, and D'Arcy hit the intercom button. "Yes?"

"Five minutes, sir."

"Right." D'Arcy hit the disconnect button and smiled at Cody. "I run this branch of the agency, but *she* runs *me*," he joked.

"There's one more thing," Cody said quickly. "I'm being tailed."

D'Arcy's smile vanished as if it had never been there. "You're sure?" he asked softly.

"Dead sure. I made him just now, on the way back to the agency from calling Callahan. And I've seen him before."

"How long?"

Cody had already cast his mind back over the past weeks, then months, but couldn't remember catching even a whiff of having been tailed until now, and he quickly recounted what little he knew.

D'Arcy assimilated this unwelcome news, trying to fit this puzzle piece in place with all the other little bits and pieces. He held out his hand, and Cody shook it. "I don't need to tell you to be careful," he told Cody. "Just remember one thing—Callahan was running the show six years ago, but this is *your* case now. The extent of his involvement is at your discretion."

"Yes, sir," Cody said.

"Keep me posted. If there's anything you need, you have the full resources of this agency at your disposal. Just ask." His eyes turned cold, and he added even more softly but with deadly intent, "I don't need to remind you what the New World Militia was capable of six years ago. If they've really been resurrected as the same organization, all the agency's special rules apply, especially seven and eight."

Cody pressed the button for the fifth floor and rode down in the elevator lost in thought. Special rules seven and eight. He knew what they were—every agent in the agency knew all eight of the special rules by heart—but he'd never had special rule eight apply to a case he was working before. It was too broad, too open to interpretation, and he didn't agree with the basic concept.

And there was a part of him that didn't agree with special rule seven, either—the part of him that had once sworn to uphold and enforce the law as a sheriff back in Wyoming. The part of him that had once bluntly told Ryan Callahan, aka Reilly O'Neill, there were other ways of taking David Pennington down…without killing him.

In the end it hadn't been possible—he and Callahan had killed Pennington together. Whether Ryan Callahan's .45 had done the deed or whether it had been the knife Cody had thrown while clinging to the side of a building nearly bleeding to death, neither of them knew, nor cared. They'd both been trying to save Mandy, held hostage by Pennington with a gun to her head and murder in his heart. The fact that Pennington had been the one to end up in the morgue rather than Mandy or Callahan was all they'd cared about in the heat of the moment.

But that didn't mean Cody was happy how things had ended, even though Pennington's death made a lot of good things possible. Cody would have preferred to go by the book: arrest, prosecution and incarceration. Long, long incarceration. It just hadn't been in the cards that night.

Deal with it, Callahan had told Cody when Cody had expressed regret about the outcome. Cody could still hear him saying it in that disconcertingly direct way he had. Callahan had been visiting Cody in the hospital while he recovered from the gunshot wound that had nearly taken his life. *You can't ever second-guess yourself,* Callahan had advised him. *Not if you want to stay alive. If you do, you'll be frozen with indecision when the chips are down. That's the quickest way I know to end up dead. Even worse, someone who doesn't deserve to die might pay the price for your screwup.*

Cody had taken that advice to heart. He'd never allowed himself to second-guess his actions in all the years since. Not until today. Not until he'd seen the bruises he'd inflicted on Keira.

She doesn't blame you, he reminded himself. *She said it herself—you did what you had to do to save her.* But after seeing the bruises on her pale, delicate skin, the reminder was cold comfort.

Cody checked the agency's intranet listing for McKinnon's phone number and picked up the phone. Then he changed his mind and looked up another number instead.

He heard a crisp "Keira Jones" in his ear, but for some reason he couldn't help remembering those two words she'd spoken to him the night they met—*I will.* He pushed the memory ruthlessly to one side and told her, "You're in."

"You're kidding," she said, and he heard the little edge of excitement she couldn't suppress in her voice. "I thought you were sure Callahan would refuse."

"He's not unreasonable, just stubborn—I should have remembered that. If you get to know him the way I do, you'll realize unpredictability could be defined by watching him."

"Is he really that good? What I mean is," she explained, "the way you and Trace and D'Arcy talk about him makes me wonder why he's not working for the agency."

Despite everything Cody was worried about, he laughed. "If you ever meet his wife, you wouldn't ask that question. Mandy is…" Pictures of Mandy flashed through his mind, from when they'd been toddlers together, through their high school years, to the last time he'd seen her after the birth of her third child, the daughter she and Callahan had been hoping for. "Let's just say any man married to Mandy could be forgiven for wanting a job that kept him home nights."

"I see."

There was an odd inflection to the innocuous words. *I wonder what that's about,* Cody thought before dismissing it as unimportant and moving on to why he'd originally called her. "Can you and McKinnon meet me down here? I've started a list of things we'll need, but now's the time for the three of us to make plans. I want to move on this as soon as possible. And there's something I just learned about that I need to share with the two of you," he added, knowing he needed to inform them he was being followed.

"I think Trace went to get coffee, but I'll round him up and we'll be down there shortly. Where's your office?"

He told her. After they hung up he started jotting down cryptic notes of the things he'd mentally listed, but then he paused, pen in hand, and stared at the phone for a few seconds as it hit him. The odd inflection he'd noted earlier but had dismissed suddenly made sense.

She didn't like hearing you talk about Mandy, he told himself as his pulse unexpectedly kicked into gear. *She didn't like it, and that must mean—*

Cody tried to shut down that train of thought. Keira was a fellow agent; not only that, she was also working for him now—that made her off-limits. Fraternization between agents was frowned upon and was strictly forbidden between supervisor and subordinate.

I'm not really her supervisor, though, he temporized. *I'm just the agent in charge.* It was a fine distinction, a legal nicety, but...it meant he could at least *think* about her without feeling he'd crossed a line he shouldn't cross.

He'd been involved with a few women since he'd left Black Rock...and Mandy. But nothing that had touched his emotions. Nothing that had made him *feel.* He'd blocked off his heart from the moment Mandy had married Ryan Callahan and had told himself he was better off that way—a lone wolf traveled farther and faster. But deep inside he hadn't really believed it. That hard, cynical edge was just a facade. Mandy had known the truth about him; but Mandy belonged to Callahan, heart and soul.

He'd finally, *finally* cured himself of loving Mandy, but he wanted a woman like her for his very own. A woman who would make him her first priority. A woman who would love him fiercely with every beat of her heart, the way Mandy loved Callahan. A woman who would kill to protect him, just as he'd kill to protect her. A woman like...

He told himself he was overreacting. That it was just the circumstances surrounding their first meeting coloring his perspective, when a vision of a woman rose in his mind. Translucent skin with a sprinkling of pale freckles; red-gold curls that made a man want to tangle his fingers in them and see if they were as soft as they looked; brown eyes fringed with gold-tipped lashes untouched by mascara—soft brown eyes that refused to cry.

And faintly pink lips without a trace of lipstick. Firm lips. No-nonsense lips. Lips that hadn't trembled even when she'd believed she was about to be raped and killed. Lips he'd give a sizable chunk of his next paycheck to discover if he could soften under his.

You've got no business daydreaming about her, he warned himself with stern resolution. He'd barely managed to relegate her to a corner of his mind when a slight movement caught out of the corner of his eye made him look up. Walking toward his office was Trace McKinnon. And right beside him was the woman with the unkissable lips Cody wanted suddenly—and urgently—to kiss.

Chapter 4

Cody stood at the firing range in the soundproofed subbasement of the agency. Safety glasses and noise-canceling headphones in place, he raised his right hand and fired his Glock 17 at the silhouette target fifty feet away until the 33-round high-capacity magazine was empty. He reeled the target in, noting with disgust that roughly half his shots weren't in the ten ring, although he had nothing outside a nine.

He liked the Glock better than the standard-issue revolver he'd carried when he'd been the sheriff of Black Rock—more accurate at a greater distance and more firepower, even without the high-capacity magazine—but guns had never been his thing. Knives had always been his first love, ever since he'd been a kid.

Cody could remember practicing until both arms were sore and aching, and then practicing some more until he was nearly as good with his left hand as he was with his right. He hadn't even stopped when his father had roughly told him that knives weren't much use anymore, not when throwing a knife left you disarmed and gave your attacker a weapon to use against you.

That had just added to the challenge. Even as young as he'd been, Cody had figured out that if you were deadly accurate, you didn't have to worry about having your own knife turned against you. A well-balanced knife in the hands of a marksman was a potent weapon.

Knives also had other uses, as he'd known when he'd used his to pry open the warped window the night he first met Keira. Using a good throwing knife as a pry bar didn't do much for its balance, but it sure came in handy.

And knives could be concealed more easily than guns.

He glanced down the line at the other two agents on the firing range. McKinnon was doing rapid, five shot strings with a SIG SAUER P226; Keira was using the two-handed Weaver stance to empty her smaller, compact Glock 19 with deadly precision.

Unlike the FBI, the agency didn't have a standard-issue firearm—each field agent requisitioned his or her own weapon based on fit and functionality, the agency's position being that what worked for one agent wouldn't necessarily work for another—but they did keep records of all guns issued.

And every field agent was responsible for staying sharp with the weapons of his or her choice. Cody was sure Keira and McKinnon didn't need today's practice rounds, but with special rule seven invoked…and it wouldn't hurt anyway; you never knew when just the tiniest fraction of an edge might make a difference.

One of the great things about working for the agency was that a lot of the bureaucracy and red tape involved in requisitioning assets for a covert operation had been minimized or eliminated entirely. And the agency had a whiz of an acquisition and supply team. Cody couldn't recall a time when he had requested something he needed for an op that hadn't been forthcoming in less than twenty-four hours.

His small team already had in their possession most of the assets the three of them had figured they might need, and he'd been assured the rest would be ready and waiting for them first thing in the morning, along with the two vehicles they'd requisitioned. Neither vehicle would be new enough, or old enough, to draw unwanted attention, he knew without asking. But under the hood—where it counted—both would be impeccably maintained. McKinnon and Keira would drive the truck with its retractable, locking tonneau cover over the truck bed, concealing their gear. Cody would drive the SUV, chosen more for its power, agile handling, corner-hugging ability and near-perfect manual transmission—things a vehicle needed in the mountains around Black Rock—than for its amenities.

Even though everything was lined up for their early departure tomorrow morning, Cody chafed at the delay. When he'd called Callahan back to let him know they wouldn't be arriving until midafternoon the following day, the other man's disappointment had been obvious.

"That the best you can do?"

"Just about, unless you tell me something more than you've told me so far," Cody said reasonably. "Which, in essence…is nothing."

"Okay." Callahan wasn't one to waste time on nonessentials. "I'll be waiting."

Mandy Callahan had just laid her sleeping daughter in her crib when she heard the front doorbell ring, and then ring again. She glanced at her watch as she went to answer it, wondering who could be stopping by way out here at this time of night. The hallway light was out, and she didn't bother turning it on. But the living room was also shrouded in darkness when she entered, and her brows wrinkled into a puzzled frown. *I thought Ryan was in here reading the paper. I wonder where he—*

A hand closed over her mouth, and her husband's arm encircled her waist. "Shh," he mouthed against her ear. "Stay here and don't move."

Mandy froze. *No!* she thought as her pulse began to race, memories of six years ago as fresh in her mind as if they had occurred yesterday—firebombs ripping her world apart, vengeful murderers after her husband. *Not again.* Her thoughts flew to the bedroom she'd just left, where her innocent daughter, Abby, lay sleeping; and the bedroom next to it, where her two sons, five-year-old Reilly and little Ryan, only three, were asleep in their bunk beds. *My babies,* she thought frantically, wanting to run back to protect them, to throw her body over them and shield them from whatever danger threatened, but she knew better than to disobey her husband when his voice sounded the way it had.

His body pressed against hers for a second more, and Mandy could tell her husband was already strapped—the leather holster and the gun it contained had once been Ryan's constant companions. But it had been years since he'd felt it necessary to be armed to the teeth in their home.

Mandy swallowed hard. She wanted to ask him why, but she was afraid she already knew the answer. Ryan hadn't said anything, but something had been weighing on his mind this past week. She'd just been so tired and distracted trying to wean Abby, she hadn't taken the time she normally would to demand he tell her what was going on. And now…now it might be too late.…

Her husband took her right hand and wrapped it around something cold and hard—the butt of a pistol. "Use it if you need to," he whispered. "I'll be right back." With that, he was gone, moving down the hallway like a shadow, slipping out the back door into the night.

Her eyes flickering every which way, straining against the darkness and starting at every creak, she waited for Ryan's return. *Not my husband, God,* she prayed as she waited. *And not my babies. Please, don't let anything happen to them. Please.*

She sensed more than heard movement on the front porch, and her heart began hammering in her breast. Then she heard a low, pained moan, and she almost screamed, thinking it could be her husband making that sound. She darted to the front door, stopping herself just in time as she remembered what Ryan had long ago trained her to do. She flattened herself against the wall beside the door but not too close to it, then waited, gun hand up and ready, counting seconds.

"It's okay, Mandy," she heard Ryan call softly. "Open the door."

She twitched the dead-bolt lock and threw the door open. A large shadow walked through carrying something even larger in its arms. "Shut the door and lock it," her husband said. She did as he bade her, then followed him as he carried his burden through the dark hallway into their lamp-lit bedroom and gently lowered it onto the bed.

"Oh, my God!" Mandy covered her mouth with one hand to prevent herself from saying anything more. She barely recognized the young man bleeding on their bed as Steve Tressler, their nearest neighbor. His face was a bloody mask, as if it had taken a terrible beating. And there were three wounds she recognized as gunshots tracing across his chest.

She dropped the gun she was holding onto the bed and stumbled to the bathroom, grabbing towels off the shelf and knocking a couple onto the floor in her haste. When she got back to the bedroom, Steve had a death grip on Ryan's shirt. Ryan was bent over, Steve's other hand in his and his ear pressed to Steve's lips, which were moving between gasps for air. And then she saw it—one long, shuddering breath, and Steve's body went limp.

"No!" she whispered, appalled.

Ryan stood up, his face hard, cold and deadly, the way she'd seen him look six years before. Blood stained his shirt where Steve had gripped it, and he slid something into his jeans pocket, but she couldn't see what it was.

"Pack some clothes and things for the kids," Ryan ordered in a voice she hadn't heard in six years, and it sent icicles down her spine. "You've got ten minutes."

Mandy didn't hesitate. She'd been there when her home had been turned into a raging inferno by members of the New World Militia. She'd been there when Ryan and Cody had confronted and killed David Pennington, the militia's founder. And she knew when Ryan looked and sounded like that, questions—and answers—would have to wait.

They drove through the stillness of the night, the children fast asleep in their car seats. "Where are we going?" she asked finally.

"Walker's cabin."

"Why there? Why not Sheridan or Buffalo?"

Ryan didn't answer at first. Then he said, "Because I need to get you and the kids out of harm's way. And because Walker will be there tomorrow, with a couple of other agents."

Mandy felt the stirrings of anger. "How do you know that?" she asked, trying to keep a lid on her temper. "What haven't you told me?"

Ryan's voice was harsh in the darkness. "I called him this afternoon and asked him to come up here."

She breathed deeply. The fear-induced adrenaline that had kept her going at fever pitch for the past hour had finally drained away, and she felt weak and shaky. But not too weak to remind her husband, "Six years ago you swore you'd never keep secrets from me again. So you'd better start talking—fast."

Cody jolted awake when the phone rang beside his bed. He fumbled the receiver to his ear and darted a quick look at his alarm clock. *After midnight,* he thought. *Who could be call—*

A deep growl sounded in his ear. "DEFCON One." A click at the other end told him the caller had hung up. But he knew that voice. And he was pretty sure he knew what the code phrase meant.

He bunched a pillow behind him and lay back against it, staring at the phone in his hand, deeply perturbed. Callahan wouldn't call him at this time of night unless something had happened, something deadly important he needed to warn Cody about.

Cody looked at the phone in his hand, then punched in a number every agent in the agency had memorized, but which few had ever been called upon to use. Cody never had, either, until now.

The phone rang for a few seconds before it was answered by a crisp voice, unmuffled by the dregs of sleep. "D'Arcy."

"It's Special Agent Walker, sir. Sorry to wake you, but you did say to keep you posted, and something has come up."

"That's okay. What is it?"

"Callahan just called me. He said two words—*DEF-CON One*—then hung up."

There was a distinct growl at the other end. "How soon can you get up there?"

"It's a six-hour drive, but we don't have everything we requisitioned yet. I was told we'd have it first thing in the—"

"Get your team mobilized and be at the agency in one hour. I'll make a call—if everything you need will be ready in the morning, it can be ready and waiting for you now."

"Yes, sir."

"I'm also going to send up two more teams—one to Buffalo and one to Sheridan—as backup, just in case. They'll be a few hours behind you, so I don't want you to wait for them, but don't hesitate to call for help if you need it."

"Yes, sir."

"And, Walker, one more thing." There was a pause at the other end. "I know you don't agree with special rule eight."

Cody was surprised into asking, "How did you kn—"

"It's my job to know everything," D'Arcy replied. "You might not agree with it, but I also know you'll follow it…if you have to. Go with your gut."

"Yes, sir."

"Get going," D'Arcy said. "You've got fifty-seven minutes."

Cody's team assembled in the ready room on the fifth floor, just down the hall from his office. He noted with approval that despite the late, or rather, early hour, both Keira and McKinnon were alert and sharp, as if they'd had eight hours of uninterrupted sleep. They were both dressed casually in jeans, sweaters and sturdy hiking boots, as he was, with the warm jackets they'd need in the mountains when they got close to Black Rock thrown over the backs of their chairs.

Both agents already had their Bluetooth earphones in place, and Cody fitted his in his ear as he briefed them quickly. He really didn't have a lot that was new to share, other than Callahan's warning and D'Arcy's order, but he reiterated the plan they'd come up with earlier that afternoon, making one change.

"Two vehicles and three drivers means we can drive in shifts, and each of us can get a little sleep on the way," Cody said. "McKinnon, you've got the GPS coordinates for my cabin already loaded?" McKinnon nodded. "I want to drive one of the vehicles on the last leg—I don't care which one. Even with a GPS it won't be easy finding the turnoff, so I might as well lead the way. You two sort out who drives when."

They left just before two in the morning, Cody driving the SUV and McKinnon driving the pickup truck, with Keira trying to sleep in the cab of the truck her partner was driving. Cody had been very careful to make sure no one followed him from his apartment to the agency, and he did the same thing now, just in case. He drove with part of his mind on the road and making sure he had no tail, but another part wondering what could have happened to make Callahan call him in the middle of the night. And what did that mean for Mandy and their three children?

They stopped to switch drivers at a gas station about a half hour before Wheatland, Wyoming. McKinnon quickly downed a cup of black coffee and said, "I'm still good. I'll sleep on the last leg, if that's okay with the two of you."

Cody nodded, finishing his own coffee and tossing the cup in the trash. Keira came over to the SUV and got into the driver's seat. "You might want to stretch out in the back here," she told Cody. "The truck's not all that comfortable for sleeping."

Cody did as Keira suggested, but found it impossible to sleep—his mind was still trying to analyze Callahan's cryptic warning and plotting out ways and means; and the backseat of the SUV wasn't wide enough to stretch out in, either, not for someone as tall as he was. And there was something else on his mind, too. After ten minutes he broke the silence. "I wanted to thank you," he said.

"For what?" Keira glanced at the rearview mirror.

"For telling D'Arcy the whole story about what happened last Friday night," he explained.

A long silence followed his words. "I owed it to you" was all she said finally.

"Maybe so, but I appreciate it. Not everyone would have done it."

She seemed uncomfortable talking about the subject. "He told you, I take it?"

"Yeah." Cody thought about his conversation with Nick D'Arcy, then added quietly, "He also said you offered to resign."

"He told you that, too?" From the tight way the words came out, he knew she was embarrassed.

"Only in passing and only because I had to tell him Callahan knows about how you and I met."

"Great." The one word spoke volumes, her tone conveying not only embarrassment but deep humiliation.

Compassion for her welled in him. *It can't be easy for a woman in a man's job,* he thought. "I had to tell Callahan," he explained. "It was the only way to convince him to keep you on the team."

She didn't respond right away, and when she did she

said drily, "I would have thought telling him that story would have the opposite effect."

Cody cast his mind back to his conversation with Callahan. "That's where you're wrong about him. He might be a throwback where women are concerned, but he respects courage and quick wits." Then he added, "I also told him you remind me of his wife."

The silence was electric, and Cody knew somehow he'd said the wrong thing. But all she said was "I guess that's a compliment." There was just a hint of something in her voice he couldn't put a name to, and he realized anew that Keira had picked up on his onetime attachment to Mandy...and didn't like it.

Putting his theory to the test, Cody said, "If you meet her, you'll understand just how much of a compliment it really is," adding more warmth to his voice than he would otherwise have done. "Mandy Callahan and I grew up together."

"I see."

She didn't say another word, and the silence in the SUV was deafening. Cody lay back, pillowing his head on one arm, using his jacket as a blanket. He had a million and one things to worry about, not the least of which was how he was going to keep his team safe if all hell broke loose as it had once before with the New World Militia.

But a tiny smile played over his lips as he dozed off in the darkness.

Chapter 5

An hour outside Buffalo, Wyoming, they switched drivers again, Cody taking the wheel of the pickup while McKinnon moved to the passenger seat. "You could try the backseat of the SUV," Cody offered. "I won't mind."

"That's okay," McKinnon said, stretching out his legs and reclining back against the passenger door, bunching his jacket behind his shoulders as a cushion. "I probably won't sleep much anyway. Besides," he added, "I want to talk to you before we get there, without Keira around."

Cody didn't speak, just drove up the on-ramp to the highway, watched to make sure the SUV was following him and waited. Eventually McKinnon said, "She told me what happened last week."

There was an edge to his voice that Cody sympathized with. A man's relationship with his partner could sometimes be closer than his relationship with his wife, especially when he trusted that partner with his life. And it was a two-way street. Anything bad that happened to a man's partner was conversely a reflection on him. Cody wasn't sure exactly how much Keira had confided in McKinnon, but he sensed the other man was berating himself for not being there when his partner needed him. Cody made a noncommittal sound that could have meant anything. No way was he going to reveal what he knew, not even to Keira's partner.

"I saw the bruises," McKinnon said softly. "Did you have to hurt her like that?"

Cody kept his face impassive, but it was an effort. There was just a hint in McKinnon's voice that betrayed the fact he wasn't *sure*; he was fishing, and Cody wasn't rising to the bait.

"Don't know what you're talking about." He kept his eyes on the road, knowing McKinnon was watching him like a hawk for any sign he knew more than he was letting on. He signaled a lane change and passed a slow-moving diesel truck on the left, then steered back into the right lane.

Eventually McKinnon sighed and said, "Maybe you don't at that." Then he slipped in a question so neatly Cody almost didn't see the trap. "So, how do you know her?"

He almost answered that he'd met her in the agency cafeteria, or something innocuous like that, but then he remembered Nick D'Arcy had mentioned the day before that Cody and Keira already knew each other, and how would D'Arcy know that unless it was related to a special op, or…?

And Keira's partner since she joined the agency would know Cody hadn't met her on a special op. "Sorry," he lied, making light of it. "That's classified."

"Mmm-hmm." The sound conveyed that McKinnon unmistakably knew Cody was lying, but wasn't going to pursue it further.

Both men were silent for so long Cody thought McKinnon must have fallen asleep, but when he glanced to his right, he saw the other man was wide-awake. "I was surprised when I heard you worked for the agency," he said on the spur of the moment. "I thought you were a fixture in the U.S. Marshals Service."

McKinnon laughed a little. "I heard your name mentioned within the agency last year in reference to a couple of cases that earned you a commendation, and I figured it had to be you—how many Cody Walkers can there be out there? But before that, the last I knew, you were in the DEA. How long since D'Arcy recruited you?"

"Just over four years."

"Going on five for me, ever since the agency debuted." He was silent for a moment. "My wife didn't want me to take the job, but...I've worked for D'Arcy ever since I got out of the service, and when he asked me I couldn't tell him no."

Cody spared him a quick look. "I didn't know you were married."

"I'm not." McKinnon's tone was dry. "Not anymore."

"Sorry to hear that," he replied automatically.

"Yeah, well, you know how it goes. Most women want a man home nights and don't understand this job isn't a nine to five you can just leave at the door." Cody laughed with wry understanding. "And when I teamed up with Keira," McKinnon continued, "that was the last straw as far as my wife was concerned."

Cody suddenly wondered if... But McKinnon answered the question before Cody could voice it. "Not that there was ever anything between Keira and me, not the way my wife suspected."

"You've been with her three years. Isn't that what she said yesterday?" Cody asked in a casual tone he was far from feeling.

"Yeah. We've closed some tough cases together. I've never had a better partner, but that's as far as it goes."

Cody glanced in the rearview mirror, noting the lights

of the SUV that had been following him at a safe distance for the past half hour, ever since he'd pulled onto the highway. There were no other vehicle lights in sight, so he knew they weren't being tailed—covert tailing at night on a long, lonesome stretch of highway was nearly impossible.

"What can you tell me about her? As a special agent," he added quickly, not wanting to reveal his personal interest in Keira to the other man.

McKinnon shifted positions, adjusting the jacket behind his shoulders and settling back against the door again. "She's got a knack for figuring things out that has come in handy more than once. I've never known anyone better at putting a few pieces together that don't seem to fit and solving a riddle that has everyone else stumped. Except D'Arcy, of course. Nobody can touch him."

"I know what you mean." He was quiet for a moment, then asked diffidently, "What else can you tell me about Keira?"

Cody could feel the other man's eyes on him in the darkness. *That was a mistake,* he acknowledged. But he hadn't been able to help himself. He wanted to know more about Keira, about what made her tick. Who better to ask than her partner?

"She's twenty-nine, served two tours of duty overseas—she was in the Corps, just like you and me—military police. Then she came back to the States and got a degree in criminal psychology. She joined the agency right after college, three years ago," McKinnon rattled off.

Then he added, "She comes from a large family—four brothers, all older, all former marines, too. Maybe that's why she has a thing about wanting to do her job as well as, or better than, a man could. Maybe that's why she jumps at every chance for a field assignment, even though her strength is research and analysis. And I know that's why it galls her, what happened last week."

McKinnon's not stupid, Cody thought. *He knows I'm interested—he wouldn't be sharing personal information about Keira otherwise. And he suspects I know something.*

"You keep referring to something that happened last week. What's that about?" he asked, lying through his teeth.

"If you don't know, it's not my place to tell you," McKinnon replied. "Keira can tell you if she thinks it's important. But it won't interfere with her job performance. That much I *can* tell you."

"Fair enough."

"I just have one more thing to say, and then I'll keep my thoughts to myself," McKinnon said slowly, and Cody stiffened at the tone in the other man's voice. "I'm curious—how *did* you get those scratches on your cheek?"

Cody had no answer.

Shortly after eight Friday morning, Cody drove the pickup truck toward a dead-end clearing at the end of a winding muddy road that still had traces of snow in the ruts even though it was nearly the end of May. Then he braked so abruptly the SUV following him almost rear-ended the truck—another vehicle was already reverse-parked in the clearing, a large four-by-four.

"Wait here," he told McKinnon softly and saw the other man reach for his SIG SAUER. Cody drew his own gun. He left the engine running and got out, signaling to Keira to stay in the SUV with his left hand.

Eyes flicking left and right, Cody approached the

abandoned vehicle with caution. A quick glance inside at the two car seats in the middle row told him everything he needed to know, and he relaxed his guard a fraction. *Callahan's here already,* he realized. *Who else could it be? Who else knows where this cabin is located?*

He sheathed his Glock and quickly returned to the truck. "Callahan's here," he told McKinnon briefly. "Let Keira know, will you?" *If you can get cell-phone reception in these mountains,* he thought but didn't say. If they couldn't, they had other communication equipment in the back of the truck they could substitute, but it wouldn't be as convenient.

McKinnon tapped a button on his Bluetooth earphone and relayed the message to his partner as Cody shifted into gear and drove the truck forward, then reverse-parked it next to the four-by-four, just in case they needed to make a fast exit. The air had an early-morning mountain chill as both men got out and were joined by Keira, who had parked the same way and was now shrugging into her warm jacket, although she didn't zip it up.

"You were right," McKinnon admitted. "I don't think the GPS could have found this place."

"And we're not even at the cabin yet," Cody confirmed. "It's about fifty yards in that direction," he said, pointing. "But the fact that Callahan's four-by-four is here already isn't a good sign. One of us had better stay with the gear while we reconnoiter." He started to give Keira the assignment, but instantly thought better of it. "You stand guard, McKinnon," he said. "Keira, come with me."

Cody led the way along the rough path he could have followed blindfolded. He used to come here often when he lived and worked in Black Rock, but his visits had been sporadic ever since he'd moved away. Still, he couldn't bring himself to sell his cabin, especially after the economy took a downturn and the real-estate market headed south with it. *Damn good thing I didn't sell after all,* he told himself. *It was a bolt-hole for Mandy and Callahan six years ago, and it looks as if it's being used for the same thing again.*

The path narrowed in a couple of places, so they were forced to walk single file, but eventually it widened, then opened into a clearing, and Cody's split-log cabin suddenly came into view. Snow still clung to the roof, and patches of snow were scattered around the clearing. There were footprints in the snow leading up to the front porch, too, none of them fresh.

Cody stopped and put a hand on Keira's arm. "Hang tight," he said. Then he called out, "Callahan!" He waited a few seconds, but there was no response from the cabin, so he called again. "Callahan!"

"Right behind you," said a soft, deep voice.

Cody and Keira whirled. Keira's Glock was in her hand before she realized she'd drawn her weapon; she had only a split second to notice that Cody hadn't drawn his. And only a fraction of a second later Cody's left hand came down on her gun hand, making sure she didn't shoot the tall, dark man confronting them with a Smith & Wesson semiautomatic.

Then she realized the semiautomatic wasn't aimed at them, and Cody was holding out his hand to the other man. When Cody said, "Callahan," Keira slowly holstered her own weapon, but kept a watchful eye on the other man's gun until he sheathed it in his shoulder holster.

"Walker." The two men shook hands before Callahan turned his eyes to Keira, his brows raised enquiringly.

"Special Agent Keira Jones—Ryan Callahan, sheriff of Black Rock. Among other things."

Callahan shook her hand and glanced back at Cody, a look of approval in his eyes. "She's quick, but not reckless" was all he said, but Keira knew she'd passed some kind of internal test on Callahan's part.

In an undertone she told Cody, "That's dried blood," nodding in the direction of the dark splotch on Callahan's shirt.

"Yeah," Callahan said. "And the body it came from is lying in my bed at home." Cody raised one eyebrow in a question that Callahan answered with a slight shake of his head before adding, "Our nearest neighbor—he lived about a half mile away. He showed up at our door late last night, already bleeding out. He was dead before Mandy and I could do anything to save him." Keira had never heard a colder, harder voice, and Callahan's face matched his voice. "That's why we're here."

Keira assessed the man in front of her in a way that was second nature to her now. He was older than Cody—somewhere in his mid-forties, she estimated, although it wasn't always easy to judge ages with men, especially this man. He was tall, too, just a shade shorter than the man beside her. He was as dark as Cody was fair, and there was an alert, wary watchfulness in his tawny eyes that told her he took no risks where he hadn't already calculated the odds. And while many men his age had started to let themselves go physically, he was as lean and muscled as Cody was—a memory flash of Cody's lean, muscular frame holding her prisoner the night they'd met made her heart skip a beat.

Callahan looked to be a formidable ally, but looks could be deceiving. And was he as impressive as Cody had already proven himself to be? Keira couldn't be sure until she saw him in action. She knew from firsthand experience that Cody was incredibly strong, but he was also quick off the mark, with courage to spare. He'd already risked his life for her once, and—

"Where's McKinnon?" Callahan asked, interrupting Keira's memories of that night a week ago.

"Guarding our escape route," Cody replied. "I figured that was your four-by-four, but I didn't want to take any chances, especially not with the gear we brought with us."

One corner of Callahan's mouth twitched into a grin. "You know, Walker, for an amateur you're not half-bad." His tone and words were deliberate provocation, but Keira realized Cody wasn't responding to it. He merely grinned back, the unexpected smile slashing across his face the way she remembered it doing once before.

Callahan was speaking again, and Keira took herself sternly to task. *Stop thinking about Cody and focus on why we're here.*

"Mandy and our kids are in the cabin," he was saying. "She'll be relieved to see you—she's been terrified ever since last night that something will happen I can't handle on my own." Keira was quick to note the way his voice softened when he mentioned his wife and children. "There's coffee already made. Why don't you go in and let Mandy know you're here while I help McKinnon unload the truck?"

Cody glanced at Keira. She read his unspoken message and turned away to call McKinnon on her Bluetooth earphone, relaying the news that Callahan was on his way there. Then she followed Cody through the muddy, semifrozen clearing toward the cabin. As they picked their way carefully, avoiding the worst of the mud, Keira asked, "Want to tell me what that was about?"

"What?"

"That remark about amateurs. He knows you work for the agency, so I don't get it."

"Long story. I'll tell you sometime." He smiled at her as they mounted the porch steps. He reached for the front door and opened it without knocking.

"Cody!" One of the most serenely beautiful women Keira had ever seen raised a relieved and thankful face from the baby nursing at her breast to greet them as they entered the one-room cabin. The woman slid something beneath her thigh before adding, "Thank God you're here."

Keira felt an unexpected wave of…not envy, exactly. More like wistfulness. Not for the other woman's classic features and all-American blonde beauty, but for the expression Keira caught on Cody's face before he controlled it and dropped a quick kiss on the top of the other woman's blond head. *No man ever looked at you that way,* a little voice said inside her head. It hurt. And that surprised her. She'd chosen her life deliberately, so it made no sense for her to now long for other things. Soft things. Man-woman things.

Mandy had a small towel draped modestly over her breast as she nursed, and it puzzled Keira until she saw the two other children still asleep on the double bed behind her. Boys, both of them, with hair as blond as Mandy's. *That must be why she's covered up—in case the boys wake up.* The pink-and-yellow outfit on the dark-haired baby in Mandy's arms was a dead giveaway the baby was a little girl.

Keira could no more help assembling random bits of data into a clear picture than she could help breathing. *Three children in six years,* she thought, remembering what Cody had told her about Mandy and Ryan Callahan. *That's some serious commitment between them.* She wondered why the knowledge lightened her mood immeasurably.

Mandy smiled a welcome at Keira before glancing inquiringly up at Cody, who quickly introduced them. Then she adjusted the towel and deftly switched the baby to her other breast. "Sorry about this." She indicated the nursing baby and gave Cody and Keira a rueful look that held only a trace of embarrassment. "I've been trying to wean Abby, but we left in such a rush last night I didn't have time to pack any formula or baby food." Her face turned troubled. "Did Ryan tell you what happened?"

"Not all of it—not yet—but enough." He moved away from Mandy's side and headed to the kitchen area to pour himself a cup of coffee, and Keira was unaccountably glad.

"He didn't tell *me* until last night, after Steve—" She caught her breath, but went on. "We were already on the way here before he told me he called you." Her blue eyes darkened. "I gave him hell for keeping this thing a secret from me, after he promised…" She stopped, a hurt expression on her face, and then started again. "Don't be like him," she begged Cody. "He can't help being who he is—it's the way he's made. But you're not like him. Don't keep me in the dark. Not this time."

Cody swallowed coffee from the mug in his left hand and grimaced, and Keira wasn't sure if it was in response to the coffee or Mandy's statement. Then his right hand briefly touched his left shoulder, and Keira remembered Cody referring to a bullet hole, Mandy and a lack of trust. Mandy had shot Cody, and she knew it hadn't been an accident. She only knew what Trace had told her—that Cody and Mandy had been best friends growing up, but that she'd shot him the night David Pennington had been killed, thinking she was protecting Callahan. But there was more to the story. A hell of a lot more. Keira was sure of it.

Chapter 6

The thud of boots on the front porch warned them all, and as Cody reached for his gun, he saw Keira doing the same. When Callahan walked in the front door followed by McKinnon, Cody relaxed and dropped his hand. He quickly downed the rest of his coffee and glanced at the pot on the stove, unsure whether he wanted another cup or not.

The two men stacked the loads they were carrying on and beneath the kitchen table beside him, then turned around and headed back the way they'd come. "One more trip should do it," Callahan told Cody laconically as they passed him, "if you help."

Cody chuckled silently to himself as he followed Callahan out. As clearly as if Nick D'Arcy was standing beside him, he could hear him saying, *Callahan was running the show six years ago, but this is* your *case now. The extent of his involvement is at your discretion.*

At some point he was going to have to draw the other man aside and let him know—privately—how things stood. But not in front of witnesses. He owed Callahan that much. Callahan had saved his life after Mandy had shot him, even though he'd known by then that Cody had once slept with her.

She hadn't been Callahan's wife at the time, but Cody

knew that hadn't made it any easier for the other man to accept…or forgive. Saving Cody's life despite that said a lot about Callahan's integrity. Or maybe by then he'd already known he had nothing to fear from Cody where Mandy was concerned.

Cody acknowledged there was probably more than a hint of truth in that assessment. Mandy had never loved him and never would. He'd known it even when he'd made love to her all those years ago that New Year's Day. *But desperate men do desperate things,* he reminded himself.

For just a moment his thoughts turned to Keira, wondering what it would be like with her. She was so different from Mandy in so many ways. He remembered the feel of her body pressed up against his that first night. Strength. Determination. A fierce will. No, she wouldn't make it easy for a man to take what she wouldn't willingly give, but…if she gave willingly, a man would *know* he was something special.

He breathed deeply as he followed Callahan and McKinnon through the woods, taking the crisp, clean air deep into his lungs, feeling the stillness of the mountainside soak into him. Even as part of him turned inward, another part of him was alert and watchful, looking to the left and right automatically, and occasionally checking behind him. He really didn't think they had anything to fear, not here. But nothing was certain, not where the New World Militia was concerned.

Michael Vishenko's office phone rang, and he picked it up automatically. "Yes?"

"We have a slight problem," the voice at the other end said.

"I see," he said. "Thank you for calling." He hung up

and limped to the door of his office, closing it firmly. Back at his desk he pulled a cell phone from his center drawer, waited five minutes, then dialed a number. When the call was answered, he said, "What is the problem?"

"There was a small leak."

"How small?"

"Minor. And it has been contained."

"Collateral damage?"

"Minimal."

"Still on goal?"

"Yes."

Vishenko breathed deeply. "Thank you for calling," he said and hung up. He stared at the cell phone in his hand for a minute, decoding the code words the caller had used. It was worrisome, but the caller had reassured him they were still on target. That was the most important thing.

In the cabin Keira watched Mandy in silence. When the other woman finished nursing her baby, she averted her gaze, giving Mandy a little privacy to adjust her clothing back to normal. Then, for something to say, she asked, "What are your boys' names?"

Mandy placed the towel over her shoulder, lifted Abby onto it and began burping her. "Reilly," she said softly, casting a backward glance at the two boys still sleeping on the bed behind her. "He's five. Little Ryan is three." She chuckled softly. "I have to stop calling him *little* Ryan. Even though they have my hair color, they both take after their father in just about every other way."

"Reilly?" Keira asked, remembering what Cody had said. "Wasn't that your husband's alias, Reilly O'Neill?"

Mandy's smile faded. "One of them," she replied, and

there was an expression on her face that told Keira this wasn't a subject to pursue.

Suddenly uncomfortable, Keira looked around for someplace to sit down. But other than the bed and a couple of kitchen table chairs over in the corner, there wasn't anything to sit on, so she leaned against the wall, watching the other woman in renewed silence until baby Abby fell asleep on her mother's shoulder.

Keira wanted to dislike Mandy, this beautiful woman Cody loved. But there was just something so basically *nice* about her, something in the way she loved her children so unreservedly. And then there was the way she looked at Cody. Or rather, the way she *didn't* look at him. Keira wasn't blind. Cody might be in love with Mandy, but in Mandy's eyes he was only a good friend. That was all he would *ever* be, and Keira felt a sense of relief.

Cody doesn't belong to you, she chided herself mentally, but that didn't stop how she felt. If was as if a bond had been formed between them that first night—on her part, anyway—when she'd known instinctively she could trust him with her life. The possessiveness she felt toward him was something new—and she didn't like it.

The sudden sound of boots on the front porch made Keira reach for her Glock even though she'd been expecting to hear it at any moment. But she wasn't taking any chances. She put a finger to her lips, motioning Mandy to silence, and moved swiftly behind the door.

Cody walked in, followed by Trace, with Callahan bringing up the rear, and Keira took her hand away from her gun. She closed the door behind the men.

"That's everything," Cody told her, and Keira knew from his eyes he'd seen—and approved—her reactions as par for the course for a good agent, which she was. He glanced over at Mandy, his eyes widening. Keira's gaze followed his, her own eyes widening as she saw something she hadn't seen before. The other woman was holding her baby with her left arm. Her right hand was holding a gun.

Where did that come from? Keira wondered, her admiration for Mandy growing.

"Going to shoot me again?" Cody teased, making light of the situation.

"Sorry," Mandy replied, tucking the nine-millimeter beneath her thigh again. "I couldn't be sure it was you, and I wasn't taking any chances."

Movement on the bed behind her made Mandy turn around, and Keira saw the younger boy stretching awake. Callahan had already dropped the load he'd been carrying beside the kitchen table. Now he moved to the bed and picked up his son.

He murmured something to the boy. Keira couldn't catch the words, but the change in his tone was amazing. There wasn't a trace of the hardness she'd noticed earlier. And the expression on his face betrayed him, too—he was completely vulnerable where his children were concerned. *Where his wife's concerned, too,* she amended as she saw the private look that passed between Ryan and Mandy Callahan.

Keira had never loved anyone as much as Mandy obviously loved her husband and children, but a sudden yearning inside her caught her by surprise. She wanted to. And she wanted to be loved in return, the way Callahan wholeheartedly loved Mandy. *To be loved like that,* she thought, hiding her unexpected emotions behind the tough, professional mask she'd learned the hard way to assume years ago in the Marine Corps. *What would it be like to be loved like that?*

Involuntarily her gaze moved to Cody, standing with

Trace by the kitchen table. The pain in her heart as she watched him was another shock. *Cody would love like that,* she realized. If he gave his heart, there would be nothing held back.

Some joke passed between the two men, and Keira saw Cody's quick grin flash across his face. Cody wasn't anywhere near as handsome as Trace, but there was something especially appealing about his angular features, something that spoke about the inner man. And Keira, who appreciated her partner's excellent qualities as well as his darkly handsome movie-star appearance, had never felt her pulse quicken with him the way it did just being in Cody's presence.

She couldn't help remembering Cody's rough treatment of her the night they'd met, the bruises he'd left on her body, but she knew that wasn't how he normally was with a woman. No, something told her he would be gentle and caring, the seducer, not the aggressor. She wondered what it would be like to…

Keira dragged her gaze away from him and brought her thoughts under control. *This isn't the time to be thinking about that,* she warned herself. *Not with an op going down. You've got to stay focused.*

She glanced back at the bed and saw the older boy was finally awake. Callahan was sitting on the bed now, a boy on each knee, holding them protectively in his arms as he talked softly to them and to his wife. Mandy was leaning close, holding baby Abby, and Keira realized from the other woman's expression that Callahan was telling her something she didn't agree with. Keira strained her ears to hear what they were saying.

"I'm *not* leaving you," Mandy was saying fiercely.

Callahan just looked at her, and it was all there in his eyes, everything he wouldn't say in front of the others.

A pang of envy twisted through Keira, combined with compassion for what the other woman had to be going through. "Somebody has to be with the kids," Callahan said in his deep voice. "Somebody has to make sure they're safe. And that somebody has to be you. You know it and I know it. Besides, I'll be stronger once I know you and our children are out of harm's way."

"That's not fair," Mandy said in a choked voice.

"No," he agreed. "It's not." As Keira watched, he leaned over and brushed his wife's cheek with his lips.

Keira turned away, shaken by the raw emotion she'd witnessed on the faces of Mandy and Ryan Callahan, and saw Cody and Trace walking toward them.

"It's time," Cody said, and Keira's eyebrows rose in a silent question that was also an accusation. Apparently the men had discussed some plan when they'd been outside together, a plan they hadn't bothered to clue her in on.

Cody caught Keira's expression and said, "McKinnon's taking Mandy and the children to the agency's safe house in Casper. He'll rejoin us after that."

Keira hadn't thought about that before, but it was the smart thing to do. Even though it appeared Mandy could protect herself, the three young children were at risk, so it made perfect sense to whisk them out of the way to safety. She was surprised Cody had picked Trace for the job, though. She would have expected him to give that task to her, the woman on the team.

Then she knew. *Callahan,* she thought with a wry twist to her lips. He probably voted to have Trace, the known element, protect his family, leaving what he probably considered the weaker link—herself—with Cody and him. And Cody had gone along with it.

A burning sense of injustice swept through Keira, but

she suppressed it. *I'm not the weaker link on the team,* she told the two men in her mind. *You think I am, but you'll see.*

Trace knew better. Her partner knew what she was capable of, and Keira drew some comfort from that knowledge. But she couldn't *tell* Cody and Callahan—they wouldn't believe her. She could only show them when she got the chance. *If* she got the chance.

Callahan and McKinnon had left to take the suitcases out to Callahan's four-by-four, which the team had decided was the best choice for McKinnon to drive, since the children's car seats were already set up in it.

Mandy was fitting her daughter, Abby, into the baby sling to make it easier to carry her along the rough path. When she was done, she touched Cody's arm to get his attention. "I'm trusting you," she said. "Don't let anything happen to Ryan. I'll never forgive you if—" Her voice broke, but she didn't have to finish the sentence.

Keira read the expression on Cody's face and knew he didn't want to make promises he might not be able to keep, especially not to Mandy. She saw compassion there, and something more, something that twisted her insides when he told Mandy in a deep voice, "I'll do my best."

"That's not good enough," Mandy whispered. She glanced down at her two boys, then put a protective arm around the baby slung in front of her. She raised her face to Keira's, tears she couldn't prevent springing to her eyes. "Please," she said as if her heart was breaking. "Please, take care of Ryan."

"I will," Keira promised her, ignoring the frown on Cody's face and the slight shake of his head. This was between Mandy and her. If Keira had anything to say about it, Ryan Callahan would return to the wife who loved him more than her own life. Even if it meant Keira had to sacrifice her own.

Callahan and McKinnon returned just then. Each man picked up one of the boys, and Callahan put his arm around his wife, ushering her toward the door. "I'll be right back," he told Cody and Keira without a backward glance.

Once the others had left, Cody told Keira, "Probably wasn't a good idea to lie to Mandy."

"I wasn't lying," she replied coolly. "Special rule seven, remember?"

"Yes, but…" He didn't know how to explain without offending her. Cody had seen Callahan in action, back when he'd gone by the name Reilly O'Neill, and Callahan could almost assuredly take care of himself. If he couldn't, then it was a fair bet no one else on the team would be in a position to do it for him. All in all, it wasn't likely that Callahan would need Keira's protection.

He caught a flash of something in Keira's eyes, but all she said was, "Let's hope it doesn't come to that." Then she asked casually, "So, did the three of you discuss anything else while you were outside, other than who was going to take Callahan's family to safety?"

Cody almost answered without thinking, then caught himself. But he knew from her expression that Keira somehow already knew the answer to the second part of her question without him confirming it in words.

"Did Trace object at all?" she asked gruffly.

McKinnon *had* objected, Cody remembered. He'd told both Cody and Callahan, *You've got Keira figured all wrong.* But he couldn't tell Keira that. And he couldn't tell her what Callahan had responded, either.

She walked toward the stack of gear on the kitchen

table and asked, "So, did Callahan tell you how he knows the New World Militia has been resurrected?"

"No." At least he was on solid ground with that answer. "McKinnon said he should wait until you were there."

"Well, that's something anyway."

"Keira…" Cody began, then stopped.

She whirled to confront him. "Why am I here?" she demanded. "If you and Callahan don't think I can pull my own weight, why did you even bother including me on the team? What's the point?"

Her eyes were flashing again, and it was anger Cody saw in their brown depths. *If you're honest,* he thought, *you'll admit you deserve it.* He nodded. "I guess there's a touch of old-school in me, too—more than I realized," he said, acknowledging the validity of her accusation.

The corner of her mouth twitched, as if she were trying not to smile. "You mean you're more like Callahan than you thought?"

"Yeah. I guess you could say that. But it won't happen again," he promised. "Not on my part anyway. I can't speak for Callahan."

She must have read the sincerity in his tone, because she nodded and said, "Okay. I'll accept that." She allowed herself a small chuckle. "Trace said the same thing—he couldn't speak for Callahan. And now that I've finally met him, I realize *no one* speaks for Callahan…except him."

"You got that right" came a soft, deep voice from the back door.

Chapter 7

Cody and Keira both whirled. Just as Callahan had crept up unnoticed behind them outside the cabin earlier, he'd managed to enter the cabin from the back entrance without them hearing him.

"Good way to get yourself killed," Cody told him as his hand dropped to his side.

"True," Callahan replied, moving into the center of the room. "But it's also a good way to hear what other people might not want you to hear." He bent a hard gaze on Keira. "You're right, and I apologize. I shouldn't have agreed to let Walker bring you unless I was willing to accept you all the way. Your partner told us we had you figured wrong. Walker and I should have listened to him."

"You heard what I said?" Keira asked him.

Callahan nodded. "I heard you ask Walker why you're here." He drew in a deep breath and let it out slowly, as if trying to figure out where to start. "You're here because I called him yesterday. I'm sure he's already told you what I said on the phone—that I *know* the New World Militia is back in business. What I didn't tell him is *how* I know—my neighbor, Steve Tressler."

"Your neighbor," said Keira, quickly making the connection. "The one whose blood is on your shirt?"

Callahan nodded and glanced over at Cody. "I knew

something was up. I didn't know what, but my instincts were telling me something wasn't right for the past week every time I saw Steve—I just couldn't get anything out of him. Then he came to me yesterday morning. Confessed he'd been recruited by the organization a year ago. They talked a good line, but then, they always did. *You* remember," he told Cody.

"Yeah."

"Anyway, Steve said he hadn't realized what he was getting into. He was a decent kid—stereotypical computer nerd, but likable nevertheless. Just a little naive at times, and didn't always use common sense. He was always playing those online war games. He didn't say it, but I suspect he joined the militia for the thrill of it, thinking it was like one of his computer games. He just didn't realize it wasn't a game."

He drew another deep breath. "It all came down on him when he accidentally stumbled across an elimination list a week ago, and—"

"He saw your name was on it," Cody said softly.

"Top of the list." Callahan smiled coldly. "I don't know if it has anything to do with ancient history between the militia, Pennington and me, or if it's just because I'm the local sheriff—Steve didn't know. All he knew was he'd seen six names on a hit list, and that was something he wanted no part of. But it wasn't that easy."

Cody looked over at Keira. "I don't know how much McKinnon told you when you started on this assignment…"

Keira's soft brown eyes hardened. "Enough to know no one just walks away from the New World Militia. At least, not the one from years ago."

"Right," Callahan said. "I doubt that's changed, and I wasn't taking any chances. He wouldn't tell me how he came across the list, or who had it, or *anything*. He said he didn't want to get anyone in trouble." His face showed his frustration.

"Since I couldn't get anything more out of Steve, I told him to just sit tight and not let on to anyone in the organization he'd seen that list or wanted out." His face contracted as he said roughly, "He was just a kid—barely old enough to drink. And they..." He drew another deep breath and put a tight rein on his emotions. "I told him I was going to call in the cavalry—your agency," he said, indicating Cody and Keira with one controlled gesture. "Which I did, first thing."

"But now he's dead, and any proof he had died with him," Cody said.

"Not quite," Callahan said. "But that reminds me. I can't just leave his body where it is. Not to mention his truck is parked at my house—he left it in the driveway in front, and I moved it behind the house last night before we left. But I didn't have time to do anything about the blood trail leading right to my front door."

"D'Arcy is sending backup teams to Buffalo and Sheridan," Cody said. "They're a few hours behind us, but I can have one of them handle it. They're not official crime-scene investigators, but they'll preserve any evidence, just in case. And they'll clear away any trace he was there, if that's what we want. We just need to decide if we want to make Tressler's death public yet."

"It depends on the original crime scene," Callahan said. "If he was shot in his cabin...I'm thinking that's where we'll want his body discovered. Whoever beat him and then shot him will be expecting us to find him there."

"Good point," Cody said. He glanced at Keira for her input, and she nodded her agreement. "What's the address? I can arrange for the backup team to check it out and handle moving the body back, if necessary."

Callahan told him, and Cody jotted it down. "That settles that. But what are you going to do?" he asked Callahan. "You can't just disappear from sight. I think the wrong people might start to wonder if the sheriff just up and disappeared, especially since your name is on the hit list."

"You're right." Callahan ran one hand over his unshaven face. "I'm too tired to think straight. But I'll have to go back to work, act as if Steve never told me anything."

"Can you do that?" Keira asked.

One corner of Callahan's mouth quirked in a faint smile. "Now that my family is out of danger—no problem."

For the first time Cody noticed the lines of tiredness on Callahan's face. *The man must have an iron constitution,* he thought, *but he's human like the rest of us.* "Did you get any sleep last night?" he asked, knowing the answer before he heard it.

"I couldn't take that risk."

Cody pointed to the bed in the corner, the one Mandy and the children had used. "Why don't you get some sack time now?" he asked with rough concern. As Callahan started to protest, he added, "You're all in. We at least had some sleep last night before you called," he said, indicating Keira and himself, "and we switched off driving on the way up, so we dozed then, too. Maybe you can go day and night, but you won't be at peak efficiency. And that puts the whole team at risk." He threw that last statement in, knowing it was the one argument the other man couldn't ignore.

"Maybe I will at that."

Keira asked, "Do you need to call your office first?"

Callahan shook his head. "I already thought of it, but I'm not on duty until tomorrow. Memorial Day weekend is always bad—lots of drinking, lots of bar fights, and lots of people on the road too drunk to drive and too stupid to know better. There's also a big Memorial Day party at the VFW hall in town on Monday. That's why I scheduled myself on duty for the whole three-day weekend." He smiled wryly. "Mandy wasn't happy about it, but…" He shrugged. "It's my job."

"Memorial Day," Cody said thoughtfully. "Do you think it has anything to do with this?" he asked. "Do you think there's something going down on Monday?"

Callahan considered the question. "Anything's possible. But Steve indicated trouble wasn't imminent when he spoke to me yesterday morning." He paused, his face hardening. "But now he's dead. So, yeah. Anything's possible."

He headed toward the bed, but stopped when Keira touched his arm. "What did you mean earlier when you said not quite?" At his questioning look she explained, "When Cody stated any proof your neighbor had, died with him, you said, 'Not quite.'"

"Right." His glance moved to Cody. "I didn't tell you everything when we met outside this morning. It's true Mandy and I couldn't do anything to save Steve, but he managed to say something to me before he died." The harsh lines of his face showed his frustration. "I just don't know what it means."

"What did he say?" Cody asked.

Callahan pinched his lips together with a forefinger and thumb as he contemplated how to put it. "It sounds funny, I know, but he said something like, 'Vay-nee, vee-dee—'"

"Veni, vidi, vici," Keira said, pronouncing the Latin words with a classical *w* sound instead of a *v,* then added, "It's also pronounced with a *v*—*veni, vidi, vici."*

"That's it, that's exactly what he said."

"It's Latin," Cody explained. "It means, 'I came, I saw, I conquered.' Supposedly Julius Caesar said it."

Callahan still looked puzzled. "I don't get it. What's so important about it that Steve would die trying to tell me?"

Cody raised his brows in a question to Keira. "Some kind of code?"

She shook her head regretfully. "If it's a code, I don't know what it is. The reference to Julius Caesar could mean anything—the Ides of March, Marc Antony, the Roman legions, crossing the Rubicon. Even the month of July or William Shakespeare. Or it could have absolutely nothing to do with Julius Caesar. Sorry." She looked at Callahan. "Did he say anything else?"

"One other word at the very end, but I couldn't really understand him. That's when he—" Callahan stopped abruptly before continuing. "It sounded something like *center* or *centaur,* but I can't swear to it. And neither word has a connection to anything as far as I can tell." He thrust one hand into his jeans pocket and came out with what looked like an ordinary house key in his palm. "He had this in his hand." Callahan stared down at it, his brows twitching together as he said in a voice from which all emotion had been wiped clean, "It still has Steve's blood on it."

Cody reached into his jacket pocket and brought out a couple of small plastic evidence bags, one of which he opened and held out for Callahan to drop the key into. "Probably too much to hope for a fingerprint other than yours and Tressler's," he told the other man, "but just in case…"

"Yeah," Callahan said.

"No idea what door it opens?"

"Not a clue. His truck keys were still in the ignition, and what looked like a house key was on the key ring. But it wasn't the same key as this one—that's the first thing I checked."

Cody looked the key over, then held the plastic bag out to Keira. "What do you make of it?"

She ignored the blood and examined the key closely through the plastic. "It's a double-sided key for a dead bolt," she said. "And the maker's mark on the bow indicates it's a copy, not an original key for the lock. That's about all I can tell you." She handed it back to Cody.

"We'll need something more to go on," Cody told Callahan. "Don't get me wrong—I believe everything happened just as you said. But with Tressler dead, we don't even have a starting point."

A thought occurred to Keira, but before she could voice it, Callahan said, "I know. But like I said, I'm too tired to think straight right now." He rubbed the back of his neck. "Maybe my brain will function better after I've had a couple hours of sleep."

While Ryan Callahan slept, Cody called the agency and got the contact information for the backup team in Buffalo. He called the head of that team and arranged for the pickup on Steve Tressler's body, along with everything else. Then Keira and Cody unpacked, sorted and stacked in neat piles the assets they'd brought with them.

Cody smiled ruefully when they were done. "Doesn't look like much to take down an army."

Keira's eyes met his. "I thought we were here to investigate," she said quietly. "Not wage war."

"True. But you weren't around six years ago, so you

don't know how quickly things can heat up with the New World Militia." He drew a deep breath and let it out slowly, tiredness tugging at him. He needed sleep, too. Maybe not as much as Callahan, but... "I wonder who else's name was on that hit list."

"Could yours be on it?"

"If the list has anything to do with what Callahan calls ancient history, it's likely. I was working undercover in the militia, too...." He thought back. "Must be almost ten years ago when I started."

He smiled slightly. "Unfortunately, my name wouldn't mean anything to Tressler—he's not a local. I knew everyone around here when I was the sheriff, and the name Tressler doesn't ring a bell, which means he had to have moved here after I left. So even if he saw my name on the list..."

There was an expression on Keira's face Cody couldn't read. "Do you think whoever was following you in Denver..."

"Was there to kill me?" he finished for her. "The thought had crossed my mind. But it's pure speculation at this point." He made a face of frustration. "I wish we knew what that key is for. I wish we knew what Tressler meant."

"I wish he were still alive to tell us," Keira said softly, turning her face away momentarily, as if to hide her expression from him.

Cody realized she wasn't just regretting Tressler's death from an investigation perspective; she was thinking about the loss of a human life, the same way Callahan had, and a small pang shot through him that he hadn't. It was easy to tell himself he didn't know Tressler, and therefore his death didn't affect him except in a professional capacity, but still...

"What's our next step?" Keira asked

"I hate to say it after we've come all this way, but I don't see anything much we can accomplish here. We need information we're not going to get, stuck in my cabin—I don't even have a phone here, much less internet access. And cell-phone coverage can be spotty at times."

"What about Callahan? We can't just leave him unprotected." And Cody knew she wasn't just thinking about him as a potential witness; Keira was remembering her promise to Mandy.

"When McKinnon gets back, he can shadow Callahan. I want you to focus on the investigation side."

She opened her mouth—to protest, Cody was sure, so he added, "McKinnon told me on the drive up you've got a knack for figuring things out, putting puzzle pieces together to solve a case. That's all we've got right now—a few scattered pieces of the puzzle that don't seem to make sense. I need you to concentrate on that."

"Okay." She was silent for a moment. "In D'Arcy's office you said the New World Militia was destroyed six years ago. What did you mean? What can you tell me about it?"

He considered what to tell her, what might be important for her to know. "You know who David Pennington was, right?" She nodded. "Callahan and I took Pennington down the hard way, together." He didn't have to draw her a picture. "Pennington kept most of the real power in the organization in his own hands, so without him to run it, the militia fell apart."

"Paramilitary in name, then, but not really," Keira threw in.

Cody nodded, remembering what McKinnon had said about her military service; she knew what he meant. "Then we both testified at a series of trials of the militia's remaining top brass. That, along with the plea-bargained testimony of Carl Walsh and Larry Brooks—"

"Wasn't Walsh Pennington's second in command at one point?"

"You've done your homework." Cody felt a flash of admiration for her, and pride. *Pride?* he wondered. *Why pride?* "Yeah. He was," Cody continued, shaking off his errant thoughts. "And Larry Brooks was a federal marshal. It's a bit complicated. Brooks and your partner were both working the witness security program under Nick D'Arcy. They were supposed to be protecting Ryan Callahan."

"Trace did mention that already. He also said he and D'Arcy had to clean up the mess…after the fact," she said, referring to collecting all the evidence and witness statements related to Pennington's death and having it ruled a justifiable homicide.

Cody wasn't really paying attention to what Keira was saying. He could feel it getting to him, his memories coming alive in gruesome detail as he recounted the story. But she had to know what they were up against. She had to understand, and he wasn't going to sugarcoat it for her. "The year before Pennington was killed, Brooks was instrumental in betraying Callahan's one-time partner, Josh Thurman, to the militia. Callahan was working the inside. Thurman was working the outside. The militia kidnapped Thurman's wife and infant son after Pennington's conviction, offering to trade their hostages for information—Callahan's whereabouts."

He drew a quick breath. "But Thurman didn't know where Callahan was," he said softly. "The militia tortured him, but he couldn't tell them what he didn't know." His voice dropped a notch. "So they tortured his wife and baby in front of his eyes." He closed his own eyes for an instant, experiencing in his gut the agony the other man must have gone through. "Then, when it was obvious Thurman would tell them where Callahan was if he knew, the militia decided he really had nothing to give them. So they murdered all three of them and dumped their bodies."

A small gasp escaped Keira, and their eyes met. Hers contained the horror he'd known she would feel over the senseless murder of a baby. "If the new organization is anything like the old one, that's the kind of people we're dealing with," he told her implacably. "They believe in their cause—fanatically. Nothing is beyond them, not even the murder of children. They're domestic terrorists, plain and simple."

Chapter 8

"That's why we can't take any chances," Cody told Keira roughly. "That's why Callahan wanted his wife and children safely out of the way, where the militia can't touch them. No one knows better than him what they're capable of. He lived it."

Her face was solemn and still. "You lived it, too," she reminded him.

Cody shook his head. "Not the way he did. My involvement was more on the periphery, at least until the end."

Callahan stirred in his sleep, drawing Cody's eyes toward him. "Let's go outside," he said quietly. "I don't want to wake him."

They sat side by side on the front-porch steps. The sun shone weakly overhead, but it was still cool, and the snow hadn't melted all the way.

Cody picked up his story. "D'Arcy knew I was also undercover in the militia. He sent Callahan to Black Rock because he figured I'd be able to keep a watchful eye on him, and if Pennington's men ever tracked him here I'd hear about it in advance and could warn him. That's when Ryan Callahan assumed the name of Reilly O'Neill." One corner of Cody's mouth curled up in a smile he knew didn't reach his eyes. "That's when he met Mandy."

"I see." There was a wealth of understanding in those two words.

Cody looked down at Keira, but she avoided his gaze. "You picked up on that already, didn't you?" he asked, watching her delicate profile, drawn to her in ways that baffled him with their complexity...as well as their simplicity.

"On what?"

Her nonchalant question didn't fool him. "On how I felt about Mandy back then."

She glanced up. "Back then?" she asked gruffly. "Or even now?"

His sixth sense was telling him his answer mattered to her. "Back then," he said softly. Then he added with a complete honesty he didn't stop to question, "And for a long time afterward." He breathed deeply and let the air out slowly. "But not anymore."

In the silence that followed, Cody watched as a red-tailed hawk lazily circled the sky, then suddenly dived toward the earth. Keira's gaze also followed the hawk until it disappeared from view. Then, in a voice so casual he knew it was calculated to hide how she really felt, she asked, "Are you sure?"

Their eyes met, and Cody saw something in the depths of Keira's brown eyes that shook him, an emotion he was afraid to name. "I'm sure," he said, a second before his mouth descended on hers.

If anyone had told him his thirty-seven-year-old body could react to a simple kiss as if he were seventeen, he wouldn't have believed it. But then, it wasn't really a simple kiss. And his body was rock hard and hurting before he knew it.

Those firm lips, lips he'd once thought of as unkissable, melted beneath his. His arms slid around her, drawing her close, and closer, as the kiss went on. In some part of him he knew he should stop, but when she moaned softly deep in her throat and her hand came up around his neck, all rational thought deserted him.

They broke apart to breathe, but he couldn't let her go. His blood was pounding in his veins, and his breath rasped in his throat. He wanted...wanted...

His lips found hers again. His hands threaded through her red-gold curls, and they were just as soft as he'd imagined they would be. Then his hands were cupping her face, and he was kissing her eyes, her cheeks, the hollow beneath her ear. And she was kissing him back. He might have been able to stop if not for that. At least that was what a corner of his brain said, but he knew it was a lie. Kissing Keira was rapidly becoming an obsession.

And not just kissing her. He desperately wanted to touch her in other places—soft, secret places. He wanted to know if she would melt there for him, too, the way her lips did. He wanted to taste every inch of her skin, to fill his senses with her, to hear her call his name when he brought her to the peak...and beyond.

She was still wearing her jacket, and he needed to feel her, to touch her everywhere. He whispered her name and pulled away slightly, his right hand sliding between their bodies to fondle her breast beneath the open jacket. Her unexpected whimper stopped him cold.

He drew back from her. She averted her face from his, but he caught her chin, forcing it up. Her eyes gave her away, and he *knew*. His face contracted in pain, and he cursed himself silently. "Keira, I..." He swallowed hard. He leaned his forehead against hers. "God, I'm sorry. I don't know my own strength. I didn't realize I..."

She shook her head slightly. "You told me to scream, but I couldn't, so..."

Cody remembered the way he'd roughly assaulted her the night they'd met, the way he'd ripped her blouse open and groped her until she screamed, and was devastated. "I didn't mean to hurt you," he whispered brokenly.

"You did what you had to do to rescue me—to rescue both of us," she maintained fiercely, defending him and his actions. "It was the best way you could think of at the time. And I already told you I bruise easily." Her face softened suddenly; her eyes softened even more as her right hand captured his left one and brought it to her right breast. "You can touch me here," she invited in a breath of a whisper.

But the spell, or whatever it was that had gripped Cody, was broken. His desire ebbed, replaced by self-recrimination. He pulled abruptly away from her and stood, putting distance between him and temptation.

"Why don't you just call me a son of a bitch and get it over with?" he asked, his anger at his earlier behavior forcing bitterness into his voice that was aimed at himself.

But she misunderstood. He could see it in her expression as she wrapped her arms around herself protectively. Despite that, she said firmly, "Because I don't think of you that way. How many times do I have to tell you?"

He gazed at her and realized she wasn't just trying to make him feel better; she actually believed it. But it didn't make any difference in how he felt about what had happened. Guilt made him say, "I should never have touched you."

She flinched but held his gaze. "Then? Or now?"

"Both."

He saw his answer sink in, and only the slight crinkling of her eyes betrayed that he'd hurt her...again. He wanted to take the word back, but it was too late. She stood up quickly and dusted off the back of her pants, then mounted the three steps to the porch and put her hand on the door. He watched her—he couldn't help himself—wishing with all his heart he hadn't been the one to hurt her. Not then. And certainly not now. He hadn't realized just how much or how easily she could be hurt, emotionally as well as physically.

She turned back, and her face was a frozen mask he scarcely recognized as the same woman he'd just kissed. "It won't happen again," she said in a flat, toneless voice. She slipped through the door and closed it firmly behind her.

"Damn!" The word released some of his tension, but nowhere near enough. He wanted to hit something. Hard. But not Keira. Never her. Himself.

He looked at the door through which she'd just disappeared, wishing he hadn't driven her to escape, wishing he could explain... *Explain what?* he asked himself, uncertain what he thought he could explain. *Explain that the minute you kissed her you forgot everything, including why you're here? That you've wanted her since the first time you touched her?*

He remembered the way she had responded to his kiss just now, and desire flickered back to life. In his head he heard the soft moan she hadn't been able to hold back, and his body hardened in a rush again, making his jeans uncomfortably tight. Then he remembered the whimper of pain...and what had caused it in the first place. But he also remembered her placing his hand on her other breast, saying, *You can touch me here.*

This time his desire didn't fade. *Great,* he thought. *Now, when it's too late. Now that she wouldn't touch you for anything you offered her and would probably scratch your eyes out if you touched her.*

He had to explain. He had to find the words…somehow. He headed for the door before he could change his mind. He owed her another apology, and he'd start with that. Not for kissing her—he'd be damned before he'd be sorry for kissing her. But for letting her think he regretted it.

He found her inside, studying the contents of the kitchen cabinet, the nonperishables he kept the cabin stocked with. They hadn't bothered to bring food with them because he'd told his team the cabin already had enough canned goods to last them several days.

He glanced at Callahan still asleep on the bed. *Good,* he thought. *I don't need a witness to this.* He walked up to Keira, determined she wouldn't misunderstand this time. He took the can of beef stew out of her hand and placed it on the countertop. "I'm not sorry I kissed you," he said, softly but firmly.

She didn't respond, just turned back to the cabinet and brought down another can, green beans this time. He took that can from her, too. "Please, look at me."

She looked in his general direction, her face that same frozen mask he suddenly realized she hid behind when she was emotionally vulnerable. But her eyes wouldn't meet his. "Okay," she said. "You're not sorry. Point taken, message received." She didn't say it, but she didn't have to—he read her thoughts. *We have a job to do, so let's move on.* Then she said something she'd said to him once before. "Forget about it. I have."

He was damned if he would. And he *knew* she was lying.

He moved, trapping her against the countertop, and her eyes flared at him as she tilted her head up, finally meeting his eyes. He'd expected anger, but that wasn't what he saw. He saw the vulnerability she struggled yet failed to hide…and something else. It was the something else that gave him hope. In a breathless voice she asked, "What do you think you're doing?"

"Kissing you again." He didn't give her a chance to escape. This time it wasn't a kiss of exploration, of discovery, of seduction. It was a kiss designed to apologize, and he put his whole soul into it. All his aching regret for every bruise she wore because of him, all his longing to prove that wasn't the way he thought of her, joined the pent-up yearning for a woman to care for him as passionately as he would her.

She resisted at first—a token resistance—but then she surrendered...by inches. Desire flooded him as her body softened against his incrementally. Then her hands gripped his shirt, and at that point the kiss changed. The yearning, the aching need rose to the top, and he pulled her closer, wrapping his arms around her as if he could make her his woman that way. As if he could stake his claim to her just by kissing her.

He wanted. Needed. Yearned. His hands clasped her hips and pulled her closer so she couldn't help but feel his desire. But this wasn't about sex. Not at all.

He wanted to lay Keira down in a field of grass with a breeze rippling through it, the wide, blue Wyoming sky arching overhead and the sun warming their skin. He wanted to undress her slowly and have her do the same to him, as if they had all the time in the world. He wanted to kiss away every bruise he'd inflicted and swear to her there would never be another. He wanted to stroke her skin, to caress her until she cried his name and pulled him close, needing him as he needed her. He wanted to watch her eyes with their gold-tipped lashes as he came into her, wanted to make her face come alive with the same desire he ached to share with her. And he wanted to lay with her afterward, his head pillowed on her breasts, passion spent but still waiting to reignite.

But all he could do was kiss her. Endlessly.

She pulled away from him so suddenly that at first he tried to force her back into his arms. Then he heard it, too—a loud yawn from the bed in the corner that indicated Callahan was waking up—and he abruptly let her go.

They stared at each other for timeless seconds, their breathing ragged. Cody saw a pulse beating in Keira's throat, and he longed to put his hand there, knowing the pulse beat for him. But he couldn't do that to her, not in front of Callahan.

She turned away first, her hands gripping the countertop for a moment before she got herself under control. He watched, amazed at how quickly she transformed from warm, vibrant Keira to cool, collected Special Agent Jones. He didn't realize he was doing the same thing, that the face he was showing her held nothing of the turmoil inside him.

Movement from the direction of the bed made him look away from Keira and watch Callahan come awake and alert; Cody realized with a jolt just how close he and Keira had been to having a witness to the interlude between them. He suppressed a surge of unreasonable anger at the other man for being there. *It's not Callahan's fault,* he reminded himself. *You had no business starting something with Keira you knew damn well you couldn't finish.*

His body didn't want to hear it. He was still hard and aching, his arousal obvious…and painful. And however much he willed it, he couldn't make it go away. With a muttered curse under his breath, Cody turned and headed for the back door, the only escape available to him. He slammed out the door, and the cool outside air washed over him as soon as he walked out, a welcome relief to his heated body.

Spring came late to the Big Horn Mountains, although earlier than to the Rocky Mountains in the western part of the state. But Cody had been here when it snowed in July, and it was only the end of May. He breathed deeply and adjusted the fit of his jeans. He tried to drag his mind off thoughts of Keira, needing to regain the control he'd let slip so badly. But it wasn't easy.

The back door opened behind him, and Cody turned to see Callahan descend the steps, stretching a little to work the kinks out. He looked better than he had before he slept, but nothing would ever make him look anything but what he was—a hard man willing to make the hard sacrifices he'd made in his life. And one of those sacrifices had almost cost him Mandy.

"Get enough sleep?" Cody asked.

"Enough for now. I'll sleep again tonight." He rotated one shoulder, then the other. "Anything happen while I was unconscious?"

Cody shook his head. He wasn't about to tell Callahan anything about kissing Keira, and other than that... "No, but I didn't tell you something you probably need to know," he said. "Something that happened in Denver yesterday." He succinctly relayed the story about being followed, about recognizing the tail as someone who'd been following him even before Callahan's call.

"Keira said— I'd already thought of it, but she suggested my name might be on the militia's hit list. That the guy tailing me might be scoping out ways of taking me down, same as you."

"I wouldn't be surprised." Callahan laughed softly.

"They love me only a little more than they love you, which is to say—not at all."

"Yeah." Cody turned away and stared at the muddy clearing around his cabin, but he wasn't seeing it; he was seeing the events of long ago. "I thought it was all over six years ago," he said honestly, "until I got your call."

"How do you think I feel?" Callahan's voice was cold. "You think I would *ever* put Mandy at risk? You think I would have let her get pregnant with one child, much less three, if I thought there was a chance—" He broke off. Out of the corner of his eye, Cody saw the other man clenching and unclenching his right fist.

Cody turned to him and began, "I told Keira—Special Agent Jo—"

Callahan cut him off. "Don't bother."

Cody bristled. "What's that supposed to mean?"

"Let's just say that when I'm awake, I'm awake. The yawn was to let you know."

Cody absorbed that statement in silence. His initial deep embarrassment over having his kiss witnessed by Callahan was overcome by a fierce surge of protectiveness for Keira. He knew he had to explain, or else Callahan might get the wrong idea about her. "It's not what you think," he said. "It just happened. She's a fellow agent and a damned good one by all accounts—D'Arcy and McKinnon think the world of her." He took a quick breath. "There's nothing between Keira and me. Not the way it might have seemed if you saw us."

Their eyes met, and Cody was surprised to see not condemnation in Callahan's face, but understanding. "It happens like that sometimes," he said softly, nodding. "I knew the first minute I saw Mandy."

Cody's immediate response was to deny Callahan's assertion, but then, unbidden, his thoughts flew to his first sight of Keira, and an intense pride in her rose in him. *She* wouldn't beg for mercy. *She* wouldn't give those animals the satisfaction of seeing her cry. No, his Keira would die fighting, the same way he would.

He stopped his thoughts in their tracks. *His* Keira? What the hell was he thinking?

"It's not what you think," he repeated, but he wasn't sure if he was saying it to Callahan or to himself.

"Try that one on someone more gullible," Callahan advised. "I saw the way you looked at her." He waited for Cody to accept that brusque statement, then added, "You can fight it all you want. It won't do you any good, but you can damn well try. I did."

Cody thought of Mandy, remembering how he'd watched her fall in love with Reilly O'Neill, and remembering also—although he hadn't acknowledged it at the time—how O'Neill had tried his best to resist her, for her own good. It hadn't mattered. O'Neill had been just as helpless under Mandy's spell then as Cody was under Keira's now.

He remembered other things, as well. How he'd tried to comfort Mandy one terrible New Year's Day when she was grieving over what she'd thought was the death of this man and the very real loss of the baby she'd been carrying back then. How she'd wept in his arms afterward as if her heart were breaking. How his heart had broken, too.

Then a startling realization swept through him—that memory no longer had the power to devastate him as it once had. Losing Mandy to Callahan was still a bruise on his heart, and always would be. But another emotion, one he recognized but wouldn't name, surged up in him—and it didn't have a damn thing to do with Mandy. "But—"

"Just don't let it get in the way of the job," Callahan

interrupted him. "You can't fight what you feel. But you *can* lock it away. I know."

Cody accepted Callahan's stricture in silence, knowing the other man was right. *Damn him!* He hadn't been able to stop thinking about Keira since that first night. He'd tried…and failed to control his growing attraction to her.

But if Callahan, who loved Mandy with a singleness of mind and heart and soul, could walk away from her to protect her, Cody could do the same with Keira. He could lock away his desire, place it where it wouldn't put her at risk. Because a man whose emotions governed him grew careless of his surroundings, as he'd already proven. And he couldn't afford to be careless, not where the team—not where *Keira*—was concerned.

"You're right," he told Callahan eventually, although he had to drag the words out. "Thanks."

The other man shrugged. "I owed you" was all he said.

Cody started to ask for what, and then he remembered. A long drive in the dead of night with this man at his side, and a promise extracted from him against his will. A promise that he'd take care of Mandy if Callahan didn't survive that night's deadly encounter with David Pennington. A promise that would have destroyed Cody because he'd known by then that Mandy would never love him, *could* never love him as she loved Ryan Callahan. But he had promised.

God had been kind—Callahan had survived, and Cody had been spared the cruelest fate a man could face. Even being shot by Mandy wasn't as bad as what could have happened to him.

And now there was Keira. He realized with a start that he finally understood where Callahan had been coming from when he'd forced that promise from him. Because if anything happened to him, if Keira was in danger and he wasn't there to rescue her as he had once before... Cody couldn't even bear to think of it.

Keira thought she was tough, and maybe she was. She could take care of herself under normal circumstances, maybe even under fire—she'd been a marine after all, same as him. But the New World Militia wasn't a normal circumstance—not by a long shot. And wanting to protect her had absolutely nothing to do with whether or not she could protect herself.

His right hand clenched as coldness descended on him. Anyone who touched Keira was a dead man.

Chapter 9

Keira dumped the contents of three cans of beef stew and two cans of green beans into a large pot, placed it on a burner of the propane stove and watched it as it heated. Most likely the men wouldn't care she'd combined the cans, and it was faster this way, less to clean up afterward.

But she wasn't thinking about the food, even as she stirred the pot. She was thinking about Cody. About his kiss. *Kisses,* she amended. The one outside that had roused her physically so that she hadn't cared about anything but having him touch her. And the one in here that had roused such powerful emotions it had wreaked havoc on her heart.

Her body still ached with unrequited desire from both kisses. She hadn't realized a woman could *hurt* that way, the way a man could. That her body could *need* fulfillment and release. And she hadn't realized how deep the well of her own passion was. Cody had done that to her, had awakened desires that didn't fit with the accusations thrown at her by back-to-back high-school boyfriends— that she was frigid, sexless. Accusations she'd come to believe and accept about herself. Until now.

Cody's first kiss had awakened her body. His second kiss had awakened her heart. And while the first kiss had taught her what it meant to want a man, strong and virile, to hold her in his arms and ignite the fire, it was the second kiss she would remember forever.

At first she had tasted his contrition, but that hadn't lasted long. Then she'd tasted his desire, and it was a potent aphrodisiac, taking her places she'd never dreamed of going. When Cody had kissed her, she'd had a vision of the two of them in the middle of nowhere, nothing but the blue sky above them. Then his golden head blotting out the sun, his vivid blue eyes alight with passion.

When he'd pulled her hips into his and she'd felt him against her softness, she had suddenly wanted to lie down with him looming over her, his lean, muscled body taut against hers. She had wanted to slide her hands across those muscles and make him tremble as he made her tremble. And she had wanted—*needed*—him inside her, driving for release, both his and hers.

Not sex. Any man could have given her that. She wanted Cody—his smile that melted her heart, as well as his passion that melted the ice. She wanted him to fill the emptiness inside, a place she hadn't even known existed until he showed her what need was. She'd been *that* close to completely losing control, not caring where they were or who else was around. Then Ryan Callahan's yawn had impinged on her consciousness, and she'd been shocked…and dismayed at herself.

Cody hadn't wanted to let her go. She hugged that knowledge to herself with a secret smile. He'd resisted her first attempt to free herself, not realizing why she was trying to put distance between them. And then…when she was finally free, his face had momentarily told her all the things she wanted him to say before he shut himself down the same way she'd done. But she still wanted him. Even though she'd regained control over her treacherous body's actions, the need Cody had engendered in her was still achingly alive.

The stew was hot; Keira turned off the flame and checked the cabinet for dishes. She found a couple of mismatched plates, three chipped bowls and a half dozen coffee mugs. She smiled. *Someone must love coffee.* It was a little thing, but she added it to her store of knowledge of Cody, which was growing hourly.

She already knew a lot about him, for a man she'd only met for the first time a week ago. Some of what she knew she owed to Trace. She'd tried to word her questions as they'd driven together in the wee hours of this morning so he would think she was only interested in learning what she could about the New World Militia, but she hadn't fooled him. Her partner knew her too well, and he had been unexpectedly forthcoming.

Trace hadn't asked, and she hadn't volunteered, why she also wanted to know whatever he could tell her about Cody from a personal perspective. Now she listed the things she knew about him in her head.

He was thirty-seven. Trace had given her that little tidbit along with the information that Cody had gone to work for the DEA after leaving Black Rock. That was a thankless job, she knew. Like trying to empty an ocean with a thimble. A couple of her friends from the Marine Corps had gone to work for the DEA when they got out. Neither man had lasted a year. She wondered how long Cody had lasted there. Trace hadn't known and couldn't tell her.

He'd been in the Marine Corps, too, like her brothers, like her partner. And like her. *Semper Fidelis.* People who hadn't been in the Corps didn't realize the bond it created—"Corps and Country" *wasn't* a meaningless phrase. Not to a marine. Dedication and loyalty *meant* something.

He carried a knife in addition to his service weapon. She'd seen him use it that first night to pry open the warped window. *He didn't get that from the Corps.* As she had the first night, after she'd realized he was an agent, she wondered if he wore the knife everywhere or just when he was on assignment.

He had a good sense of humor and could laugh at himself. That was always a good sign. And he refused to take credit for someone else's accomplishments, even minimizing his own contributions. Hadn't D'Arcy said Cody was involved in bringing down the New World Militia, along with Callahan? And hadn't Cody dismissed his part as relatively unimportant? But Trace had told her enough this morning to know Callahan couldn't have done the job on his own—Cody had played a crucial role.

He also had a very strict moral code and held himself to a higher standard than most men. Despite everything she said, he still blamed himself for hurting her the night he'd rescued her. And at the same time he'd sacrificed his covert op—who knew how many hours had been invested in it—to save her, a stranger. That was part of his moral code, too, special rule seven notwithstanding.

And he had almost died six years ago. He made light of it, even joked about it with Mandy. But Trace had been there that night, after the fact, and in the truck he'd told her it had been a very near thing for the onetime sheriff.

Yes, Keira told herself with a smile she couldn't repress, *I know a lot about Cody already.*

Cody and Callahan walked in the back door just then, and Keira quickly heaped the two plates with the combination stew and filled one of the bowls for herself.

"You've got to be starving," she said, laying a spoon on each plate.

Callahan took a plate. "Yeah," he said. "Looks good. Thanks."

Cody took the other plate and told Keira, "There are only two chairs. You and Callahan can sit at the table. I'll stand."

"I don't mind," she said quickly.

"My cabin, my rules." He smiled to take away the sting.

Keira sat across from Ryan Callahan and watched him covertly as they ate in silence. From time to time she glanced from him to Cody, standing by the kitchen sink, and back again. She thought it was just habit, at first; always wanting to know what made people tick. But then it came to her. *You're trying to see what Mandy sees in him,* she told herself with a shock of revelation. *To figure out why Mandy would choose him—or any man—over Cody.*

She couldn't see it.

Oh, Ryan Callahan was physically intimidating, she'd give him that. But no more so than Cody, whose strength she'd experienced firsthand. And Callahan had impressed her earlier with his ability to move as quietly as a jungle cat. But Cody had great stealth, too. He'd slipped silently across the bedroom of the shack that first night, with her kidnappers in the next room, to pry open the window for their escape.

And whereas Callahan was saturnine and displayed a cynic's view of the world, Cody was golden-haired with an unexpected grin that lit up his face and made you want to smile, too. Somehow you just *knew* the world was a better place when Cody smiled. *No,* she thought, *Mandy must see her husband differently than I do.* She had to, if she was willing to kill her best friend—to kill *Cody*—to protect him.

Callahan stood abruptly, the chair rasping across the floor, breaking Keira's train of thought. He went to the stove to refill his plate. He offered the pot to Keira first, but she shook her head. She was nearly full and still had some left in her bowl. Cody allowed Callahan to add half of what remained in the pot to his plate. Then Callahan scraped out the last of the stew, placed the pot in the sink and ran water in it.

He didn't come back to the table, but stood next to Cody and asked as he ate, "What time do you think McKinnon will get back?"

Cody looked at his watch. "It's just over two hours to the agency's safe house in Casper—say two and a quarter. Figure another hour to get your family settled in and squared away, and a couple of hours back. Five and a half hours at the least. My guess is somewhere between three and four." He looked at Callahan. "About the same time the backup team will be done at your house."

"You're sure the safe house is safe?"

"There are no guarantees in this world," Cody said with a level stare. "You know that. But I know the agents who run that safe house. Even stayed there once on an op. You're going to *have* to trust some people unless you decide to hole up in a cave somewhere."

"Fair enough."

Cody resumed eating and said, "I told Keira while you were sleeping we need to head to where we at least have internet access. We can't do much of anything here."

"I won't be much help in that investigation," Callahan said. "Steve was my only link to the new militia, and he's dead. Unless we can figure out what his last words mean or what that key opens…"

His face expressed his frustration at not knowing as well as his desire to *do* something. Keira knew he wasn't the kind of man to sit patiently on the sidelines while others ran the football. But at this point there wasn't a lot he *could* do.

"I don't even know who else might be a member locally," he growled. "For all I know, one or more of my deputies might be involved. The militia is that insidious."

"That's why I'm leaving McKinnon with you," Cody said. He held up his hand as Callahan started to protest. "It's not open for debate. We can't afford to have anything happen to you. Not if we ever solve Tressler's murder and want to bring his killer or killers to justice. You'll need to testify."

That silenced Callahan. Keira could tell he wasn't happy about it, believed he could take care of himself now that he didn't have to worry about his family. But a man who always calculated the odds, as she'd already realized Callahan did, knew that he couldn't always be on guard, knew that he'd have to sleep sometimes.

"He'll need a cover story to stay with you," Cody said. "And you'll need an explanation for why Mandy and the kids are gone."

"I'll come up with something," Callahan said. "Don't worry." Finished eating, he turned to wash his plate and the pot in the sink. He stacked them neatly on the dish rack, and Keira thought with a tiny inward smile how incongruous he looked doing mundane kitchen chores. When Cody followed suit, her smile grew. Neither man even thought of leaving KP—kitchen patrol—for her to do, and a good thing, too.

She quickly scraped the last bite out of her bowl, washed it and followed the two men out the front door. Cody was leaning against the porch railing; Callahan was standing at the bottom of the stairs. Both men were staring outward, at the forest that surrounded the clearing around the cabin's perimeter.

Callahan was saying, "I never cared for the isolation of this place. Hated being out of my element the first time Mandy and I stayed here." He turned to face Cody and Keira, a rueful smile on his face. "I was a New York City boy...until I came to Wyoming."

With a twinkle in his eye, Cody said, "You didn't do too badly...for an amateur."

Callahan's booming laugh lightened his face, and Keira suddenly realized what Mandy saw in him. In many ways he was a lot like Cody, just more cynical in how he perceived the world. She wouldn't pick him *over* Cody, but...she could see the attraction.

"So am I ever going to hear that story?" she asked. When both men turned inquiring expressions toward her, she explained, "You rag each other about being amateurs. But you're both highly trained professionals—anyone can see that. So what's the story?"

The smiles faded from the faces of both men and Keira knew she'd asked the wrong question. *Mandy,* she thought suddenly. *It has to do with Mandy somehow.* "Never mind," she said before either man could respond, wishing she'd never opened her mouth.

"Ancient history," Cody said lightly, but Keira could tell the lightness was an effort.

"Then tell me about the New World Militia. I've heard bits and pieces from Trace and you," she said quickly, looking at Cody. "But I'm not getting the full picture. And I think I'm going to need it."

Cody glanced at Callahan. "You want to tell it?"

"How much have you already told her?"

"Just about taking Pennington down, the trials and a few other things. Your former partner, for one."

Callahan's tawny eyes narrowed, an attempt to hide a flash of pain, and Keira realized the cold exterior he projected to everyone but his family was a facade. *He cares,* she thought with insight. *Steve Tressler. Josh Thurman. He can be hurt. That's what Mandy sees in him, too.*

"It's not pretty," Cody continued. "But she needed to know the kind of people we're up against."

Callahan nodded. "Okay." His hand indicated the porch steps. "You might want to have a seat. The whole story will take a while."

The sun was well advanced in the sky by the time he finished. He told the story succinctly but well, and occasionally Cody threw in a comment or two to elaborate on some point Keira could see he felt Callahan wasn't giving enough detail on. Keira hadn't had to ask many questions.

She sat quietly afterward, her chin propped on one hand, thinking. Then she asked both men, "So if the militia was shattered six years ago, how is it possible it's been revived so quickly? Especially without Pennington's money."

"You see that, too? It's a good question." Cody looked at Callahan, who nodded.

"It all comes down to the money," Keira said. "No terrorist organization can survive without it. Look at al Qaeda. Look at the Irish Republican Army, the IRA. Look at FARC," she said. "No matter how fanatically someone believes, without money it all falls apart. Follow the money trail."

"That's first on the list as soon as we get out of here," Cody confirmed.

"We already have something on that," Keira reminded him. "Remember that super PAC I mentioned in D'Arcy's office yesterday, NOANC? In the last election every senator and congressman on the list he gave us received campaign support from it. Not direct contributions—super PACs are prohibited from donating money directly to any political candidate. But they *can* raise unlimited amounts of money from any source and spend that money to openly advocate for or against any political candidate—and they did. We *know* they were the deciding factor in at least three elections, and Trace and I had just started digging." She looked at Callahan. "Ever hear of it?"

He shook his head. "What does it stand for?"

"National Organization for the Advancement of New Ideas—NOANC."

"Sounds pretty vague."

"Yes," she agreed. "Trace and I couldn't find out much about it or what they stand for in the short time we've had to work on this. But super PACs have to report their donors to the Federal Election Commission at least quarterly. NOANC received thousands of donations from individuals all over the country, so it sounds fairly grassroots, except..."

Her eyes widened with sudden excitement as she made the connection, and she could hardly get the words out. "Except for one thing. There were huge donations every year from a limited-liability corporation—an LLC. The Praetor Corporation."

Cody and Callahan looked at each other, puzzled. "*Praetor* is Latin," she said. "Like *veni, vidi, vici*. It has two meanings," she explained, her eyes sparkling. "One of them is an elected official, a magistrate. The *other* meaning is the commander of an army." She looked from one man to the other, her face alight, willing them to follow her logic. "Don't you see? It's *got* to be connected somehow."

The two men stared at Keira, then at each other. "I think she might be onto something," Cody said, his expression reflecting his growing belief that Keira was right—there *had* to be a connection.

Callahan nodded slowly, and a tiny smile started in his eyes. "It's a good working theory anyway."

"We have to get back to Denver," Keira told Cody with a sense of urgency. "I don't just need internet access. I need access to government data banks I can't get into except through the encrypted connection at the agency." She pulled a notebook from her back pocket and started jotting down notes to herself on things she wanted to check, everything forgotten except the job at hand.

The silence made her glance up. "What?" she asked, looking at the two men, realizing they were both staring at her in rueful discovery.

Callahan answered for both of them. "Walker was right," he said softly. "Guts *and* brains. You can't beat that combination."

Keira flushed but made a quick recovery. "You're just now figuring that out?" she said, raising her chin in a challenge.

Cody cast a look at Callahan. "That puts you in your place," he said with a grin.

"Like you weren't thinking the same thing?" Callahan growled back at him.

Chapter 10

McKinnon returned just before four, and Cody quickly brought him up to speed on the revised plan. "Makes sense," he said. "But what's my cover story?"

Cody glanced at Callahan. "Whatever the story is needs to explain why he's shadowing you, but what?"

Callahan smiled at McKinnon. "That one's easy. Pick a small town from some other state, become its newly elected sheriff and say you're here to learn how to operate your department more effectively."

When McKinnon looked doubtful, Callahan explained, "We met each other at the New Sheriffs' Institute last month—I taught two of the training sessions, so that part is based in fact. Anyone who knows me, knows where I was last month. The New Sheriffs' Institute is a weeklong training program put on by the American Sheriffs' Association specifically to train first-term sheriffs from all across the country. It's an ideal cover and even explains why you're staying with me—your department's limited budget won't stretch to cover living expenses."

McKinnon looked at Keira. "Do you see anything wrong with that story?"

She shook her head. "It sounds plausible."

"Sounds good to me, too," Cody said. "Since there's nothing more we can do here, I think we'll head back to

Denver tonight—the sooner the better. We'll leave our gear and the truck with you, McKinnon, and take the SUV. We'll get in late, but we can switch off driving and nap along the way."

They left a half hour later. The sun was already setting behind the mountains, and Cody turned on the headlights before setting the cruise control for five miles above the speed limit. He drove in silence at first while Keira continued to make notes in the rapidly dimming light. When it got too dark to see, she sighed, sat back against the seat and slid her notebook into her pocket.

"How long do you expect Trace to stay with Callahan?" she asked. "That cover story won't work for more than a couple of weeks at the most."

Cody considered her question. "I don't know. It all depends on how much manpower D'Arcy is willing to assign to the case and what we can uncover about the New World Militia in that time. It's possible Tressler's death doesn't have anything to do with the militia—although I doubt it. It would be too much of a coincidence. But if Callahan and McKinnon solve the murder, then the immediate danger will be over. It doesn't resolve the issue of the hit list, but..."

"It would be a start," she finished for him.

"Yeah."

Keira yawned unexpectedly. "Sorry," she said. "I guess last night is catching up with me. Maybe I should nap now, so I can drive later."

He cast her a sideways glance and realized she looked tired...about as tired as he felt. But they still had more than five hours of driving ahead of them, so it was probably a good idea for her to nap even though part of him wanted her to stay awake so he could talk to her.

But what would he say? Callahan had told him he couldn't fight what he was starting to feel for Keira but he could lock it away, and he'd agreed it was what he should do. *You just don't want to,* a little voice inside his head told him.

Should he tell her Callahan had witnessed the kiss they'd shared in the cabin? *Bad idea, Walker.* She'd already been embarrassed enough when he'd confessed he'd told Callahan about how they'd met. She'd be devastated to learn the other man had seen the two of them in a compromising situation. Keira was so sensitive about being taken seriously as a member of the team, she might even request D'Arcy remove her from the case. And that was the last thing he wanted.

Cody let his eyes stray from the road in front of him for a second and saw that Keira was already asleep. *She must have been more tired than she would admit,* he thought with sudden tenderness. In sleep her face was soft, sweet and defenseless, and he knew she would hate it—would hate knowing he'd seen her vulnerable again.

The corner of his mouth twitched into a half smile. *Guess that will have to be my secret.*

Not quite two weeks later Cody sat in his office staring at his computer screen, but his thoughts were only partially on the document he was skimming. The other part of his mind was miles away, wondering how Callahan was holding up without his wife and children, wondering how Mandy was doing without her husband.

Callahan had been right—Memorial Day had come and gone with no trouble from the New World Militia. But he had adamantly refused to let Mandy and the children return home, insisting it wasn't safe for them, especially since McKinnon was going to have to return to Denver Sunday—his cover story had lasted for two weeks, but beyond that was going to look suspicious.

"I can take care of myself," Callahan had told him when Cody had suggested sending another agent to guard him. "But my family can't come home. Not until we know who killed Steve Tressler. Not until we know what he tried to tell me before he died and what that key opens. It's been almost two weeks, damn it, and we don't know any more now than we did then!"

The statement wasn't quite true. The backup team that had cleaned up Callahan's house had determined the original crime scene *was* Tressler's cabin, just as Callahan had surmised. They'd returned the body there but left it in his truck, as if he'd tried to drive away but died before he could. Callahan and McKinnon had "discovered" the body and had opened an investigation into his death as if Tressler had never appeared at Callahan's house, as if he'd never had a chance to utter those cryptic words.

There were more agents assigned to the case now. The original two backup teams D'Arcy had dispatched to Buffalo and Sheridan had been joined by two dozen more teams spread across the country. And Cody now spent most of his time coordinating everyone's actions and reading reports generated by the agents in the field rather than doing any fieldwork himself.

In all this time they'd managed to uncover a whole lot of…nothing. Yes, Callahan had been correct. The New World Militia *had* risen like a phoenix from the ashes of six years ago. But they hadn't uncovered any evidence to link it to illegal arms stockpiling, drug trafficking or any of the activities the militia had been involved in before. In fact, if Tressler hadn't been murdered the way he had, D'Arcy might have pulled the plug on the investigation. But he *was* dead. And somewhere there was a clue as to why. They just had to find it.

Cody was still careful, of course; he hadn't imagined being tailed two weeks ago. He alternated his route to and from work every day, so if anyone *was* following him, they wouldn't be able to latch on to a pattern and plan an ambush. And he watched his rearview mirror constantly. He'd never again seen the guy who'd been tailing him before he went to Wyoming, although he knew that didn't mean anything—the militia could easily have any number of different people switching off following him. But the urgency he'd felt when Callahan first called him was no longer there.

And he wasn't complaining about his current job, even though he'd always hated being chained to a desk in the past. There was something to be said for going home at a decent hour and getting a full night's sleep. Not to mention having time for a social life.

A social life. That was a bit of a misnomer, when the woman you were courting seemed oblivious to your overtures, and you had to resort to stratagems to spend time with her away from work.

Pathetic, Cody thought with a rueful laugh. He'd quickly learned Keira was a tigress when she was working a case, especially when she was onto something. But ever since they'd returned to Denver, he'd managed to spend time with her nearly every weeknight. The first week they'd discussed the case as they grabbed a bite to eat after work before heading their respective ways.

Then a week ago he'd surprised her with an invitation to a lecture on "Crime in the New Millennium" on the campus of the University of Colorado on Saturday afternoon. He'd carefully picked something he knew she'd have trouble turning down, and she hadn't. And he'd avoided treating it like a date, although he *had* talked her into having dinner with him afterward.

They'd had a great time that evening sharing their different takes on the lecture. But when he'd tried to get her to open up about herself, she'd steadfastly refused to go below the surface, adroitly steering the conversation into other channels when it got too personal.

Sunday he'd invited her to go to the shooting range with him, and although she'd hesitated, she hadn't refused that invitation, either. They'd made it a challenge to see who could score more points in a variety of competition rounds. Cody had been secretly amused at how competitive Keira was and how much joy she'd gotten out of beating him—joy she was hard-pressed to hide. Losing to her hadn't dented his ego. He knew if the competition had been knives instead of guns, she wouldn't have been able to hold a candle to him.

This past week she hadn't even hesitated about accepting when he'd invited her to dinner every night—she'd almost seemed to be expecting it. But now it was Thursday. One more day and the weekend loomed before him. *You're running out of excuses,* he told himself. *Maybe you'd better just tell her the truth.*

The truth. That was a good one. The truth was…he didn't know what the truth was. He just knew he wanted to be with her no matter what, even if it meant taking a desk assignment to make it possible.

He wanted to listen to her arguing with herself and him about what she liked to call "next steps." He'd shared the field reports with her as they came in, and at first she'd devoured them as he did, searching for clues that might trigger a breakthrough. But lately she'd seemed distracted, as if the information they contained wasn't crucial to the case.

He wanted to watch her face come alive as she animatedly discussed theories of the case, what she was uncovering and what it meant. Although the past few days she hadn't said much of anything, almost as if she didn't want to jinx whatever it was she was onto by saying anything about it.

And he wanted—desperately wanted—to take her to bed. That physical obsession had grown until it was now a constant ache, just barely contained. Cody was finding it increasingly difficult to lock away how he felt, especially since Keira was there…every day…just a few feet away from him at times. So close. And yet, an impossible distance away.

It was easier for Callahan, he thought. *When he let Mandy think he was dead, he didn't have her around as a constant reminder…and a temptation.*

Cody knew he'd changed over the past two weeks in ways he couldn't reconcile with his conscience. He'd never considered himself an alpha male—the leader of the wolf pack. Those were the Callahans of this world.

But ever since that day at his cabin, when he'd acknowledged that anyone who touched Keira was a dead man, he'd realized he didn't know himself as well as he'd thought. In addition to his obsession with her, he could now add a dangerous possessiveness. Dangerous, because his growing frustration was telling him to just take, whether or not she wanted to give. And that wasn't him at all. That had never been his style with women.

His protective instincts where Keira was concerned

didn't apply to him—he wanted to protect her from everyone and everything—except him.

Just tell her the truth. Right. That'll work like a charm, Walker.

Keira pressed the "print" icon to send the last document to the secure printer, then locked her computer and rose from her desk. She stood by the printer, keyed in her pass code to release the documents, then drummed her fingers impatiently as the documents printed, one by one, forming an impressive stack. She could hardly wait to show Cody what she'd uncovered. He'd be just as excited as she was, and he'd be so proud of her he'd have to—

Have to what? she asked herself sharply, knowing all the while what the answer was.

He'd *have* to respect her. He'd *have* to admit she wasn't the weak link on the team. Wasn't that what she'd been thinking in the back of her mind all this time, ever since that day in his cabin in Wyoming? Proving herself to him? Making him respect her? Making him proud of her?

And why?

Keira picked up the stack of documents and walked slowly back to her office. She sat down and sorted the documents into a logical order, stapling certain pages together before placing everything in a file folder, as if she could distract herself by focusing on the case. But that wasn't going to work—not anymore. Not now that she'd solved a major part of the puzzle.

Maybe you can hide it from everyone else, she told herself with brutal honesty, *but you can't hide it from yourself. You want him to be proud of you because...*

Because she was falling in love with him.

She stared at the folder for a minute, her stomach churning along with her thoughts. She'd managed to suppress her wayward emotions for the past two weeks, sublimating what she now acknowledged as her growing love for Cody into her investigative zeal. But in her lonely bed at night, she'd cherished every moment they'd spent together, reliving in her mind his words, his smile and the way he looked at her when he thought she wasn't watching.

Not to mention the way he'd kissed her at his cabin. The way her body ached for his touch so that she tossed and turned on her pillow every night before falling asleep and dreaming of him. The way her treacherous thoughts kept wandering down sensual pathways she'd never realized she wanted to follow.

She just hadn't let herself focus on any of those things when Cody was around, because she didn't want him to know how she felt. Not until she'd proven herself to him. Not until she regained the self-respect she'd lost when she'd needed him to rescue her.

He'd never touched her since that day at his cabin, but she knew he wanted her—she could see it in his eyes, could feel it emanating from him. And now... Keira took a deep breath as a secret smile began to form. She tucked the file folder under one arm and headed for the elevator.

Cody frowned and made a notation on his spreadsheet, a meager clue for one of the agents to follow up on. A sound made him look up from his computer. Keira was standing in the doorway to his office, a thick file folder under one arm and the expression on her face a dead giveaway...to him, at least. "You've got something," he said immediately.

"I had to pierce the corporate veil on three shell companies, but, yes, I do." She closed the office door behind her. "Does the name Michael Vishenko mean anything to you?"

Cody frowned. "No. Should it?"

"Would it mean something if you knew Vishenko was his mother's maiden name?" A tiny smile teased the corners of her lips, and her eyes were electric. She put the file folder down on his desk, facing him, and flipped it open. "Marriage certificate for Mariella Vishenko thirty-five years ago...to David Pennington."

"What?"

She turned a page. "New York birth certificate for Michael Pennington, thirty-four years ago. Parents, David and Mariella Pennington."

"Pennington had a son?"

"Mmm-hmm." The second page followed the first. "Divorce decree for Mariella Vishenko from David Pennington, thirty-two years ago, cause of action—desertion." Another page was turned over. "Petition the same year for a name change of a minor child—from Michael Pennington to Michael Vishenko. And there's nothing in the record to indicate Pennington objected."

Keira's air of suppressed excitement told him there was more. "Guess who inherited Pennington's fortune when he died? And although he stays far away from the day-to-day operations, guess who—through three shell corporations—owns the Praetor Corporation?"

"Wait a sec." Cody held up one hand. "I thought Pennington forfeited his fortune under RICO," he said, referring to the Racketeer Influenced and Corrupt Organizations Act, under which a racketeer forfeited all ill-gotten gains and any interest in a business gotten through a pattern of racketeering activity.

Keira's eyes sparkled. "Yes, but Pennington's conviction was overturned, remember? And he died before he could be retried. In essence that means he was never convicted under the RICO Act. Which means—"

"His fortune went to his heirs, not the government. Damn! Why didn't we know this?"

"The FBI knew." She riffled through several pages until she found the report she wanted, a copy of an official FBI document. "Here," she said, handing it to him.

Cody scanned it quickly. "Damn!" he said again. "What else did the FBI know?"

"Michael Vishenko has no criminal record—a clean slate as an adult. But..."

"But you found something. What?"

"A juvenile arrest, no conviction. Guess who intervened on his behalf?"

"Pennington?"

She shook her head. "No. As far as I can tell, Pennington wasn't involved much in his son's life. It was Michael Vishenko's uncle on his mother's side, Aleksandrov Vishenko. You might know him better by his nickname, Alexei Vishenko."

Cody felt himself go cold. "The Russian mob? You're telling me the New World Militia is hand in glove with the Russian mob now?"

Keira's eyes lost their excitement, and her face took on a solemn expression. "They always *were* connected to the Bratva—the Brotherhood," she said softly. "You just didn't know it."

"Oh, my God." Cody sat back in his chair, staring up at Keira, his brain racing. Disconnected facts suddenly started falling into place like a chain of dominos. Pennington resurfacing with a sizable fortune—from where, no one knew—only a few years after his release from Leavenworth after being cashiered from the Marine Corps. Arms dealing. Thefts of military-grade weapons.

Suspected ties to one of the most powerful drug cartels in the country—the Russian mob? "Why didn't anyone make the connection before this?"

Keira's eyes hardened. "Someone did," she said.

Cody froze. "Who?"

She pointed to the file on his desk. "There's an FBI report in there, dated nine years ago, detailing the possible connection. The author of the report was killed—under suspicious circumstances—three weeks later. And the report was buried." She took a deep breath. "The FBI doesn't know I have that report or any of the other reports I got from their files—at least, I don't think they do."

"How did you get them?"

One corner of Keira's mouth quirked upward. "Didn't you know the agency has a secret data link directly into the FBI's mainframes in Washington?"

D'Arcy, Cody thought with admiration, in his mind hearing his boss say, *I have my own sources within the FBI...and a few other places....*

"Do you know who suppressed that report?" Whoever had been responsible had to be involved, and Cody knew Keira was as aware of it as he was.

She spoke a name that seemed vaguely familiar to Cody, but he couldn't place it, and his eyes asked the question. "He was the SAC of the FBI's New York Field Office Criminal Division," she said, using the abbreviation for *special agent in charge.* Her voice dropped a notch. "He retired from the FBI five years ago and went into politics. He's the junior senator from New York now, one of the campaigns we already know was won through the intervention of NOANC—and the Praetor Corporation."

A web within a web within a web, he thought. "What else have you got?"

"It's all there in the file." She took a deep breath. "We need to tell D'Arcy. And I think Callahan needs to be told his name isn't on that list because he's the sheriff." Keira's dry tone conveyed that no one had really thought this, least of all her. Then she added in a voice that wasn't quite steady, "And I'd bet anything you want to stake they're gunning for you, too."

Chapter 11

"**N**o bet," Cody said lightly. He picked up the phone and dialed a number. "Special Agents Walker and Jones need to see the boss as soon as possible. Is he free?" He listened and glanced at his watch. "We'll be there. Thanks." When he hung up, he told Keira, "Have a seat. We've got an appointment in twenty minutes."

She sank into one of the chairs in front of his desk. "Are you going to wait to call Callahan?"

"No." Cody started to pick up the phone, then thought better of it. He opened his drawer and pulled out the encrypted cell phone he'd used in Wyoming, the one he hoped couldn't be traced back to him. He punched in a number. It rang and rang, but no one picked up. "Damn, where is he?" He let it ring a few more seconds, then hung up and dialed another number. This time it was answered.

"McKinnon," said a voice in his ear.

"It's Walker," he said crisply. "Where's Callahan?"

"Shift change. He's briefing the deputy going on duty."

"Tell him to call me immediately. It's urgent."

McKinnon asked guardedly, "Keira found something?"

"Yeah." Cody wasn't surprised at how McKinnon had worded the question. Keira's partner had been right about her. She'd managed in less than two weeks to pull to-gether assorted bits and pieces and assemble them into a complete—and deadly—picture. *Even D'Arcy couldn't have done a better job,* he thought. "Would you believe a tie-in between the militia and the Russian mob? And not just now—back then, too."

McKinnon cursed softly and fluently. Then he said, "Tell her— No, I'll tell her myself. I'm a lucky man to have her as my partner. I'll have Callahan call you as soon as he's free."

A click in his ear told him McKinnon had hung up. He disconnected, too, hearing McKinnon's words again. *I'm a lucky man to have her as my partner.*

Cody gazed at Keira sitting across the desk from him, her red-gold curls tousled as if she'd been running her fingers through them as she worked, and realized the truth of those words far beyond what McKinnon had intended. Any man who had her in his life in any way was a lucky man.

And he wanted to be that man. Not as a working partner—no. What he wanted was so much more. He wanted to be *the* man in her life, the only man who counted. And he wanted her as his woman, so much it took his breath away.

The cell phone shrilled in Cody's hand, and he almost answered it automatically with his last name until he remembered this wasn't his official cell phone. "Yes?"

Ryan Callahan's voice growled in his ear, "McKinnon said to call you. Said you've got something I need to know."

"Yeah. Keira found it." He quickly relayed the facts she'd uncovered, as well as the conclusions she'd drawn from them. "It all fits," Cody said. "The money, the way the militia was revived so quickly, the political tie-ins, everything."

"A nice, neat little package," Callahan agreed. "You realize what this means?"

"Yeah. It's not going to be as easy as it was last time."

"You got that right. Damn!" said the man on the other end. "If I'd known…"

Cody knew, as if he could read Callahan's mind, that the other man was thinking about Mandy…and their three children. Callahan had walked away from Mandy once to protect her. Now she wasn't the only one at risk. Now he had three children he loved as much as he loved Mandy, all of them equally in danger because of him.

"Does D'Arcy know?" Callahan asked.

"I've got an appointment to see him in—" Cody checked his watch "—nine minutes."

"Whatever it is, I want in," Callahan said grimly.

"It's not your responsibility, not anymore," Cody said. "You've done your duty."

"This isn't about duty, and you damn well know it," Callahan responded in that implacable voice Cody remembered all too well. "This is my *family* at stake."

"I'll see what D'Arcy says." But even as he said the words, Cody knew Callahan wouldn't abide by D'Arcy's ruling…unless it was the outcome Callahan wanted. "I've got to go," he said. "Keira and I don't want to be late."

"Keep me in the loop."

"You know I will."

Cody hung up, glanced at his watch and locked his computer. Then he picked up the thick file from his desk and stood up. "Let's do it," he told Keira.

As they rode up in the elevator, Keira asked, "What did Callahan say?"

"He wants in."

"You didn't have to tell me that," she said drily.

"I understand where he's coming from—I'd feel the same—but..."

"But he's a civilian," Keira finished for him.

"Yeah." Cody glanced her way. "I don't know how we'd manage to keep him out, though. If we didn't include him, he'd just go his own way. I know him."

"Then we'd better find a way to include him. Better to have him on the team than taking the law into his own hands and maybe getting in our way."

Cody chuckled ruefully. "Practical Keira," he said, smiling down at her.

She smiled back. "I try to be."

Their eyes met, and suddenly Cody wasn't thinking about the case. It was still there in the background, looming over them, but in that instant he was focused on Keira, and the way her brown eyes and her mobile mouth softened when she smiled.

She must have read something in his expression because her smile faded as she gazed up at him. Cody saw a flash of some emotion in her eyes in response before she shut it down, but he was better able to read her now. Just as he'd known earlier she'd uncovered something crucial to the case, he knew she wasn't as indifferent to him as she pretended.

He took a step closer to her just as the elevator doors opened. *Damn!* he thought. *Now's not the time.* But he resolved he wasn't going to put it off any longer. *Tonight,* he told himself. *I'll talk to her tonight.*

He just wasn't sure exactly what he was going to say.

D'Arcy was standing in the outer office talking to his executive assistant when they walked in. "Walker, Jones," he greeted them. "You're right on time. Come on in." He led them into the inner office and closed the door behind them. "Before we start on this, you'll both be happy to know we had a positive resolution on Walker's earlier case."

Cody shot a sharp glance at D'Arcy, then at Keira to see how she would react. "Thank you, sir," he said, noting the expression of relief on Keira's face. It had obviously been bothering her she'd inadvertently caused the failure of that original sting operation. "My partner did happen to mention it the other day." *Hell, I probably should have told Keira,* Cody thought, even though he knew she didn't have an official "need to know." But he should have known it had been eating at her—she was that kind of agent.

"Good," D'Arcy said. "So, what have you got on this case?"

Cody waited for him to sit behind his desk. "It's Keira's story," he said, handing the file to D'Arcy before sitting down himself. "She'll tell it better than I can."

Keira flashed him a questioning look, and Cody wondered if she thought he'd try to take credit for her work. That had never been his style, but maybe she didn't know it, so he smiled encouragingly at her. "Tell him what you told me," he said.

She did, but Cody noticed the animation she'd had in her face and her voice when she'd recounted what she'd found to him was missing. This time she was the consummate dispassionate professional agent, reporting to a superior officer.

When she was done, D'Arcy sat back, holding the FBI report from nine years ago in his hand, perusing it. He read it through twice before putting it back in the folder. "Suspicious circumstances?" he asked.

"Yes, sir," Keira responded promptly. "The author of the report was killed as he walked home from the subway. It looked like a simple mugging, but there was one thing that stood out to investigators at the time. His wallet was taken, but he was wearing an expensive gold watch and a wedding ring, neither of which was touched. The case was never solved, even though the FBI supposedly threw the resources of their office behind the investigation."

"Supposedly?" D'Arcy asked, unerringly focusing on the most crucial element of her statement.

Keira nodded. "I can't find a record of anyone in the FBI's New York office being assigned to the investigation, but...the SAC reported to *his* superiors that the investigation was ongoing."

"In other words," he said, voicing what they were all thinking, "the SAC—who is now the junior senator from New York—buried the report connecting the New World Militia to the Russian mob, arranged for the author of the report to be killed, and hindered the subsequent investigation into the murder."

"Yes, sir," Keira confirmed.

"Great. Just great." D'Arcy swiveled his chair away from Cody and Keira, staring at the far wall. "No wonder," he said softly to himself.

"Sir?" she asked.

"That was the last unanswered question I had from six years ago," he said, turning a cold face to her. "Brooks betrayed Callahan's partner, Josh Thurman, to the militia, but he never would say how he knew—that information was compartmentalized, and he shouldn't have known anything about Thurman. Now it all makes sense."

He added softly, "And here's something you might know, but maybe not. Brooks was killed in prison less than a year after he and Walsh began serving their sentences. Shanked by a fellow inmate in the prison yard.

And Walsh died—ostensibly from a heart attack—four months later."

"So, someone got to them…on the inside," Cody said. "Sounds more like the Russian mob than the militia."

D'Arcy frowned. "Doesn't matter either way. They're both dead, so neither one can add anything to the official record." He looked at Keira, then back at Cody. "So, what's your plan now?"

Keira glanced at Cody, shaking her head slightly, and he knew she was telling him she wasn't prepared with an answer. She'd uncovered the critical links, but…

"The Praetor Corporation is the key," Cody said, an idea coming to him. "Pennington's son—although he goes by the name Michael Vishenko, he's still Pennington's son—owns the company through a series of shell corporations. Keira already found the link between it and NOANC. But there's got to be a paper trail between the Praetor Corporation and the Russian mob, as well as between the Russian mob and the New World Militia. We just have to find it."

"Any ideas?" D'Arcy asked. "And how do those last words of Callahan's neighbor tie in? What about that key he gave Callahan?"

"No ideas yet," Cody told him. "We haven't figured out what Tressler's words mean, either, or what the key is for. But there's something you should know. Callahan wants in on the investigation."

D'Arcy picked up the FBI report again and looked from it to Cody. "We owe him," he said grimly. "The FBI recruited him to go undercover with the militia in the first place. He sacrificed his career and risked his life to put Pennington behind bars. He trusted us—*me*—to protect him when he went into the witness security program. We failed him." His voice was filled with savage self-recrimination. "*I* failed him."

He paused to gain control of his emotions. "The militia—or the Russian mob—had men inside the FBI, inside the U.S. Marshals Service. Because of that, Pennington had Thurman, his wife and his baby son murdered trying to get to Callahan."

His face was colder than Cody had ever seen it. "Anything Callahan wants, he's entitled to. Keep that in mind. Just remember…"

"Yes, sir," Cody said, knowing what D'Arcy was going to say. "This is *my* case. I won't forget."

It was after six when Cody and Keira wrapped up for the day. Cody called Callahan, and although she only heard Cody's side of the conversation, she could imagine what the other man was saying.

"You're in, but remember the agency is running the show. You can't let your emotions get in the way," Cody warned. "We have to be professional about this." He laughed at something Callahan said before he hung up.

Amateur, Keira thought, *I'll bet that's what Callahan said that made him laugh.*

Before she could think about it, she asked, "So, are you ever going to tell me what 'amateur' means when you and Callahan say it to each other?"

"How'd you kn—" he began, looking from the cell phone to her.

"The way you laughed," she said simply. "It's the same way you laughed before when he said it to you, and the way he laughed when you said it to him."

Cody drew in a deep breath and expelled it slowly. "It's not something I'm proud of, but I guess you have a right to know."

"Only if you want to tell me."

"Not here," he said. "Not in the office."

"Where?"

He gave her a steady, considering look. "My place?"

She thought about it for a second, then shook her head. "My condo?"

He nodded slowly. "Okay. Want to pick up some dinner on the way?"

"If you want to eat a decent meal, you're going to have to," she said with a wry smile. "I can open cans and heat up frozen dinners in the microwave, but my mom despaired of teaching me to cook."

Cody smiled back. "Let me guess. None of your brothers can cook either. Right?"

"How'd you know?"

"Ahhh, that would be telling," he teased her.

Keira's eyes narrowed, but playfully. "Trace has a big mouth."

Cody held up his hands in mock protest. "You didn't hear it from me."

"You asked him about me?" Keira was curious. "When?"

Cody's playful smile turned rueful. "In the truck on the way up to Wyoming."

"Oh." Keira's heart skipped a beat as she realized what this meant, what it *had* to mean. *Even before he kissed me,* she thought, a frisson of excitement running through her veins. *He was interested even before that.*

Cody raised a hand as if to touch her cheek, but stopped himself. "I wanted to know about you. Who knows you better than your partner?"

"You could have asked me."

Cody shook his head. "I doubt it. I've been trying to ask you for almost two weeks, but…you never tell me anything about yourself. You always change the subject." His eyes held hers and wouldn't let her look away.

"Is that what…?" she asked, her heartbeat picking up the pace. "I knew you—" She stopped herself just in time before she said, *I knew you wanted me.* "I didn't realize…"

He nodded, totally serious now. "Before we go any further, we need to talk about the agency's rule on fraternization."

"You're not my supervisor," she said quickly.

"I know that. But I *am* the agent in charge." He hesitated. "Up 'til now I've told myself the time we've spent together is related to the case. Maybe I was stretching things a bit, telling myself what I wanted to believe, but…"

"You're not my supervisor," she reiterated, raising her chin and giving him a fierce look. "That's the only hard-and-fast rule against fraternization—and we're not breaking it."

He stared down at her, one corner of his mouth teasing up into the little half grin she loved. "Okay," he said finally. "Okay. But first I need to tell you some things about me. Things you're entitled to know. Then…" He left the rest hanging, as if he wanted to leave Keira an out, just in case.

Keira searched his face, his eyes, and her breath quickened. There was so much she longed to know about him, so much she wanted to ask. Maybe tonight she'd get the answers she needed. *Maybe tonight's the night for other things, too.*

Part of her was afraid. Not of anything he might do to her, but of what she might reveal to him. And what she might learn about herself. But part of her wanted this, wanted *him,* as much as he seemed to want her. "Let's get dinner," she said before her courage failed her.

They finished the Italian take-out dinner in the small dining area of Keira's condo and tossed the trash. "Want some coffee?" she asked, pretty sure she already knew the answer if the number of coffee mugs in his cabin meant anything. "I can't cook, but I make good coffee."

"Sure."

"I seem to recall you prefer regular, not decaf."

He smiled. "Night or day, it's the same. I prefer the jolt of caffeine."

He stood in the doorway of her tiny kitchen, dwarfing it, watching as she made the coffee. "Black, no sugar, right?" she asked when the pot was nearly finished brewing, feeling just a little flustered at his looming presence...and his silence.

"Right."

She took a large coffee mug from the cabinet, filled it, and handed it to him. He took a sip and made a face of appreciation, then took a larger swallow.

"Let's go into the living room," she said, turning off the coffeemaker.

"Aren't you having any?" Cody asked.

Keira shook her head. "Not at this time of night. But it won't go to waste. I'll reheat it in the morning." She laughed at his look of horror regarding drinking coffee that wasn't brewed fresh, then led him into the living room and indicated the sofa. For a minute she was undecided whether to sit in the armchair, but then—boldly for her—sat next to him, just an arm's length away.

"Amateur," she encouraged softly. "You were going to tell me...."

Cody looked away for a minute and put his half-empty

cup down on the coffee table in front of him. His face reflected his indecision, but then his expression hardened.
"There was a time when Callahan hated my guts," he
said finally. "And I felt nearly the same about him, just
for a different reason."

His eyes met Keira's. "I'd loved Mandy all my life up
to that point—you already know that much. But I had
to watch her fall for O'Nei—Callahan—when he moved
to Black Rock through the witness security program."

He rubbed the side of his face, obviously uncomfortable with the memory. "Callahan didn't know how I felt
at the time. I don't think Mandy knew, either—not then.
Not until…" He broke off.

"Anyway, Callahan didn't hate me when he first
moved to Black Rock. We respected each other pro-
fessionally, and worked together just fine. We probably could have been friends if not for…well, anyway, he
didn't grow to hate me the way I hated him until a long
time later. I don't blame him, though—I would have
hated me, too, under the circumstances."

"Why?"

One corner of his mouth twitched into a sad travesty
of a smile. "Because I slept with Mandy."

Chapter 12

"**O**h." It hurt, more than Keira had thought possible. She'd known there was *something* between the two men. And she'd known somehow it involved Mandy. But hearing Cody confirm her suspicions caused a physical ache in the region of her heart.

"She wasn't his wife at the time," Cody continued, his lips twisting. "But I'm not making excuses. On some level I knew it was wrong...and I did it anyway. The only thing I can say in my defense is that I didn't plan it...at least not consciously."

"So, what happened?"

"It's a long story. Are you sure you really want to hear it?"

She nodded, struggling to keep condemnation or any other negative expression out of her face. "I'd like to understand...if you want to tell me."

Cody stared into the distance. "It started almost eight years ago," he said. "Some other people you know were involved, too—D'Arcy and McKinnon."

"Trace did tell me some things," she offered.

"But he couldn't tell you this story because he doesn't know it. Not the important parts, anyway."

"Then, you tell me," she said softly.

Cody thought for a moment, as if he were trying to

find the right thread to begin. "It's a bit involved. I was the sheriff in Black Rock, but I was also working undercover in the militia way back then. Some people were openly members of the militia, but I wasn't. My code name in the militia was Centurion." He laughed humorlessly. "Pennington picked the name. He thought it was clever. Maybe it was."

He breathed deeply. "D'Arcy knew I was undercover. He was responsible for Ryan Callahan, and it was his idea to send him to Black Rock after Pennington's trial, and Callahan agreed. I know I already told you D'Arcy figured if Pennington somehow tracked Callahan down, I'd get wind of it and would be able to warn him."

She nodded.

"It actually worked out better than that—when Pennington located Callahan I was given the assignment of eliminating him. But I'm getting ahead of the story."

His eyes took on a faraway expression as he looked into the distant past. "You already know Callahan came to Black Rock under an alias—Reilly O'Neill. He fell for Mandy. Hard. It was the same for her. Two months after they met, they…became lovers."

Keira closed her eyes momentarily at the pain in Cody's voice, a pain she felt twisting inside her.

"Some of this I inferred by what happened later. Neither of them actually told me, of course, but I…I had my suspicions early on. Mandy never was good at hiding how she felt. And even if she'd wanted to, I don't think she could have hidden it from me. I knew her too well."

He stopped and took a deep swallow of coffee, then stared down into the cup. After a minute Keira said, "Go on."

"Callahan had been in Black Rock about six months when Pennington tracked him there. I was ordered to kill him, but not just in any way I saw fit. Pennington was obsessed with seeing Callahan in hell—a vow he'd made after Callahan testified against him and put him in jail—so Callahan *had* to die by fire.

"D'Arcy, McKinnon, Callahan and I set it up to fake Callahan's death. We rigged his truck with explosives, and D'Arcy even arranged for a cadaver to be burned in the truck." He grimaced at the memory. "We also had a fake autopsy report all ready, identifying the corpse as Callahan, to make it more realistic."

Cody paused for a moment. "Callahan was afraid that if Pennington had tracked him down once, it could happen again, so he insisted we not tell Mandy. He said he'd rather give her up than risk having anything happen to her." A wry smile played over Cody's lips. "That's the throwback part of him. In his world a man doesn't put the woman he loves in jeopardy. Even if it means breaking her heart." The smile faded.

"We planned it for a Saturday, Mandy's busiest day at her bookstore. Neither of us counted on her showing up at the reservoir where she thought Callahan was working, where the explosion was set to go off."

Keira's gaze was glued to his face. "Why? Why did she show up?"

Cody's expression was grim. "She went there to tell him something. Something important. She just didn't get there in time."

"So, what happened?"

"She saw the explosion from the road. She thought Callahan was inside the truck. She crashed trying to reach him. She lost their baby. She almost lost her life." The choppy little sentences were spoken without emotion, but Keira knew Cody was bleeding inside.

A long silence followed, and Keira waited patiently.

Then Cody said, "Callahan had to disappear for the deception to work. D'Arcy had arranged for federal marshals to whisk Callahan away to safety immediately after the explosion. McKinnon was one of them. For security reasons, I wasn't told where he was going. But everything was in place to convince Pennington that Callahan was dead, and that I'd obeyed orders. We, none of us, considered how Mandy would take it, and Callahan didn't find out about the crash…or the baby, until a year later."

"So she lost the man she loved, and she lost his baby," Keira said, trying to imagine what Mandy had gone through. Now that she'd witnessed firsthand the love between Ryan and Mandy Callahan, the enormity of what Mandy had to have felt swept through her, leaving her more shaken than she wanted to admit. "If I were Mandy I wouldn't want to live," she whispered under her breath, but Cody's sharp ears heard her.

"Yeah, that's exactly how she reacted. I was there when she regained consciousness in the hospital. I didn't have to tell her—she already knew. But…" His eyes darkened with remembered pain.

"Part of me was tempted to tell her Callahan was still alive, but would that have made it any easier on her with him gone? To know the explosion was faked, that her desperate attempt to save him was meaningless? That her baby didn't have to die?"

Keira blinked against the prickling sensation that was a precursor to tears, and waited until the sensation subsided. "No," she confirmed softly. "It wouldn't have been any easier to bear."

"I don't know what I would have done if I'd been in Callahan's situation," Cody said. "His choices were limited. Maybe I'd have done the same thing—I just don't know. But Callahan had decided Mandy needed to be protected, no matter what. He chose to leave her, chose to let her think he was dead. He didn't know...."

He drew in his breath sharply. "Mandy says I should have found a way to tell her the truth. Callahan says he trusted me to watch over her while he led the wolves off the scent. I was damned either way."

"A no-win situation," Keira agreed.

"All Mandy's friends were worried about her after Callahan 'died,' not just me." Cody's next words came out harshly. "She lost weight. She wasn't sleeping. She looked like hell. We were all afraid she'd—" He broke off, obviously suffering with the memory.

"Suicide?" Keira asked, feeling she already knew the answer.

Cody nodded reluctantly. "She'd tried once before, in the hospital right after it happened. I don't think she really intended to...but...we were all still afraid for her afterwards." He fell silent, and Keira knew he was back in that time, reliving the events as they occurred.

Then he picked up the thread of the story. "It started snowing the day before New Year's Eve—a real three-day blizzard. As sheriff, I always checked on the local residents when there was bad weather, especially the most vulnerable ones, the ones who lived alone."

Keira could see where this was heading. "So you went to check on Mandy."

"Yeah. New Year's Day. I should have sent one of my deputies," he said roughly, "but I...didn't."

"What happened then?"

"Mandy had downed the remains of a bottle of whiskey the night before. She told me she just wanted to sleep for once without having nightmares. She wasn't drunk that next morning, but she was in bad shape emotionally." Cody's gaze was turned inward, and Keira knew he blamed himself for everything that followed.

"There's some excuse for Mandy—Callahan was dead, or so she thought. I knew he was alive—there's no excuse for me." His eyebrows drew together in an expression that combined both self-condemnation and honest bewilderment. "Callahan once accused me of planning it. I've gone over it in my mind a thousand times since then, and I don't think I did, but...who ever really knows why we do what we do?"

He swallowed hard. "Mandy was grieving, and I loved her. I just wanted to...but it was the worst mistake of my life. Afterward, she wept as if her heart was breaking. God!" he said. "I never want to hear a woman cry like that again, especially if I'm the cause."

He was silent for so long Keira finally asked him, "Then what?"

"Then Callahan returned for Mandy almost a year after his 'death.' He'd had plastic surgery to disguise his face, but he had no way of knowing his cover was already blown, that his 'death' had already been revealed as a fake. Pennington's conviction had been overturned by the appellate court, the prosecutors were panicking because without Callahan there was no case left to prosecute, and D'Arcy had no choice but to disclose to them that Callahan was still alive, still available to testify."

He looked at her, his eyes bleak. "Remember what I told you, and what D'Arcy said about Larry Brooks betraying Callahan's partner, Josh Thurman? D'Arcy still didn't know Brooks was in the militia, and he dispatched Brooks and McKinnon to bring Callahan in. As soon as he heard Callahan was alive, Brooks informed Pennington, and I had to do some fast tap dancing to explain how it came about I *hadn't* killed him the year before."

Keira thought about asking him how he escaped Pennington's wrath, but decided against it. She wanted to hear the end of this story first.

"Brooks firebombed Mandy's house on Pennington's orders to get Callahan. It almost worked. Everyone thought Mandy was dead—only Brooks and Pennington knew the real target was Callahan, and they thought he was dead, too. Callahan figured it was safer for Mandy and him to play dead until he could work out a plan. They hid out in my cabin—just as they did after Tressler's death." He sighed. "Most of the rest of the story you already know. But Callahan and Mandy almost didn't reunite...because of me."

Keira knew she had to ask. "Who told him?"

"I think Mandy intended to, but before she could find a way, he guessed. He confronted us, and...I...I told him the truth." He shook his head and added softly, "He deserved to know. It wasn't right not to tell him—I know how I would have felt. But he's a proud man. Very possessive of Mandy."

"That had to hurt him where he was most vulnerable."

"Yeah." Cody's tone indicated this was a gross understatement. "Even worse, he still needed my help setting the trap for Pennington. It galled him—I know that—but he didn't have much of a choice. It wasn't just his life at stake. It was Mandy's, too. And despite everything, he still loved her."

Keira carefully digested what Cody had told her. While it still hurt to think of how much he had once loved Mandy, she honestly believed he hadn't planned to seduce her that fateful New Year's Day. Cody just wasn't that kind of man. It happened; he regretted it; he accepted his responsibility. But he couldn't change it— he just had to live with it. He could even put himself in the other man's shoes and say he didn't blame Callahan for hating his guts.

But Cody wasn't quite finished. "Callahan still loved her. And she…she never loved anyone but him. So I told him," he added in a low voice.

Keira turned a perplexed face toward him. "Told him what?"

Cody smiled crookedly. "The other truth Callahan deserved to know."

"I don't get it."

"I told him Mandy cried…after I made love to her."

"Oh, Cody." Her tender heart, the one she hid from the world, ached for him, for the wound to his pride… and his heart. But she was also fiercely proud of him. What other man would have done it? What other man would have pocketed his masculine ego, suppressed his own love for a woman, to atone for something he hadn't planned but still blamed himself for? She couldn't think of any man…except for him. It was another reason to love him. Another in an ever-growing list of reasons.

She wanted to cry for him, but tears were one of the things she'd denied herself for years. And besides, tears weren't what he needed right now. He needed to know she understood. She put her hand on his, curling her fingers and squeezing to let him know she empathized with what he had gone through. His hand turned so that it was clasping hers, and she stared at it for a moment. Her hand looked so small wrapped in his hand.

But there was still something she didn't get. "You've told me this whole story," she said, with a puzzled expression on her face, "but you still haven't explained what 'amateur' means."

Cody's smile turned rueful. "Six years ago we were so caught up in the hostility between us we both acted like amateurs. Not once, but twice. We knew better, and we knew it could have gotten either or both of us killed, along with Mandy. But it didn't stop us. It's just a subtle reminder, that's all."

His smile faded away. "Callahan doesn't hate me anymore—he's forgiven me. So has Mandy. And I've forgiven myself."

Keira wasn't sure this last part was true. Cody would always carry that scar on his conscience—it was the way he was made.

"And I no longer love Mandy," Cody went on. "At least…not that way. She'll always be a good friend—you can't wipe out thirty-seven years of friendship—but that's all. So I don't hate Callahan, either." He hesitated, drew a deep breath, and exhaled slowly. "I just envy him."

A tiny sound of pain escaped Keira, and she drew her hand away as she averted her face, wanting to hide from Cody how much it hurt to think….

"No," he said, capturing her chin and forcing her to look at him. "I don't envy him *Mandy*. Not anymore." His blue eyes darkened. "I just envy what he has with her. It's what I've always wanted, but never thought I'd find after I lost her."

He released Keira's chin, and his fingers slid up, over the curve of her cheek, brushing the curls away from her face before sliding back and tracing the shell of her ear. Keira shuddered at the unexpectedly sensual touch and caught her breath. She wanted to close her eyes, to let herself just *feel,* but something in his eyes held her spellbound.

"And then…" he whispered, his voice dark and deep, his fingers trailing down her neck to the hollow of her throat where a pulse beat wildly. "And then I met you. And I realized that's what I want to have…with you."

Keira couldn't take it in at first, but it was all there in his face. Love and longing, possessiveness and…hope. She caught her breath again, and this time her eyes closed against the tumult of emotions that swamped her. *He loves me,* she told herself, and the moment was sweeter than she'd ever imagined it could be.

She leaned toward him, but he didn't kiss her as she'd expected. He didn't even draw her into his arms. Her eyes flew open, and she saw he was waiting—waiting for a word from her that she felt the same way.

Cody had bared his soul to her. Could she be any less honest with him? "When I first met Mandy," she confessed in a low voice, "all I could think about was how much I wished I could have what she had. That I could love someone the way she did. Then later, when I saw Callahan with her, saw the way he loved her with nothing held back, I thought to myself, 'Cody would love like that.' And even though I wouldn't admit it to myself then, I wanted to be loved that way…by you."

She knew her heart was in her eyes, but somehow it didn't matter. If she could trust him with her life—and she did—she could trust him with her heart. "Love me," she whispered. "Please…"

Then she was in his arms, and it was like the first time he'd kissed her. Desire flashed to life, and Keira exulted in the knowledge that he wanted her this much, but that he'd been strong enough to hold himself back…until now.

He stood, pulling her to her feet with him, just looking down at her for a long moment, his hand caressing her cheek. Then he bent and swept her into his arms. At her faint protest he smiled at her, his eyes blazing, and carried her into her bedroom. Keira's hands crept up around his neck, and for the first time in her life, she accepted that it was okay to feel small and helpless—but only in Cody's arms. He laid her on the bed and followed her down, his body hard and urgent.

Chapter 13

Cody's hands were caressing her everywhere. Strong hands, but curiously gentle at the same time, and Keira knew he was remembering the bruises that had long since faded, determined there would never be another. Not from him.

She didn't care about that. She just loved what it said about him.

Since he couldn't be, she became the aggressor, tugging his shirt from his jeans, popping the buttons free with an impatience she didn't recognize in herself, but didn't question. She wanted his bare skin beneath her hands, wanted to glide her fingertips over his taut muscles, wanted to make him tremble as he fought for control…and lost it.

His belt was next, then the zipper of his jeans. She couldn't suppress a gasp as she freed him: hard, throbbing and impossibly large. She stroked him, hesitantly at first, but with a stronger, firmer grip as she gained courage, loving the way he swelled even larger and the way her touch made his breath rasp in his throat.

His hand caught hers and pulled it away. "Don't," he said in a strangled voice, and Keira knew he was dangerously close to the edge.

"I want to," she whispered, her breath deserting her

as she thought about making him come this way, about making him lose that iron control.

"Not this time," he managed, making it a promise for the future. Their future. Then he was undressing her, and it was the seduction she'd imagined, only more. While his hands caressed, he whispered in her ear everything he wanted to do to her. His words as much as his hands aroused her to the point where she ached to have him inside her, to assuage the need he'd created.

Her hands tugged at his hips, telling him what she wanted without the words she was suddenly too shy to say. But he wouldn't be hurried. His fingers parted the petals of her womanhood, and she gasped, arching toward him.

She knew he could feel the dampness there, so she didn't understand why he still held back. Instead, one long finger slid inside her, then out again, drawing the dampness up and over the unbearably sensitive nub he found. He rubbed up and down, again and again, occasionally dipping back inside and out again.

Keira couldn't bear it. Her nipples were so tight they ached, and the pressure building in her loins, in her whole body, was so unexpected she moaned. He soothed her with soft whispers. "Shh. It's okay. Let it go." His lips captured one nipple, and his tongue rasped against it, circling around and around, sending shards of electricity throughout her body.

His fingers were still weaving their magic, and she moaned again. This time his lips captured hers, swallowing that moan and the ones that followed. Her breathing grew shallow and hurried, and still his fingers kept stroking her unbearably. She wanted…she wanted….

Then everything her body had been building toward suddenly exploded, and she arched against the seductive hand that had done this to her, clinging to Cody's arms and crying out his name as the throbbing sensation went on forever.

She floated down to earth, her one thought that she couldn't bear any more, that her body couldn't take it. But she was wrong. Blood pounded in her ears, and her breathing was ragged as Cody removed his hand and fitted himself in place. He whispered her name, and her passion-drugged eyes opened—she hadn't realized they were closed until that moment. He gazed down at her with that same expression of love and longing, joined by a fierce, possessive desire held firmly in check.

"Tell me," he demanded in a voice made harsh by passion.

How could she hold back the words that trembled on her lips...and in her heart? She reached up to cradle his face in her hands. "I love you, Cody," she whispered.

He drew a long, shuddering breath. As if he'd waited only for her avowal before continuing, he surged into her. Then froze. His shocked eyes met hers for a second before they squeezed shut in contrition.

The slight pain of his entry was already receding, replaced by the incredible sensation of having him embedded deep inside her, stretching her, hot and hard and throbbing. Keira didn't want him to stop. She'd die if he stopped. Her hands grasped his hips and pulled him closer. "Please," she begged. "Please..."

His blue eyes stared down at her, pain in their depths, and she could read his thoughts. So she said the only thing she could think of in that instant. "You'll only hurt me if you stop," she breathed. One hand slid down and touched him intimately. "Please...please, don't stop..."

His mouth descended, his kiss telling her everything she needed to know about how much he wanted her...

needed her. Instinctively she contracted her inner muscles around him, again and again, and he made a rumbling sound deep in his throat. Then he began driving into her, shallow strokes and deep, setting a pace she struggled to keep up with.

Without warning she caught fire again, and then she was racing ahead of him toward something just outside her reach. It grew bigger and bigger as Cody's tempo increased, and her body was out of her control. She'd wanted to make *him* lose control, but instead… Her hips thrust up at him to take him deeper as he held tightly and pounded into her. Then everything shattered, and she arched against him one last time as she cried his name, feeling him empty himself inside her.

Keira couldn't catch her breath. Her body was trembling, and she couldn't prevent it. Her inner muscles throbbed around his manhood, milking him in a way that seemed both foreign and natural to her.

And Cody lay in her arms, completely spent.

Time stretched out endlessly as she held him, and she smiled secretly to herself. She loved him, and now he was hers. He hadn't said the words, but they weren't important—they were just words. He'd shown her his love with his body, taking her to the mountaintop with him, but first letting her soar.

Keira's secret smile slowly grew until she could no longer keep it from her face. Her breathing finally slowed, and she began to doze off. Her high school boyfriends had been wrong about her, she thought as sleep claimed her. She wasn't frigid—in Cody's arms.

Cody came to only minutes after passing out. Keira was already asleep, but her breathing was shallow, so he knew she hadn't been asleep long. She whimpered slightly when he withdrew from her body, as if she missed him the minute he was gone. But she didn't waken.

He slid quietly from the bed and made his way to her bathroom. He stepped into the shower for a minute, quickly washing himself. Then he dried off with her towel. He ran the water in the washbasin until it was hot, held a washcloth under the stream, then wrung it out and brought it back to the bed with him.

He gently placed the warm, damp cloth between Keira's legs, and she caught her breath in her sleep. She made a little sound deep in her throat when he tenderly washed her, but it wasn't a sound of pain, and he was relieved. He obviously hadn't hurt her as he'd feared when he'd taken her virginity.

No, he corrected himself. *You didn't take it. She gave it to you.*

When he was done, he took the washcloth back to the bathroom. There was a smear of pink on the cloth, and Cody stared at it for a long minute before he held it under the running water and washed the blood away along with everything else.

She couldn't know what a priceless gift she'd given him. Not her virginity, but by calling his name both times when she climbed the peak. For a man whose heart and ego had been savaged when the only woman he'd loved called him by another man's name in bed, it was healing to know that Keira was only thinking of him at that moment. She wanted *him.* Only him.

Cody padded softly back to the bedroom and slid in bed next to Keira. He watched her sleeping for a minute—her face so unlike the usual one she showed the world when she was awake. And there was a tiny smile on her lips. Whatever she was dreaming, it made her smile. And that made him feel damned good.

He suddenly needed to hold her even if it meant waking her. He propped himself up against the pillows, then drew her unresisting body into his arms, cradling her against his chest as he pulled the covers around them. Her curls tickled his chin, and he breathed in the unique scent that was Keira—plain soap and water and warm woman. He wanted to hold her this way forever, especially now that he knew she loved him. Especially now that she was his.

He admitted to himself he had wanted her ever since that first night. Hadn't been able to erase the memory, even though he'd told himself time and again he had no business remembering anything about that episode other than the basic fact that it had happened. It hadn't done any good. His body had a mind of its own. It had remembered...and wanted.

He chastised himself sternly for the thrill of exultation that coursed through him now. It was primitive. Archaic. Sexist. He couldn't help it. Part of him was saying, *Mine. No one else's, ever. Mine.*

He didn't know why she'd still been a virgin at twenty-nine, but the reason paled in comparison to his primal male response to the fact. No other man had ever held her this way. No other man had known the soft, warm place between her thighs. No other man had ever heard her cry out in ecstasy. She'd given herself to him, and to no other. She was only and ever his.

Then and only then did it dawn on him he hadn't worn protection when he'd made love to her. His brows drew together in a sudden frown, and he cursed under his breath. Not because it mattered to him, but because it most certainly would matter to her...when she came to her senses.

He didn't think she was on the Pill or any other contraceptive. *Not likely, since she's not sexually active,* he thought. *At least she wasn't until you came along.* But it wouldn't hurt to ask. Still concerned about what this could mean for both of them, he watched as she woke up by degrees: first her eyelashes fluttered, then her nose crinkled, then her eyes flew open, and she blinked at him, as if she'd dreamed him.

"What time is it?" she asked.

He raised his wrist and squinted at his watch in the dim light.

"Nine-thirty-two. Plenty of time."

"Time for what?"

"Time to talk."

"Oh." She sounded disappointed, as if she was expecting a repeat performance already, and Cody smiled to himself.

He toyed with her curls for a minute, then idly let one curl coil around his finger. "Why didn't you tell me?"

She didn't pretend not to understand. "I didn't want you to know," she said in a small voice.

"Why?"

She didn't answer at first. Then she said, "I was... embarrassed. I didn't want you to think..." She shifted restlessly and added so softly he had to strain to hear, "My two boyfriends in high school...they called me a freak. They both said I was...frigid. Because whenever they touched me...that way, I froze. I don't know why, but I just *couldn't* bring myself to..."

She drew a sharp breath. "Then I went right from high school into the Corps. The only men I knew then were my fellow marines. I had enough trouble proving to them I was just as tough as they were. I wasn't about to let one of my hyper-sexed macho mates take me to bed…and then brag about it."

"Hey," he said softly, his hand pausing as he stroked her bright curls. "Not every marine brags. I never did."

She cuddled against him. "If I'd known you back then…maybe I could have…. But as it was, I just couldn't risk it."

"And then?" he asked in a deep voice.

"I spent four years in the Corps, so when I finally went to college I was four years older than most of the guys in my classes. They all seemed so young, so…callow… it just never felt right with any of them."

"And then you joined the agency right out of college," he filled in for her.

"Right. And you know how this job is. Odd hours, last-minute changes of plans. There aren't a lot of guys on the dating scene who'll put up with that for any length of time." She rubbed her cheek against his bare chest. "And besides…" she said softly.

"Besides?"

She laughed a little self-deprecating laugh. "Besides, every guy I went out with, I knew I could take him down, one on one." She laughed again, softly. "No woman really wants a man she can control that way."

"Oh, ho!" Cody teased. "The truth comes out. Do I hear the old-school double standard coming out of *you*?"

She hid her face with her hand. "I shouldn't have told you."

Cody's smile faded, and the teasing light left his eyes. He gently drew her hand away from her face and made her look at him. "I'm glad," he said. "Not just that you told me, but that…you chose *me*." He wanted to tell her how deeply he was affected, how much it meant to him that she had never given herself to any other man, just him, but he didn't know how to put it into words without offending her somehow. Instead, he said, "I just hope I can live up to your expectations."

"You did," she whispered, the love and admiration in her brown eyes confirming it. "You do." She sighed, a deep sound of contentment, and snuggled closer, as if she wanted to melt into him and stay part of him forever. She breathed words Cody didn't catch, but when he asked her to repeat them, she hesitated. Finally, reluctantly, she replied, "I said I'm not...frigid...with you."

"You're not frigid at all." The answer was so clear to him he marveled it hadn't occurred to her before. Maybe she'd been too young and too hurt by that pejorative term when it had been thrown at her, she hadn't seen the truth for what it was. "You just needed to find a man you could trust, that's all." And in his head he heard himself telling her that first night, "Trust me." And her immediate response, "I will."

She trusts you, he told himself. *That's the difference.* And the proof of her trust was just as sweet and precious to him as having her call his name when she climaxed. He swore in that instant she would never have cause to regret giving him her trust...or her love. He needed both more than he'd ever thought possible.

He allowed his hands to wander down to her breasts, cupping them, toying with the nipples until they tightened for him, and he smiled possessively before moving his hands down to the swell of her hips.

He loved her body. She hid her compact curves inside clothes that denied her sexuality, wanting to be taken seriously in her job. But they were there. And they were enticing to him. Never again would he see her in clothes and not remember this moment and the ones that had gone before. He would always remember the way her first orgasm had taken her by surprise. It made him feel both powerful and curiously humbled.

And until his dying day he would remember the little catch in her voice when she'd begged him not to stop. He hadn't wanted to—a primal part of him had wanted to keep going, no matter what, to possess her body in that most basic way—but he would have tried…if she hadn't pleaded with him not to.

She trusts you, he told himself again. *And she loves you.*

He stirred at the thought, swelling against her hip. He knew she could feel it, too, because her hand slipped down and touched him there. Then her fingers were stroking him, and he swelled even more. "Don't start—" he began, but then he groaned when her fingers encircled him and squeezed. "Keira…"

"Let me," she said. "I want to."

He let her have her way for a minute, and another, and another. Then he caught her hand. "Not yet," he said. "We still have to talk."

"About what?"

"About birth control. Or rather, the birth control we *didn't* use earlier."

"Oh."

"You wouldn't by any chance be using anything, would you?"

"No." She shook her head, then thought for a moment, her lips moving soundlessly as if she were mentally counting something. Then she said, "But we should be okay. I'm… It's not…"

Cody chuckled softly, pulling her tightly against his shoulder. "You know, doctors have a word to describe women who rely on the rhythm method of birth control."

"What's that?"

"Mothers."

"Oh, I…" She chuckled, too. "I see. Very funny."

He put his other arm protectively around her. "I wasn't planning this. I hope you believe that."

"I know you weren't." Her voice was soft as a sigh.

"I don't carry condoms with me everywhere I go. I know a lot of single guys do, just in case. But I don't."

She wouldn't look at him. "I didn't think you were that kind," she said gruffly, toying with the hair on his chest.

"So I need you to promise that if something happens—something we didn't plan on—you won't keep it from me."

She didn't answer right away, then said in a low voice, "I promise."

There was an ache in the back of his throat, and in his heart, and it didn't have anything to do with extracting a promise from her not to keep him in the dark if she ended up pregnant. The ache was for the sudden, unexpected yearning to see Keira with his child in her womb. Where had that yearning come from?

And was it something she wanted, too? He didn't know, and it didn't seem the right time to ask. But the more he thought about it, the more he longed for it to be true. He was thirty-seven, long past the time most men fathered their first child, but until now it hadn't been a priority. It hadn't even occurred to him. *Keira's baby,* he thought, tenderness and possessiveness warring for dominance. *Our baby.*

A savage surge of desire shot through him with unexpected force, and he was shocked to realize he didn't just want to make love to her because he needed her warmth and passion to bring him to life. And it wasn't just because he needed her love. A primitive, elemental part of him wanted to plant his seed deep within her, marking her as his territory so no other man would even *think* of touching her.

Cody had never felt this possessive before about any woman, and his lips compressed into a thin line as the sharp awareness tugged at his conscience. Keira didn't *belong* to him...not in that way. She was her own woman. She'd given herself to him, but that was *her* choice, not his. He'd always firmly believed it was a woman's choice whether she slept with a man or not. But that didn't stop the primal urge to claim her as his.

He clamped his jaw shut, restraining the primitive desire, and instead told her, "We're in this together. We'll work it out. Okay?"

"Okay."

But it wasn't okay with him. Not by a long shot. A savage, inner voice—the alpha wolf howling on the hillside—still insisted that Keira was *his,* damn it! *His* woman. His mate, body and soul. The future mother of his children. He wanted to put the stamp of possession on her so she'd know, so *everyone* would know.

She belonged to him. And he'd kill any man who tried to take her from him. It was that simple.

Chapter 14

Michael Vishenko limped to the plate glass window in the library of the Long Island compound he'd inherited from his father, and stared out into the night. Everything was finally coming together. "Six years," he whispered to himself. He'd waited six years to avenge his father, and even though it had just begun, the taste of it was already sweet.

His first impulse had been to hunt down his father's murderers himself all those years ago. But his uncle Alexei had talked him out of it. "You are not the man to do it," Alexei had said with brutal honesty. "You can kill some of them, yes. Any man can be killed. But you would not be able to kill them all before you were caught, convicted and sentenced to death."

His second impulse had been to ask his uncle to take care of it—the Bratva had men who killed in the blink of an eye. But he'd discarded that idea, too, as an admission of weakness. The indignity of the physical deformity he'd suffered since birth was bad enough. He had always refused to let that deformity define him—he would not let it define him in his uncle's estimation.

No, this way was best. It had taken longer, far longer than he'd wanted, but this way was sure. His father's money had smoothed the path, but his own brain had devised the means, his own determination had brought it about. Though other hands would do the actual deeds, the vengeance was his.

It had cost him a substantial sum to uncover the names involved, and even more to track them all down and keep constant surveillance on them, but it was worth it. From the federal prosecutors who'd first put his father in prison, to the men who'd murdered him, to the men who'd covered up the murder, the list was now complete. Soon they would be eliminated.

Callahan and Walker, DeSantini and Brockway, D'Arcy and McKinnon. Vishenko smiled coldly. Each one would die by fire. A deserving end—one his father would have appreciated and approved. He'd been a silent witness in the courtroom when his father had wildly shouted the words, "I'll see you in hell!" to Ryan Callahan. But it wasn't enough to just send Callahan to hell. The other five needed to join him in the inferno.

Then and only then would Michael Vishenko's father be avenged. Then and only then could he take back the name on his birth certificate—Michael Pennington—the name his mother had stolen from him the same way she'd stolen him from his father. Because then and only then would he have earned the right to bear his father's name.

Keira watched in silence as Cody dressed. More than anything she wished he didn't have to go, wished she could fall asleep in his arms and wake up the same way. But she knew he had to go back to his apartment. He needed to change for work tomorrow, if nothing else— he couldn't show up in the same clothes he'd worn today. Not that people noticed what men wore the way they noticed what women wore, but still…

She lay there with the sheet pulled up under her arms,

and as she watched him dress she realized there was something so elementally *male* about his actions. Men didn't dress themselves the same way women did—at least Cody didn't. There was an economy of motion to the way he shrugged his shirt on and tucked it into his slacks before decisively closing the zipper and buckling his belt.

He looked up and caught her watching him, and he grinned in that boyish way she'd come to love. He didn't say anything, just continued smiling as he sat on the bed to pull on his socks. When he picked up his boots and removed something from one of them, Keira saw it was a knife sheath.

"You *do* wear it everywhere," she said. "Not just on an op. I wondered."

He stopped short. "You wondered?" he asked. "Since when?"

"Since that first night," she confessed. She took a deep breath and admitted, "And like you, I asked Trace about you in the truck driving up to Wyoming."

The smile on Cody's face spread at her revelation. "I'm glad," he said, holding her gaze before turning his attention back to his boots. He tugged them on and slid the knife sheath neatly in place before he answered her original question. "Doesn't do me any good if I'm not wearing it when I need it," he explained, and she knew he was remembering that first night, and the use he'd put the knife to in their escape.

"Doesn't it bother you, though, wearing it in your boot?"

He shook his head. "I'm used to it. If I didn't wear boots it might be difficult, but as it is…" He shrugged.

"How…?" She wasn't quite sure what she was asking, but he seemed to know.

"I've been fascinated with knives ever since I was

a kid," he said. "My father gave me a shotgun for my twelfth birthday, but long before that I was teaching myself to throw knives. I know it's an arcane skill, like archery, but there's something satisfying about it I can't explain, so I don't even try."

He smiled faintly, and—not bragging, just stating a fact—said, "It might even be that I saved Mandy's life that way six years ago, and Callahan's, too. No way to know for sure—Callahan's pretty sharp with his .45, and he fired almost at the same time I threw my knife. But a knife has one thing a gun can't match, even with a silencer—it's whisper-quiet. And just as deadly."

"In the right hands," Keira qualified.

"Yeah," he agreed, and Keira knew even without him saying it that his hands were the right ones...and she wasn't just talking about knives.

He leaned over and kissed her, a long, lingering kiss that made her heart kick into overdrive. He gently tugged the sheet down, his gaze sliding down, too, and Keira's nipples tightened automatically. His lips brushed first one nipple, then the other, and he said, "No bruises. Good." His hand followed his lips, and as she watched, his expression changed from possessive satisfaction to intense desire.

Keira felt herself flushing, hating the way her complexion betrayed her at times. But she didn't try to tug the sheet back into place. What would be the point? And besides, a very female part of her reveled in the enjoyment he derived from her body. It was a powerful feeling, even if it took her by surprise. She knew she was softening, melting, her womanhood responding to the firm, masculine hand caressing her. And she loved the way Cody made her feel almost as much as she loved him.

"I have to go," he said finally, regret coloring his

words; she knew they were aimed at himself even more than they were aimed at her.

"I wish…" she began, but then stopped herself.

"Me, too." He smiled at her, a soft, intimate, and very male smile that held more than a touch of possessiveness. "But not tonight." He pulled himself away and stood up. He slid his shoulder holster in place and buckled it before shrugging on his jacket to cover it. "Come, lock the door behind me," he said.

Keira slipped out of the bed and snagged the khaki-colored T-shirt she always wore in place of a nightgown from where it hung on a hook in her closet. The U.S. Marine Corps logo was on the back, and *Semper Fi* was emblazoned across the front. She scrambled into it as Cody watched.

"Not bad," he teased, tracing the lettering across her chest with one finger. "I like the way you think."

"Once a Marine, always a Marine," she answered promptly.

"Yeah, but none of my marine buddies looked like this in a T-shirt." His hands slid beneath the hem, curving around her bare bottom and pulling her closer. "Damn!" he whispered before his mouth descended for a long, drugging kiss.

"No more," he said when he finally raised his head. Keira knew he was fighting himself…and she knew why. He wasn't going to make love to her again until they addressed the birth control issue, and she resolved to make an appointment with her doctor tomorrow. In the meantime, there was a drugstore just down the street….

Cody whistled tunelessly to himself as he rode down in the elevator. He couldn't help but feel good about his life, despite Keira's revelations earlier that day about the connection between the New World Militia and the Russian Brotherhood. The agency had a long, tough job ahead of it putting together a prosecutable case. And the ever-present threat of danger to anyone who had been involved in bringing down the militia six years ago still lurked.

But somehow those things didn't matter right now. All he cared about in this instant was Keira. Life couldn't be anything but good for a man when Keira loved him.

He exited Keira's building, his eyes automatically sweeping the street, alert for danger even though part of him dismissed the possibility. He saw nothing to worry about, but when he walked to where his truck was parked, he stopped dead in his tracks even before he clicked the electronic unlock button on the key fob. Something wasn't right.

He couldn't have said what it was at first. A cursory inspection under the streetlights indicated his truck didn't appear to have been tampered with. But then he realized it was too clean. The thin film of dust that should have been on the hood...wasn't.

He slid his hand inside his jacket for his gun, drew it and backed away, hoping whatever explosive device had been wired inside his truck was ignition or accelerator detonated, and not remotely detonated by someone watching nearby. But nothing happened, and he breathed a small sigh of relief. When he reached the entrance to Keira's building, he buzzed her condo, his mind racing.

Someone had followed him here.

Someone had followed him, waited for him to enter the building, and rigged his truck with explosives. Someone who had known they'd have enough time to finish the job. Someone who had followed him before...and had seen him with Keira.

"Cody?" Keira's voice came through the intercom. "What's wrong?"

He realized then that the building's entrance was wired for video as well as sound. He glanced up, and sure enough, there was a camera in one corner. "Buzz me in," he said.

When the buzzer went off, he opened the door and headed for the elevator, holstering his gun at the same time. Then he changed his mind and took the stairs. *Elevators can be death traps,* he reminded himself as he opened the door to the stairwell.

If they'd followed him to Keira's, she might very well be in danger even though the building seemed to have decent security. But he knew any security could he breached, and his face hardened as he jogged up the eight flights to Keira's floor. He rang her doorbell, only slightly winded, and when she opened the door to him he hustled her inside and locked the door behind them.

"What is it?" she asked, her eyes wide.

But she wasn't frightened, Cody saw. Just alert. And her Glock was in her right hand. A thrill of pride shot through him as he remembered his one-time wish for a woman who would kill to protect him, just as he'd kill to protect her. He smiled and kissed her fiercely before moving to the phone in the living room.

His voice was grim. "Somebody tampered with my truck." He picked up her phone and dialed the agency. It only took a couple of minutes to arrange for an explosives team to come check out his truck, and he gave them his cell phone number to contact him, not wanting to give out Keira's number.

When he hung up she asked him, "How do you know?"

Cody laughed without humor. "You wouldn't believe

it if I told you." He looked at her, still clad in nothing but her *Semper Fi* T-shirt; but her hair was damp, so he knew she'd taken a shower after he left. He said, "You'd better get dressed. I'm going to call Baker Street." He dialed a number from memory he'd already used once this month, and watched as Keira headed for the bedroom.

The phone rang only a few times before it was answered. "D'Arcy."

"It's Special Agent Walker, sir. I hope I didn't wake you."

"No. What is it?"

Cody told him, quickly and concisely.

"Let me know when you get confirmation from the explosives team," the other man said. "I want the specifics." Cody noted he didn't even question Cody's reading of the situation. Any other man might have said "if." But D'Arcy, who never said what he didn't mean, who never used one word when he meant another, said "when." It was a little thing, but that positive assessment of his judgment was something Cody needed right then. Especially since he'd had to tell D'Arcy about....

"I will, sir," Cody promised.

"And stay where you are for now, unless something happens. I'm going to send a team to protect the two of you until we can talk about this tomorrow morning. I am *not* going to lose an agent if I can help it."

"Yes, sir."

"Have you warned Callahan and McKinnon?"

"My next call."

"Good. Keep me posted."

Cody hung up when D'Arcy did. He pulled out the disposable cell phone he used exclusively to contact Callahan, and when the phone was answered he didn't even bother to identify himself.

"Someone tampered with my truck earlier tonight." Keira came back into the room just then, fully dressed, including the jacket he knew hid her shoulder holster. He mouthed the word "Callahan" to her before continuing. "An explosives team is on their way, but I wanted to warn you."

"Since you're calling me, I can safely assume it didn't go off?" Callahan said dryly.

Cody was surprised into laughing. "Yeah. Go figure."

"How'd you manage that?"

"Dust," Cody said. "That wasn't there."

Callahan grunted his approval. "You know, Walker," he started, but Cody beat him to the punch line, laughing.

"For an amateur, I'm not half bad. Yeah, I hear that a lot." Then he turned serious. "Watch your back, okay? Mandy would never forgive me, if…" He didn't have to finish.

"I've got McKinnon," Callahan said. "He's enough for now."

"Just do me a favor and double-check everything, okay?" Cody didn't wait for Callahan's response. He disconnected and pocketed the cell phone, then told Keira, "At least he's warned. He says McKinnon is enough for now, but…"

"What did Baker Street say?" she asked.

"He wants us to sit tight. He's sending a team to protect us until we can figure out what we need to do. And he wants to see us first thing tomorrow."

A stricken look came over her face. "You *told* him?" she whispered. "You told him about us?"

Cody stiffened and smothered the slash of pain her words engendered. *Is she ashamed of loving me?* he wondered, before he said, "I didn't tell him the specifics, but, yes, I told him where I was and how long I was here."

He gazed down at her. "I *had* to, Keira," he said softly with just a hint of pleading in his voice, willing her to see the necessity. "He needed to know—it's relevant to the situation."

"I…" She threw him a wounded look. "I had to tell him about you rescuing me," she said, and he saw her swallow visibly. "What will he think of me now?"

Cody thought he understood then. "That you're human, like the rest of us?" he offered.

"You don't understand."

"I understand more than you think I do."

"You can't. You're not a woman."

"Then tell me so I'll understand." Cody knew the issue was more than just a lack of understanding; he knew somehow he was fighting for Keira herself. If they were ever to have a future together, if their relationship was ever going to be more than just fantastic sex, he needed to understand where she was coming from…and she needed to understand him, too.

Something McKinnon had said to him weeks ago suddenly came back to him. *She comes from a large family— four brothers, all older, all former marines, too. Maybe that's why she has a thing about wanting to do her job as well as, or better than, a man could…*

"This is about your brothers, isn't it?" he asked quietly. "About your family?"

She drew a sharp breath and turned away from him, and Cody knew he'd hit the bull's-eye on the first try. He walked over to her and slid his arms around her from behind. She resisted at first, standing stiffly in his embrace, but when he didn't do anything but hold her, she relaxed her guard just the slightest bit.

"I never told you what I said to Callahan when I was trying to convince him you could be trusted, did I?" he asked conversationally, breathing in the scent of her but refusing to succumb to the temptation.

"You told him how we met," she said gruffly. "And you told him I reminded you of his wife."

"Yes, but that's not all I told him."

"Something about guts and brains?" she asked. "He mentioned you'd said that, too."

"Yeah, but that's still not all of it." Cody thought for a moment, trying to remember his exact words. "I told him that physically you're no match for a man, but you've got guts and brains. I said you'd fight to the death, if that's what it takes, and he couldn't ask for much more than that."

She turned in the circle of his arms, facing him, her eyes betraying her emotional uncertainty. "You didn't even know me then," she whispered. "How could you know that about me?"

Cody gazed down at her. "I knew that about you in the first five minutes," he said simply, his eyes forcing her to remember that first night and the way she'd fought not only him, but her kidnappers.

When she continued to stare at him in disbelief, he added, "And when I told Callahan you reminded me a lot of Mandy, I also said you'd shoot me if you had to. That was the clincher. And it was the truth, too."

Her eyes crinkled at the corners, in the way he was coming to know meant she was emotionally hurt. "Not now," he clarified with a faint smile. "I don't think you'd shoot me *now*...unless I completely misheard you earlier."

She laughed a little at that, as he had intended her to do. He pulled her closer. "Being a woman doesn't have anything to do with the kind of agent you are. Everyone who knows your work thinks the world of you, including me."

His voice dropped a notch. "But, Keira, you're a woman," he told her. "Don't be ashamed of that." He took a deep breath, letting his pain creep into his voice. "And don't be ashamed of what you feel for me."

"I'm *not* ashamed of loving you," she said fiercely, her hands gripping his arms.

"Then don't be ashamed of being a woman. My woman."

She drew a sharp breath. "I'm not. It's just—"

He never got to hear what she was going to say, because a buzzer sounded just then. Keira pulled out of his arms abruptly and together they went to the view monitor. Two men stood in the vestibule below. They had that watchful look of agents, but neither Keira nor Cody was going to let them in without identification.

"Yes?" Keira said into the speaker.

Both men held identification badges up to the camera. "Special Agents Sabbatino and Moran. Baker Street sent us."

Calling D'Arcy Baker Street was even more convincing than their ID cards, and Cody nodded at Keira as her hand hovered over the buzzer that would let the two men in.

Chapter 15

The hands of the clock stood at 12:17 a.m., and Keira was curled up in the armchair almost asleep, when the phone call came on Cody's cell. He listened intently, and jotted down a couple of things on the notepad he pulled from his pocket. "Thanks," he said at the end. "I owe you guys."

Keira blinked owlishly at him. "What was it?"

"Gelignite," he said. "Beloved of terrorists the world over."

She caught her breath. "How?"

"Rigged to the accelerator. Turn the key, step on the gas and boom," he said lightly, although part of him was still shaken at how narrowly he'd cheated death. If he hadn't noticed the dust missing from the hood…

Keira squeezed her eyes shut for an instant, as if she didn't want to think about what might have happened. Cody glanced at Sabbatino and Moran, sitting quietly in the little dining area, hoping for her sake they hadn't seen Keira's reaction. For himself, he didn't care if the whole world knew—except for the terrorists who were gunning for him.

"Why don't you get some sleep?" he asked her. "I've got to call Baker Street—he wants the details—but there's no reason you have to stay awake, too. Not with bodyguards in the next room."

Keira stood up. In just those few seconds her face had been wiped clean of emotion. "Maybe I will." Her voice was flat, toneless.

Cody knew that expression. It was the same frozen mask she'd worn after the first time he'd kissed her, but now he was all too aware it was her way of hiding deep pain she didn't want the world to see. And he knew that voice—he'd heard it before, too, the same time she'd told him it wouldn't happen again, referring to their first kiss.

This wasn't his Keira, this cold, emotionless automaton. His Keira was warm, animated...and a fighter. For her to shut down this way had to mean she cared so passionately she couldn't deal with it any other way.

She loves you.

She'd said the words when they were making love earlier. And he'd believed her. But now he knew it went far deeper. He wanted to take her in his arms and comfort her, reassure her that he was safe for now, but the presence of the other agents stopped him. He knew she wouldn't want them to know...anything. All he could do was let his eyes tell her what he couldn't show her. But she wouldn't look at him, and the message didn't go through. She slipped quietly into the bedroom, and Cody watched her go silently, wanting to call her back, willing her to turn around. But she didn't.

Keira closed the bedroom door behind her and stood for a minute, her back to the door as her gaze fell on her bed. The sheets and blanket were all rumpled, and in her mind's eye she could see Cody and her there earlier, their bodies entwined. She could still hear the echoes of their passion. She could still feel him deep inside her.

Then she heard Cody saying, *Turn the key, step on the gas and boom*. She shuddered and covered her face with her hands. All her earlier excitement and pride at solving a big piece of the puzzle—figuring out who had revived the New World Militia and how, uncovering the link between them, NOANC and the Praetor Corporation, uncovering the connection between them and the Russian Bratva—all that was gone.

Turn the key, step on the gas and boom.

Her hands dropped to her sides and formed impotent fists. Solving the puzzle hadn't protected Cody. It was a miracle he wasn't dead or gravely injured. It was a miracle he'd noticed—how had he put it to Callahan? *Dust...that wasn't there*. Sometime while they'd made love tonight, maybe even at the moment she was confessing her love to him, someone was planting explosives in Cody's truck. Someone who wanted him dead. And not just dead—someone wanted him to die a horrible, agonizing death by fire.

Something niggled at the back of her mind. Something to do with death by fire. But another thought crowded in, pushing everything else aside. *Cody's name is on that list,* she knew with certainty. *Maybe right beneath Callahan's.*

And she had failed to protect him. That was the bottom line for her. The man she loved had been in danger, and she'd let him walk out of her bedroom without a second thought for his safety. All she'd cared about was keeping him with her, not because it was dangerous for him otherwise, but because she selfishly wanted to fall asleep in his arms. And when he said he couldn't stay, she hadn't argued, she'd just let him go.

Turn the key, step on the gas and boom.

If Cody had died tonight, how could she live with that knowledge?

Mandy suddenly came to mind. Mandy, who had witnessed the explosion she thought had taken the life of the man she loved, the father of her unborn child. Mandy, who had attempted suicide when she lost both the man she loved and the child he'd given her—her last link to him. Mandy, who had shot Cody, thinking she was saving Callahan's life.

When Cody had told her those stories, Keira had sympathized, but she hadn't *empathized*. Now it was different. Now she understood, *really* understood.

Keira shuddered again, but this time it wasn't because she could have lost Cody so soon after finding him. No, this time was because she acknowledged a primitive part of her was desperately praying she'd conceived his child tonight.

Psychologically she understood. Faced with the threat of sudden death, the human response was to cling to life. Not just for oneself—for the next generation, as well. But that didn't explain her desire for Cody's child. Not entirely. She wanted to be the one to give him the immortality only his child could give him. She wanted it for herself, too.

That's not just old-school. It's archaic, she told herself sternly. But she couldn't deny it. She wanted Cody's child with an intensity that shocked her. And she wanted that part of him to love and cherish, if…

"No," she whispered, her face hardening, and this time her right fist clenched with purpose. Then her hand slid inside her jacket to touch the comforting stock of her gun in its leather holster. Nothing was going to happen to Cody. She wouldn't *let* anything happen to him. No matter what she had to do.

* * *

Early the next morning Keira drove Cody to his apartment so he could shave, shower and change after sleeping fully clothed on her sofa the night before. Sabbatino and Moran followed close behind them. Sabbatino went upstairs with Cody, while Moran waited with Keira.

She was grateful Moran didn't say anything, just leaned against the outside of her car, his eyes on the alert, his head constantly pivoting. She wondered whether he and Sabbatino were thinking...well, thinking the truth. She'd tried not to show anything of her feelings for Cody in front of them, either last night or this morning. But still...if she were in their shoes...she knew it wouldn't take much imagination to figure out what Cody had been doing at her condo.

She'd told Cody the truth last night when she'd said she wasn't ashamed of loving him. She wasn't. And she didn't think she was *ashamed* of being a woman. That wasn't it. But he still didn't understand. She wished she could explain to him she'd fought all her life for respect— first from her father and her four brothers, then from her fellow Marines in the Corps, and now in the agency. That's all she wanted. Respect.

She smiled ruefully as she heard Aretha Franklin singing in her head. The smile faded. Aretha had first sung that song in 1967, long before Keira was born, and things hadn't changed all that much in the years since, not in Keira's line of work. But could she make Cody understand?

Keira had finally earned her father's grudging respect after she'd joined the Corps, but she hadn't had much time to bask in it because he'd died during her first tour of duty overseas. She remembered flying back for the funeral, standing by his coffin with her weeping mother, holding back her own tears because she knew her father would have condemned her tears as a weakness. He would have lost respect for her if she'd cried, so she hadn't. Not at the funeral. Not even in the privacy of her old bedroom at home.

And then there were her brothers. She loved them and they loved her, but she had always been their baby sister. She'd always been so much smaller than they were, and not just because they were all older. She'd gained their respect, too, when she'd followed them into the Corps. Her job with the agency was also a badge of respect in their eyes. Even though her brothers had jobs that took them all over the world and she seldom saw them, they were still family, and their opinion of her still mattered.

Respect from the important men in her life—was it wrong to want it? Need it?

Her partner respected her, she knew that. He hadn't at first, not until she'd proven herself to him by taking down a cold-blooded killer who'd had Trace in his sights. Now Trace trusted her as well as respected her. Would he feel the same if he knew she'd become involved with a fellow agent? Or would he see her as weak?

And what did D'Arcy think of her now? She'd hated being forced to confess the story of her kidnapping and subsequent rescue by Cody to him, although she'd felt she had no choice at the time. But now that D'Arcy also knew—well, she wasn't quite sure exactly what he knew, but she could hazard a guess—would he still say she was an excellent agent? Would he still say those words she'd treasured, that he didn't want to lose her? Or would he lose all respect for her as an agent now?

And there was Cody himself. More than anything, she yearned for his respect. Oh, yes, she wanted his love, *needed* his love. And now that she'd slept with him, she wanted that, too, wanted those incredibly passionate feelings only he could arouse in her body—and only he could assuage. But if she had to choose one thing, she would choose his respect and sacrifice the rest.

Could she make him understand?

Moran straightened just then, and Keira looked up. Cody and a watchful Sabbatino were walking toward her car. Cody didn't say anything to her when he got in and buckled his seat belt, just told Sabbatino, "Thanks. We'll see you at the agency."

Keira started the engine and waited for the other two agents to get into their car, then signaled and pulled out into traffic, Sabbatino and Moran right behind her. They drove in silence for a few minutes before curiosity got the better of her. "Did Sabbatino say anything to you?"

Cody glanced at her. "Yeah. He said, 'Nice view.' My apartment's on the top floor and faces the Rockies."

Keira knew she shouldn't ask, but she couldn't help it. "He didn't say anything else? Anything about…us… being together last night?"

He gave her a level look. "Nope. All he said was, 'Nice view.' Why? Did Moran say something to you?"

She shook her head. "Not a single word the whole time." But she wouldn't look at Cody, just focused on the traffic.

"So, why do you ask?" he said softly. "Whatever they're thinking, why do you care?"

"Because…" She didn't have an answer for him, not one she could put into words.

"You told me last night you weren't ashamed of loving me."

She darted a glance at him. "I'm not."

"Sure seems like you are." There was an edge to his voice.

"It's not that," she said quickly, and when she stole a peek at him, she saw his jaw was set and there was an expression on his face that gave her a pang to see. Almost as if she'd hurt him if she admitted...

"Then what is it?"

"I don't want them to lose respect for me," she said in a low tone.

He was silent for a moment. "Is that what this is all about? Respect?"

Keira nodded. "It's different for men. A man doesn't lose respect for another man because he sleeps with a woman. But a woman...especially an agent..." She couldn't finish, but she didn't have to.

"In other words, the double standard is alive and well...in your mind."

"Not just in my mind," she defended hotly. "It's still the way things are, even after all these years—don't deny it."

Cody didn't say anything, and Keira knew he was considering her statement. After a while he sighed and said, "Maybe you're right. I don't like admitting it, but..."

Keira saw the agency's fenced parking lot ahead of her and signaled a turn. Then she fished in her purse for her ID badge and saw Cody take his out of his pocket and clip it to his jacket's lapel. They both flashed their badges to the guard on the gate, who waved them on through and wished them a nice day. The car containing Sabbatino and Moran was right behind them.

All four of them badged into the building, one after another—"tailgating" wasn't allowed. Not only did the agency want to restrict access to those who had the electronic ID badges, they also kept track electronically of who was in the building when, so employees had to badge out to exit, as well as badge in to enter.

"Might as well go right up," Cody said, once all four of them had passed muster with the security guards in the lobby. Sabbatino and Moran rode up with them, then delivered them to D'Arcy's outer office.

Baker Street's executive assistant told Cody and Keira, "He's waiting for you."

Sabbatino and Moran took seats, prepared to wait as long as it took. Cody knocked once, then opened the door to the inner office and ushered Keira through.

"Walker. Jones. Good to see both of you…alive," D'Arcy said. He was sitting at his desk, and he waved them over. "I just finished reading the explosives team's report on your truck," he told Cody. "Nothing new there beyond what you told me on the phone last night. But there's been another development." There was a grim set to his mouth as he handed copies of another report to both of them.

Keira skimmed through her copy. "Oh, my God," she said. She glanced over at Cody, who had read his copy just as quickly, and was looking at her with a disturbed expression on his face.

They both turned to face D'Arcy when he said, "The FBI has already sent an official inquiry through channels requesting whatever information we have on this."

"But we don't have any, sir," Keira said faintly.

"No, not directly, but you can't tell me there isn't a connection between this and Walker's truck last night." He looked from Keira to Cody. "In case you don't remember, Brockway and DeSantini were—"

"The lead prosecutors on Pennington's trial eight years ago," Cody finished for him. "Yes, sir, I remember." His face hardened, as did his voice. "Callahan's in danger. Maybe his family, too."

"I've already dispatched a team to bring him in, along

with McKinnon. And another to bring Callahan's family to Denver. The safe house in Casper is well enough under normal circumstances, but not for this."

"Callahan won't trust the team you've sent unless I warn him in advance," Cody said. "You know how careful he is."

"Then call him," D'Arcy said. "Now." He glanced at his watch. "I sent the team by helicopter. They should be there soon."

Keira watched as Cody drew the cell phone from his pocket and walked to a corner of the room, punching in a number. She looked back at D'Arcy. "What are you going to tell the FBI, sir?" she asked.

"As little as I can," he said. "I have to tell them about what was found in Walker's truck—the circumstances are too similar to what happened to Brockway and De-Santini. And there could be an evidentiary tie-in. But I'm not giving them the file you compiled," he said, pointing to the thick file folder in the center of his desk.

"Sir?"

"Two reasons," D'Arcy explained. "First, I don't want them to know this agency has access to their computers. Second, if the SAC of the FBI's New York Field Office Criminal Division was a member of the militia or on the Russian mob's payroll before he resigned five years ago, there's no telling who else in the FBI might be involved. I'm not going to risk it. I've already got one agent on the militia's hit list. I'm not adding your name to it."

Startled, she said, "I didn't think of that."

Cody walked back at that moment, his face grim. "Callahan's halfway to Casper. McKinnon's with him. McKinnon called my secure cell—it must have gone to voice mail," he said, glancing at the phone for confirmation before continuing. "They found explosives rigged in Callahan's official sheriff's SUV early this morning, parked right outside his house. They didn't wait to collect the evidence—you can notify the FBI to do that, sir. Callahan was determined to get to his family as soon as he could."

"Damn." The word was softly spoken, and D'Arcy picked up the phone and punched a number. "Get someone to radio the chopper on its way to Black Rock," he said with cold urgency. "Tell them to divert to our safe house in Casper. Callahan and McKinnon are on their way there." He listened for a minute. "That's right. And tell that chopper team Callahan will be expecting them." He raised his eyebrows inquiringly at Cody, who nodded. "Okay, thanks."

"Four attempts," Cody said. "Two dead."

D'Arcy nodded. "They're batting .500."

"No sir," Keira said swiftly. "They're batting .333. As far as we know, at least." When both men looked at her, she reminded them, "There were six names on the list, not four. That's what Callahan reported Tressler told him."

"That's right," Cody said, snapping his fingers. "Brockway, DeSantini, Callahan and me—that's four. Who are the other two? They've got to be connected to Pennington in some way."

D'Arcy said, "Those four are easy. Brockway and DeSantini—they put Pennington in jail the first time. Callahan testified against Pennington. He also killed him, with your help," he told Cody.

"It can't be Walsh and Brooks," Cody said. "They're already dead—no reason for their names to be on a hit list now."

Something was nudging Keira's brain, but she couldn't think what it could be. Something told her she knew whose names should be on that list—she just couldn't put her finger on it.

Cody was still speaking. "The other two names depend on whose list it is. Since Tressler was in the New World Militia, we've assumed the list was related to that, but it doesn't seem to fit somehow. Callahan—yes. And me. We were both undercover in the militia, and we betrayed the organization. So I see the connection there."

He paused, as if marshaling his thoughts in order. "But Brockway and DeSantini—that's more related to David Pennington personally, not to the militia per se. Especially after all this time. If their names were on the list—a reasonable assumption since they were killed in the same way the attempt was made on me—then the list has to be Michael Vishenko's. Pennington's son."

"That's it," Keira whispered as everything coalesced in her brain. "It's the only thing that makes sense."

Cody glanced at her. "What?"

"You're right—it's Vishenko's list," she confirmed. "And the other two names on the list have to be Trace's name...and yours, sir." She looked D'Arcy straight in the eye.

D'Arcy looked at her sharply. "Why do you say that?"

"Trace told me that after Cody and Callahan killed Pennington, the two of you had to collect all the witness statements and physical evidence relating to his death, and get it ruled a justifiable homicide."

She looked from D'Arcy to Cody. "Don't you see? It's the only logical conclusion. If Vishenko wants revenge for his father, it's not just the men who put his father in jail, and it's not just his father's killers he wants dead. It's also the men who helped his father's killers—Callahan and you—get away with...murder."

Cody's brows drew together in a frown, and he opened

his mouth as if to deny the allegation, but she spoke before he could. "I know it wasn't murder," she said. "But you have to look at it from Vishenko's perspective. In his eyes it was murder, and the men who helped you get off the hook for it are just as responsible."

She looked at D'Arcy again. "Walker told me Pennington was obsessed with seeing Callahan in hell. I can't think of anything more hellish than an agonizing death by fire, and if I were Vishenko looking for revenge…" She took a deep breath. "I think you have to accept that someone will be coming after you, too, sir, the exact same way…if they haven't already. You and Trace."

D'Arcy picked up his phone and dialed a number. "I need an explosives team at my house now." He gave the address. "I suspect something was done to my car similar to what was done to Special Agent Walker's truck last night, so be extremely careful." He gave the make and model, and a license plate number. "It's parked in the driveway. Let me know what you find."

He put the phone down. He was breathing a little faster than normal, and there was an expression on his face Keira had never seen there. "My car was low on gas when I got home last night," he explained, "but it was late and I figured I'd fill up on the way to work. Then I got your call last night. My wife is visiting her sister in South Carolina. I knew her car had a full tank, so I drove her car this morning."

Keira caught her breath. Her first thought was for her partner, and she turned concerned eyes on Cody. But before she said what she was thinking she realized her mistake and she relaxed a little.

"Trace hasn't been home for two weeks," she said, "because you assigned him to bird-dog Callahan. His car has been in the secure parking lot here at work all this time, ever since the three of us went to Wyoming. If not for that, I'd bet anything you want to stake you'd find his car rigged to explode, just like your truck."

"No bet," Cody said. And there was something in his eyes that told her she'd earned his respect…again.

Chapter 16

"I'm putting you under twenty-four hour guard," D'Arcy told Walker. "You don't step outside the agency without security. Understand?"

"Yes, sir. What about—"

D'Arcy cut him off. "I'll do the same for McKinnon once he gets back. Callahan and his family, too—that goes without saying."

Cody's gaze traveled to Keira, then back to D'Arcy. "What about Keira?" he asked.

Keira said quickly, "My name isn't on the list."

"Neither is Callahan's family," Cody answered. His jaw tightened, but he held D'Arcy's gaze. "If they followed me to her condo, if they knew they had time to rig the explosives…" He didn't say anything more, but he knew from D'Arcy's eyes he was getting the message.

"Separate? Or together?"

Keira gasped, and Cody knew she was aware what D'Arcy was asking. Did he need to post separate sets of bodyguards on Cody and Keira, or would one set suffice for both?

Cody didn't look at Keira before answering. "Together."

Keira made a faint sound of protest, but Cody didn't care. She'd told him last night and again this morning she wasn't ashamed of loving him, and he wasn't going to lie to D'Arcy—he needed to be with her. Not just because he wanted her, but because he wanted to be there to protect her if anything happened.

The rational part of his brain told him that agency bodyguards could protect her, probably better than he could. They were as highly trained as the Secret Service that guarded the president. But one president in recent memory had been killed and another seriously wounded despite the Secret Service's best efforts. So, placing agency bodyguards around Keira was no guarantee, and that wasn't good enough. He needed to be there, too.

D'Arcy looked from Cody's set expression to Keira's distressed one, and nodded. "Okay, that's how the orders will read." He changed the subject. "When Callahan and McKinnon get here, I want a sit-down with them and the two of you. We need to map out a plan."

"Yes, sir," Cody and Keira responded, almost at the same time.

As they were walking out of the office, D'Arcy stood up and said, "One more thing, Walker."

Cody told Keira, "Wait for me," and turned back.

Keira looked from Cody to D'Arcy, her brow wrinkling in a question, but D'Arcy smiled reassuringly at her and said, "This will just take a minute. Please, close the door on your way out." He waited until the door had closed behind Keira, then asked Cody softly, "I hope I don't have to worry about a sexual harassment claim."

Cody had known the question—or something similar—was coming, but even though he was prepared for it, it still wasn't easy to answer. He looked D'Arcy straight in the eye and said, "No, sir. You don't have to worry about that. You can ask her yourself if you want. She'll tell you the same thing." Then he waited.

D'Arcy glanced down at his desk for a moment, then back at Cody, and Cody could see he was torn. "I don't want to take either of you off this case," he said finally. "But if I have to, I will."

Cody knew the decision was hanging in the balance. The only thing in his mind was that it would destroy Keira if D'Arcy removed her. She'd put her heart and soul into this case, and had uncovered things no one else had uncovered. She had earned her spot on the team, and then some. "I hope it won't come to that, sir. But if you remove anyone," he said, "remove me, not Keira. I'm replaceable. She isn't."

D'Arcy made a face of frustration. "I should probably replace you anyway, since you're a target." He held up one hand as Cody started to protest. "But I'm a target, too—Special Agent *Jones* convinced me of that," he added, using her last name deliberately. "And I'm not about to recuse myself. Especially if they find something in my car."

After a long minute he sighed, then bent a hard gaze at Cody. "I'm just going to have to trust you to do the right thing, Walker. Trust you to tell me if you can't be objective. And I'm not just talking about the New World Militia and the Russian Brotherhood."

Keira's name hung unspoken between them.

"You have my word on that, sir." Cody shifted his stance slightly. "There's one other thing. Keira was upset I told you about us last night. She said, 'I had to tell him about you rescuing me. What will he think of me now?'" His voice roughened. "She's the most conscientious agent I know. I would hate to think this would affect her career."

D'Arcy didn't say anything at first. Then he smiled slightly. "It's almost funny," he said. "When she told me you rescued her, she was determined to defend your career with the agency, no matter what happened to hers. And now you're defending hers the same way." He nodded. "You've made your point. I'll keep it in mind."

Cody took that for a dismissal, turned and walked out. Keira was waiting for him in the outer office, along with Sabbatino and Moran. He knew from her face that she had questions—not to mention a protest he could see she was dying to lodge. But she wouldn't say anything, not in front of Sabbatino and Moran. He knew her well enough to know that.

"I don't know about you," he told her, 'but I'm starved." He included Sabbatino and Moran in his invitation. "Let's grab some breakfast in the cafeteria before we do anything else."

Michael Vishenko listened dispassionately to the voice on the phone speaking in code phrases. "One and two— failure. Three and four—success. Five and six—no data yet."

"Thank you," he said, then hung up. Even though the house was swept daily for listening devices, even though the men reporting to him were supposed to use disposable cell phones as he did, the lessons learned by the New World Militia years ago, along with his uncle's training, stayed with him. The FBI could easily have him under surveillance, electronic and otherwise. Vishenko wasn't risking anything being said that could incriminate him.

Three and four—success. He already knew about De-Santini and Brockway. The internet was a wonderful tool for getting news about anything, anywhere, anytime. He'd found the short articles on the explosions in New

York and New Jersey, and the deaths of the two men, a half hour apart, late last night. He hadn't even tried to repress the sense of exultation that had swept through him as he read the articles.

There had been a much longer article this morning that attempted to tie the two deaths together—some smart reporter had tracked the high-profile cases the two federal prosecutors had worked on, and had questioned the FBI about whether there was a connection between their deaths and the sensational trial of David Pennington eight years ago. The FBI's "No comment at this time" response didn't mean anything, but he wasn't worried. Not yet.

One and two—failure. Those failures hurt. DeSantini and Brockway were secondary targets, as were D'Arcy and McKinnon—five and six. Callahan and Walker were the primary targets. They had murdered his father in cold blood six years ago. Not to mention both men had betrayed his father's organization, the New World Militia, through their undercover activities, and by Callahan's testimony at his father's trial.

Not that Michael Vishenko cared about the New World Militia and the cause it espoused. The militia was just a tool. He knew there was little chance of a successful military overthrow of the United States government. But there *was* a way to power. The way he was pursuing through NOANC.

He smiled coldly and let himself be distracted for a moment. NOANC had been a brilliant idea. Super PACs were the way to go, he'd realized, even before his father had been murdered. Power—real power—only came through controlling the political process.

Even his uncle Alexei acknowledged that money and ruthlessness alone weren't enough. The Russian Bratva couldn't survive in this country without the payoffs to various government officials that allowed it to operate with impunity.

So Michael Vishenko had used his father's fortune to resurrect the New World Militia for one purpose and one purpose only—as a means of obtaining legal donations to NOANC. NOANC "owned" the politicians it had helped get elected. And he—through the Praetor Corporation—controlled NOANC.

He was only thirty-four, but already his power was spreading. Congressmen, senators, judges. And…soon… if he played his cards right, perhaps even a president would owe NOANC—and Michael Vishenko—the election. *No, not Michael Vishenko,* he corrected himself with a grim smile. *Michael* Pennington. *Because by then I will have reclaimed my rightful name.* He would be the power behind the throne, his dream ever since he'd been old enough to recognize his physical deformity would limit his own political aspirations.

His smile faded. But first, he needed to avenge his father. Failure was unacceptable. If he couldn't even manage to kill Callahan, Walker and the other two, he didn't deserve to succeed elsewhere.

With a halting step he walked to the library window and stared out into the garden, but he wasn't seeing the imposing statuary his father had acquired years ago; he was wondering how his primary targets had evaded elimination. He needed data from the men on the ground, data that couldn't be transmitted through code phrases. And then he needed to modify his plan.

His targets were smart—he didn't underestimate them. That was one of the reasons he'd waited this long, to lull them into a false sense of security. All the deaths had been timed to occur within twelve hours of each other. But now he had to assume the deaths of DeSantini and Brockway would put the other targets on the alert. His new plan would have to take that into consideration.

Five people sat around the conference table in D'Arcy's office. Keira had watched D'Arcy's greeting of Callahan with a tinge of surprise. They hadn't just shaken hands; the two men had embraced before sitting down at the table next to each other. Not only that, they'd addressed each other by their first names. Knowing Callahan, as she was beginning to, and knowing D'Arcy, as she'd known him by his reputation since she joined the agency, she realized the two men had to be closer than they'd let on before. Was that related to the time Callahan had spent in the witness security program, when D'Arcy had been responsible for him? Or was there something else?

D'Arcy turned to Keira and Cody. "Bring them up to speed."

Cody glanced at Keira. "Go ahead," she said.

"Tressler told you there were six names on the elimination list," he said, facing Callahan, "but he only recognized yours. We had already surmised my name was on the list, and the attempt on me last night seems to confirm it. We think the other four names were Darrel Brockway, Al DeSan—"

"DeSantini," Callahan broke in. "I remember them. They were the lead prosecutors when I testified against Pennington. Smart guys."

"Yeah, well," Cody said flatly, "they were murdered last night. Same M.O. as the attempt on me," he said, meaning *modus operandi,* or method of operation. "And from what you told me on the phone, it sounds like the same M.O. as the attempt on you, too. We won't know for sure until the FBI deconstructs your SUV, but we'll assume it is unless we hear otherwise."

D'Arcy handed Callahan and McKinnon copies of the report on Brockway and DeSantini he'd given Cody and Keira that morning. Cody waited until the other men had a chance to read them before continuing. "We brainstormed about this, and we think the hit list doesn't really come from the New World Militia. We think this is Michael Vishenko's personal hit list to avenge his father." He looked at Keira, and she took her cue from him.

She turned to her partner. "Trace, remember when you told me you and D'Arcy had to clean up the mess after Pennington was killed?"

He frowned and glanced at D'Arcy, then at Callahan, obviously regretting the wording he'd used to describe that situation. "Yeah. So?"

"From Vishenko's perspective, Callahan and Walker murdered his father. And you and D'Arcy covered it up, helped them get away with it. That puts the two of you on the hit list. It's the only thing that makes sense." She took a deep breath. "Six names, two of them dead."

D'Arcy spoke up. "Out of five attempts we know of— they found my car at home rigged the same way. It's a miracle I'm not dead." He quickly explained the circumstances to Callahan and McKinnon. Then he added, "I'm placing both of you in protective custody. Neither of you leaves this building without armed protection."

Callahan shook his head, his voice implacable. "That's okay for my family, but I have to be able to operate on my own."

Keira saw D'Arcy's face change and knew a fight was brewing. She said quickly, "What if the four of us operate as a team?" The men at the table looked at her, then at each other. "You're all targets," she explained. "I'm not." Cody frowned, and she emphasized, "My name isn't on the list."

She looked at D'Arcy. "All of us have been working this case already. Trace and I are partners. Walker and Callahan have worked together before, as have Trace and Callahan. Between the four of us, I think we can guard each other and not get in each other's way in the investigation."

"It's a risk," D'Arcy began, but Callahan spoke up.

"I'd go for that."

Keira cast him a grateful look before turning her eyes to her partner. "Trace?"

"If you and Callahan think it's a good idea, I'm fine with it."

Keira turned to Cody. "What do you think?" She could tell by his expression that he was torn, and her eyes pleaded with him. *Please, don't,* they said. *Please, don't object. I love you, but, please, don't humiliate me. Not again.*

Cody glanced down at the notepad in front of him, and when he raised his eyes to hers again she saw pride and respect overcoming his fear for her. "Fine by me," he said lightly, and only Keira knew what it had cost him to say it.

She turned back to D'Arcy. "Sir?" He gave her a long, considering look, and she remembered her private interview with him just under three weeks ago. "I took your advice, sir," she said as if they were the only ones in the room. "I've moved on."

He smiled slightly, acknowledging her point. Then he nodded. "Okay." His eyes encompassed everyone at the table. "You are all responsible for each other. And each of you is answerable to me."

Keira knew Cody's eyes were on her, knew he wondered what she meant by her statement to D'Arcy that she'd moved on. But she also knew he wasn't going to ask. Not when anyone else was around.

She allowed herself a tiny smile, remembering that morning and the questions she'd been burning to ask him but couldn't because Sabbatino and Moran had been there all through breakfast. And then afterward, Cody had made sure they were never alone, so she hadn't been able to ask him why D'Arcy had wanted to speak to him privately. *Two can play that game,* she thought. *Now maybe he'll understand what it's like.*

At least he hadn't humiliated her just now, the way he'd done this morning when he'd told D'Arcy they could be guarded together. She had wanted to contradict him then, but something had held her back. Maybe it was the way he had refused to look at her before he answered. Maybe it was the way his jaw hardened in profile. Or maybe it was because he'd told her this morning in the car that she seemed to be ashamed of loving him, and she didn't want him to think that. Whatever the reason, she'd held her tongue, and she was glad now.

Cody was speaking to Callahan. "We've had more than two dozen teams working this investigation, and in two weeks we haven't found *anything* indicating the New World Militia is a threat. Not the way it was when Pennington was running it. No illegal arms. No drugs. Nothing of that nature."

He held up a hand as Callahan started to speak. "I know, I know. Tressler's dead. I'm not ignoring that. But what if that was something separate—maybe still connected to the militia—but not directly related to the big picture?"

"It's possible," Callahan admitted.

"The militia *has* been resurrected, no question." His

voice dropped a notch. "But what if it's a blind? A cover-up hiding the real scheme?"

Keira *saw* the light come into Callahan's eyes, saw him make the connection Cody was leading up to. She didn't get it yet, but she knew Cody and Callahan were somehow on the same wavelength already.

Cody was smiling, and his eyes blazed with the same light as Callahan's. He turned to her. "Didn't you say that super PAC, NOANC, has received thousands of smaller donations from across the country?" he asked her.

"Yes," she answered, glancing at her partner, hoping for a sign he knew where this was leading, but he shook his head. "Trace and I saw the donors lists filed with the Federal Election Commission going back to its inception."

"Grassroots," Callahan said softly. "Wasn't that the word you used?"

Then she got it, and her eyes widened. "The militia? Vishenko's using the militia to fund his super PAC?"

"Not entirely," Cody said. "The Praetor Corporation still has to kick in big-time. But it fits beautifully. If the super PAC was only funded by one company, that would be a red flag. But with thousands of individual donors across the country…NOANC flies under the radar."

"And Vishenko's hit list?" she asked.

"Personal, just as we thought. Nothing to do with the New World Militia."

Trace spoke up. "What about Tressler's death?" he asked. "Maybe it's not related, but can we take that chance? There still could be a connection somehow, something we're not seeing."

Callahan nodded and looked at Cody. "He's right. We can't completely ignore it. Steve was dying, but he didn't drive to the hospital. He drove to my house to warn me.

To tell me whatever it was and to give me that key. It was important enough to him, that…" He drew a deep breath and let it out slowly, and Keira realized again that he wasn't as cold and uncaring as he appeared to be.

He couldn't be, she thought suddenly. *Or Cody wouldn't care about him the way he does.* And Cody *did* care about him. It wasn't just Mandy and her children he'd been worried about, it was Callahan, too. What had Cody said last night? "We probably could have been friends if not for…" *If not for Mandy. That's what he almost said. But Cody doesn't love Mandy anymore. He loves me. And Ryan Callahan* is *his friend, whether he realizes it or not.*

D'Arcy had been listening quietly this whole time. Now he spoke. "I've seen the autopsy on Steve Tressler, same as you. He didn't die from those gunshot wounds— not directly. None of them hit a vital organ. He died from loss of blood."

Callahan looked grim. "Other than the fact he was beaten before he died, and that the evidence clearly points to the crime occurring at his cabin, we don't know a hell of a lot. And I can't think of anyone who might have had it in for him…other than the New World Militia."

"They recovered three .357 slugs from Tressler's body," D'Arcy told him, "two of which are in good enough shape for a match. *If* you find the gun. And there's something else. Whoever shot him made two crucial mistakes, which means—"

"He's not a professional." Callahan interjected. "Yeah, I'd already thought of that. He should have made sure Steve was dead…*and* he should have searched the body to make sure Steve didn't have any incriminating evidence on him." He smiled, but the smile didn't reach his eyes. "Those mistakes will cost him."

"Black Rock is a small town," Keira said. "Has anyone given any indication they know something about his death? What I mean is," she clarified, "has anyone expressed undue concern about his death who shouldn't? Or on the other hand, has anyone who *should* be worried about his death *not* shown it?"

Callahan shook his head. "No, and in the past two weeks I've interviewed just about every resident of the town in some way. Nothing has seemed out of kilter, and I haven't gotten even a hint of anybody hiding anything. Everyone knew him, and everyone seems duly shocked. Either his murderer is an incredible actor, or I haven't talked to him."

"What about his employer?" Keira asked.

"Steve didn't have a real job, not the way you mean. He was smart enough, but he didn't want to be tied down to a regular nine-to-five job. He made just enough to get by doing odd jobs—yard work, handyman kind of stuff in the summer. And in the winter he did snow plowing—he had a snow plow attachment for his truck. He used to plow a lot of the parking lots for the businesses in town on a regular basis, including Mandy's store, but he also did one-off plowing or shoveling jobs for people when they called him."

Keira darted a glance at Cody, and she could see the same thought was occurring to him. Before she could say anything, he said, "When we were up at my cabin the Friday before Memorial Day, there were still patches of snow on the ground. When did it snow last?"

An arrested look came over Callahan's face. "The week before," he said slowly. "Right around the time I started getting vibes from Steve that something wasn't quite right. Right around the time he must have seen that hit list."

Chapter 17

An agency helicopter took the four of them to Casper that night, where they picked up Callahan's four-by-four from the safe house. From there they drove to Black Rock.

Callahan drove, and Cody sat in the passenger seat. Keira and Trace sat in the middle row, after the child car seats had been removed and stored in the back. Cody heard Keira tell Trace, "You have no idea how glad I am you're okay. Once we figured out your name was on that list, I was worried until I realized your car was at work, and they couldn't get to it."

Cody suppressed the unreasonable shaft of jealousy that rippled through him. *McKinnon's her partner,* he told himself. *Of course she cares about him. But McKinnon told you there's nothing between them, and never was. Not that way.* Besides, he knew it himself—she loved him. But that didn't stop the sudden flare of possessiveness.

He glanced over at Callahan. "Did you see Mandy and the kids before we left?"

"Yeah." The word wasn't much more than a growl. "For about fifteen minutes." Then Callahan added, "If we've got this thing figured correctly, at least I don't have to worry about their safety. But I won't relax until we know for sure."

Cody remembered the last time he and Callahan had driven together through the darkness, six years ago. He'd been at the wheel then, with Callahan in the passenger seat. They'd known that either or both of them could have ended up dead that night. And Callahan had extracted that promise from him regarding Mandy.

Six years, he thought. *An eternity.*

He looked over his shoulder at Keira in the row behind him. Her face was turned away now, staring out the window into the night, so all he saw was her profile in shadow. As he watched her he realized, all told he'd only known her three weeks. *Three weeks. Another eternity.* But this eternity had changed his life even more profoundly.

He smiled to himself, remembering...was it only last night? Remembering the way she'd listened to his story without judging him, the way she'd clasped his hand, the way love and admiration had shone from her eyes. He hadn't told her that story to gain her sympathy—or her love—he'd just felt she needed to know those things about him before they took the next step in their relationship.

But she had surprised him once again—it seemed as if she was constantly surprising him. When she'd confessed she wanted to be loved by him the way Callahan loved Mandy, something that had been broken inside him six years ago had been healed. He saw that now.

Then she had given herself to him—physically and emotionally. A surge of desire swept through him as he remembered the way she'd called his name...twice. He would never tire of hearing his name on her lips that way, just as he'd never tire of making love to her. Just as he'd never tire of lov—

Keira turned her head at that moment and caught his eyes on her. Her face was solemn at first, but then she smiled slowly, and it was a smile for him alone. It warmed him from the inside out.

He heard again in his head the faint sound of protest she'd made when he'd told D'Arcy they could be protected together. But she hadn't denied him. That hadn't been easy for her—he knew that. Just as it hadn't been easy for him to consent to her plan this afternoon. As much as he wanted to protect her, he knew that part of what made Keira so special to him was her dedication to her job, the same dedication he had. Their jobs were dangerous, but vital to the safety of their country.

Once a Marine, always a Marine, she'd said to him last night, and it was another bond between them. So many bonds. They were inextricably linked. She belonged to him, and he…he belonged to her. *Semper Fidelis*—Always Faithful. It was more than just the Marine Corps motto now. It was a personal pledge between them.

He smiled back at her in the darkness.

Callahan pulled up in front of his house and parked, but before anyone got out, he turned around and said, "Hang on a sec. Let me check first. You never know, and I don't want to take any chances."

"I'm coming with you," Cody said, opening his door before Callahan could protest. They hadn't taken more than three steps toward the house before floodlights hit them from all directions. "Freeze!" barked a voice from the darkness. "FBI."

"Damn!" Cody glanced across at Callahan, realizing they'd both said the same word at the same time. They both raised their hands and froze, neither wanting to give any trigger-happy FBI agent an excuse to open fire. But Cody called out, "Hold your fire! I'm Special Agent Cody Walker, and this is Sheriff Ryan Callahan. Special Agents Keira Jones and Trace McKinnon are with us."

FBI agents swarmed around them, and at first it seemed as if the Fibbies didn't care who they were. But then the man in charge let Cody—very slowly and carefully—show his identification and his badge. When Callahan was allowed to do the same, the order was given to the other FBI agents to lower their weapons.

"Sorry," the man in charge said as he holstered his gun. "The agency, huh?" And Cody could tell by his tone that the FBI's agent in charge wasn't impressed. *Only natural, I suppose,* he thought. *They don't like us any more than we like them.*

Out of the corner of his eye he saw FBI agents opening the doors of Callahan's four-by-four, and ordering Keira and McKinnon out. He suppressed the instinct to go to Keira's side, knowing she could take care of herself in this situation, and instead pocketed his credentials.

"What are you doing here?" Callahan asked as he put his wallet away. He didn't add, "on my property," but he might as well have since his tone indicated that's what was in his mind.

"Sorry," the FBI agent said, but this time his apology was sincere, and Cody smiled to himself as he thought, *The FBI doesn't want to tick off the local sheriff.* "I'm Agent Jeff Holmes, from the FBI's resident agency in Casper. We were notified by *his* agency," he said, jerking a thumb in Cody's direction, "that there could be a link between an attempt on your life and the murders of two federal prosecutors on the East Coast last night."

"Yeah." Callahan glanced over at Cody. "I take it you found one?"

Agent Holmes nodded. "The SUV that was in your driveway, we took it apart and found what we think are the same explosives and wiring device. The lab has them now, and they're being analyzed to see if we can tie them together forensically, but in the meantime, our working assumption is that there *is* a connection. So, what can you tell me?"

Cody shot Callahan a sharp look and got a confirming look in return. Callahan wasn't about to reveal anything more than he had to. Not to the FBI.

"Not much, other than the fact I knew both men," Callahan said laconically. "I was a witness in a trial they prosecuted eight years ago, but I haven't seen or talked to them since then. *His* agency—" Callahan hooked a thumb toward Cody, just as Agent Holmes had done "—seems to think there's a connection, but that's about all they told me. *And* they dragged me all the way to Denver to tell me that much."

Cody had to admire the way Callahan told the truth… but concealed almost everything of importance. He'd revealed only what he wanted to reveal, and made it sound as if the agency was overreacting. *Throwing the Fibbies off the scent,* he acknowledged. *Nice job, Callahan.*

"So, did you search my house?" Callahan asked.

"Uh, we got a search warrant for the car, but we couldn't get one for the house," Agent Holmes said.

Doesn't mean they didn't search, Cody thought, knowing Callahan was thinking the same thing.

"I was just wondering if it was safe to enter. If there were explosives in the SUV, they could have done something to my house, too—I've been gone all day."

"Want us to check for you?" Agent Holmes asked.

He was just a little too eager, and Cody and Callahan exchanged glances. "That's okay, I've got these guys babysitting me," Callahan said, indicating Cody, Keira and McKinnon. "I'll let them check it out." He held out his hand. "So, if that's all, I'll say thanks and wait to hear from you regarding when I can get my SUV back."

Cody hid a grin at the masterful way Callahan had dismissed the FBI. Jurisdictionally the FBI was on thin ice as it was, since no connection had as yet been established between the explosives found in Callahan's SUV and the ones that had killed the two federal prosecutors. Callahan was the local sheriff and hadn't requested FBI assistance, and since technically they *were* trespassing on his property, Agent Holmes didn't have much choice but to shake the hand offered, gather up his team and their equipment, and depart with as much good grace as he could muster.

Cody waited until the FBI vehicles were out of sight before he started chuckling. "Remind me never to get on your bad side," he told Callahan.

Callahan didn't smile. "It went against the grain not to cooperate with him, but I can't trust the FBI the way I used to." His gaze moved from Cody to Keira. "Not since you uncovered what you did on that New York SAC." He shook his head, a grim look settling on his face. "It's a hell of a situation when I can't trust the FBI."

"Sorry," Cody said, meaning it. "Just a little interagency rivalry. They've always resented the agency, which is why they only grudgingly share information with us. And I guess we're not much better. But when we don't share, we usually have a damn good reason."

"Like the junior senator from New York?" Callahan asked dryly.

"Yeah. Like that."

Keira and McKinnon had been listening quietly, but now McKinnon spoke. "I don't know about the two of you, but I'm tired and hungry. What say we go in and you continue that conversation some other time?"

Dinner was long since over, and the four of them sat in the living room, discussing their plans for the next day. Keira hadn't said much, just listened to the three men with part of her brain while the other part was trying to puzzle out the meaning of Steve Tressler's last words to Callahan. *Veni, vidi, vici. Centaur.* Or *center.* Or... or what? *If Callahan couldn't figure it out, what makes you think you can?*

Two weeks ago she'd been convinced there was a link between the phrase *veni, vidi, vici* and the Praetor Corporation. Now she wasn't so sure. *Why didn't you research that more when you had the chance?* she berated herself. She *had* researched the phrase, but she couldn't find a link to the Praetor Corporation. The only thing she had been able to come up with was an online video game, so she'd put it aside to consider later. Then, when she'd started following the trail of David Pennington and his wife and son, she'd never gone back to it.

Veni, vidi, vici—*I came, I saw, I conquered.* It was a motto of some kind. Like *Semper Fidelis*—Always Faithful—was to the Marine Corps. But nothing she'd read about the Praetor Corporation, or NOANC for that matter, said anything about a motto for either organization.

Maybe it was a holdover from the old militia. David Pennington had seemed to have a thing for Roman history. Hadn't Cody said something about that? She cast her mind back. It was there, on the tip of her tongue. She closed her eyes for a minute to block out her surroundings, and then it came back to her. *My code name in the militia was Centurion. Pennington picked the name. He thought it was clever. Maybe it was.*

Centurion. A professional officer in the Roman army. Not just anyone could be a centurion, she remembered. She'd read somewhere that centurions had to meet strict guidelines, including having already served a few years in the military. Was that how Pennington had seen his militia, a reincarnation of the Roman army? Or was it just a coincidence?

Veni, vidi, vici...Praetor...Semper Fidelis...Centurion...

When the Latin words and phrases started running together in her mind, Keira realized she was dozing off. She blinked, trying to force herself awake. She glanced at her watch and saw it was late. They'd been up late last night, too, waiting to hear from the explosives team investigating the tampering with Cody's truck.

"That okay with you, Keira?" Trace said, his voice breaking into her thoughts.

She took a deep breath. "Sorry," she said, "I wasn't listening. I was thinking of something else." She wasn't about to admit she'd nearly fallen asleep.

"I said I've been sleeping in Callahan's guest room, but you can have it. Walker and I can use the boys' bunk beds."

Keira's gaze flew from Trace's face to Cody's, and a small part of her wished...but not with the other men there. There was no way. She glanced back at Trace. "Fine with me," she said with a smile for her partner. "Thanks."

As she stood up her earlier question came back to her, and she asked Callahan before she forgot, "You were pretty close to Pennington at one time, weren't you?"

Callahan's face went cold, and Keira rushed to clarify. "What I mean is, you knew him fairly well when you were undercover, didn't you?"

"Yeah."

The one word made her shiver, but she said, "I'm trying to get a picture of him in my mind. Do you know if he was interested in Roman history?"

Callahan considered her question for a few seconds, then said, "Maybe. He never mentioned it that I recall, but he had a couple of statues in the garden of his Long Island compound. I couldn't say if they were Greek or Roman, but they looked like warriors in those old gladiator movies—you know what I mean. Swords and shields and helmets—that sort of thing."

"But you never heard him use the phrase *veni, vidi, vici.*"

It wasn't a question, but Callahan answered anyway. "No."

Cody asked her, "What are you thinking?"

She shook her head. "I'm not sure yet. When I know, I'll tell you."

She walked over to where her duffel bag sat by the door and picked it up. She looked at Trace. "Where's the guest bedroom?"

Keira was so exhausted she fell asleep almost as soon as her head hit the pillow. But her sleep was disturbed by dreams. At first she dreamed of Cody and the way he'd looked at her as she'd passed him in the hallway, heading back to the guest bedroom after she'd showered and brushed her teeth. He hadn't said anything, but his eyes…his eyes had spoken volumes, and she'd known just what he was thinking, because she'd been thinking the same thing.

Then her dream changed, and she saw Cody dressed in the Roman garb of a centurion, sword in one hand, shield in the other. He looked so totally unlike himself, but his eyes...his eyes were the Cody she knew. And he was gazing at her the way he had Thursday night when he'd demanded she tell him she loved him—with love and longing, and a fierce, possessive desire.

Veni, vidi, vici...Praetor...Semper Fidelis...Centurion...

The key... Where was the key? She *had* to solve the puzzle. Cody needed her to solve it. His life was at stake. Other lives were also at stake: Trace's, Callahan's and D'Arcy's, too. But Cody was the only one who had come close to dying. *Turn the key, step on the gas and boom.*

There it was again. Key.

Key...lock... There was something about a lock....

Her dream dissolved into another scene, and now Cody was sitting at his desk, concentrating on his computer as she walked up to his office door. She stood there watching for a moment, savoring the secret knowledge that she was finally going to prove herself to him, that he would *have* to respect her.

Like snapshots in a slide show, pictures flashed through her dream. *Click!* Now she was giving him the folder with everything she'd uncovered. *Click!* Now Cody was calling Baker Street's executive assistant and making an appointment to see him. *Click!* Now Cody was talking to Callahan. *Click!* Now they were in the elevator, and Cody was gazing down at her, taking a step toward her as if he were going to—

Stop! her dream self said. There was something wrong with the slide show memories. She knew it. She'd missed something. Something important. A small thing, but crucial.

She restarted the slide show from the beginning, examining each frame minutely. No, nothing wrong with the first one. Nor the next, nor the next, nor the next. *Back up,* her dream self said. *Back up to right before the elevator.* And then she knew.

Cody had locked his computer with his personal password. That was standard procedure in the agency—you logged on to the agency network with a password, and you locked your computer for security with that same password whenever you were going to be away from your desk. She'd done it herself right before going to pick up the printouts from the printer, the ones she was going to show Cody.

Password?

Callahan suddenly appeared in her dream, holding a blood-stained key in his hand. *It sounded something like* center *or* centaur, *but I can't swear to it.*

Center...centaur... A computer password? Could it be that simple? If so, where was the computer? What did it have to do with the bloody key? And what about *veni, vidi, vici?* Cody had wondered if it was some kind of code, but that didn't make sense. Tressler had to have known he was dying—why would he speak in code? The answer was right there, just out of reach. What had Callahan said?

He was a decent kid—stereotypical computer nerd, but likable nevertheless.... He was always playing those online war games. He didn't say it, but I suspect he joined the militia for the thrill of it, thinking it was like one of his computer games. He just didn't realize it wasn't a game.

Online war games...

Veni, vidi, vici...

No, not a code...an online *video* game...

Chapter 18

Cody woke from an erotic dream of Keira. She was torturing him with her mouth and hands; her soft little moans of pleasure joined by the ragged sounds torn from his throat as she—

"Trace," he heard Keira say in an urgent whisper. "Trace!"

No, that's not right, Cody thought, disoriented for a moment. Keira was supposed to be calling *his* name, not her partner's name. He sat up abruptly in the upper bunk, almost hitting his head on the ceiling before he realized where he was and that the woman of his dreams was kneeling beside the lower bunk bed, shaking McKinnon's arm.

"Keira? What's wrong?" McKinnon was instantly awake.

Cody slid lightly from the upper bunk to the floor, saying at the same time, "What the hell is going on?"

Startled, Keira caught her breath in a gasp that was loud in the quiet room. "Cody! I didn't mean to wake you." She was fully dressed.

"What time is it?" he asked her.

She wasn't wearing her watch, but she said, "It's early—maybe four-thirty?"

Cody grabbed his jeans from the back of the chair

he'd laid them on last night and donned them hastily. As he zipped up, then turned on a lamp, he heard Keira say to Trace, "I have to ask you something. When you and Callahan searched Tressler's cabin, did you find a computer?"

McKinnon shook his head. "We found a box for a laptop in the garage," he said, "and there was a DSL line in his living room. But no laptop. That was one of the first things we checked."

Keira tapped a fingernail on her teeth as she considered this. "No," she said finally. "I don't think so."

"No what?" Cody asked.

"Callahan said Tressler was a gamer," she explained. "Gamers usually prefer desktops because the graphics processors necessary for high-detail, high-resolution gaming are a lot more expensive in a laptop than a desktop. Not to mention the RAM. Tressler might have had a laptop for other uses—although I doubt it—but for gaming, I'm betting he had a desktop."

"How do you know all that?" McKinnon asked.

Keira chuckled softly. "I don't have four older brothers for nothing," she replied. "Every one of them went through the video gaming phase."

"Well, if Tressler had a desktop computer," McKinnon maintained, "whoever killed him took it, because there wasn't one."

"Maybe." Keira didn't look convinced.

"What are you thinking?" Cody asked.

"I'm thinking about that key he gave Callahan," she said, her eyes staring off into the distance. "I'm thinking about where a man would stash a computer he wanted to hide. A computer that contains a deadly secret."

"Hide in plain sight?" said a deep voice from the doorway. Cody turned and saw Callahan standing there, his hair rumpled and looking as if he'd dressed hastily.

"Sorry," Keira said. "I didn't mean to wake you."

This was said so perfunctorily Cody knew she didn't really mean it. There was a repressed excitement about her that reminded him of the way she'd looked on Thursday, when she'd brought him the file folder of things she'd uncovered about Vishenko.

"I thought of something while I was sleeping," she told Callahan now, her eyes giving her away. "I just wanted to ask Trace—"

"I heard," Callahan said as he advanced into the room. "He's right—we didn't find a computer, but now that you mention it, I think that laptop was a red herring. I went through all of Steve's papers, piece by piece, and found a receipt for that same type of laptop dated four days before he was murdered."

"You didn't tell me that," McKinnon said with a frown.

"Four days?" Cody asked. "That was before he talked to you about the militia."

"Yeah. But *after* he started acting strangely." Callahan's gaze transferred back to Keira. "I didn't think about it at the time, but now…"

"Was there anyone he was particularly close to?" she asked urgently. "Someone he'd trust. Family, maybe, or a girlfriend?"

"No family, no girlfriend." A speculative look crept into Callahan's eyes. "But he *was* close to one person— Betsy Duggan." He glanced at Cody. "Remember her?"

"Roland's wife, Betsy?"

"Yeah. Roland passed away…must be close to three years ago now. Steve used to do yard work and plowing for her at a discounted rate—she's close to seventy, you know, and doesn't have any family around now that Roland's gone. He didn't leave her much other than the house outside Black Rock—she gets by on just her Social Security. Steve let her pay him a little to keep her pride, but I found out by accident just how little that actually was." His gaze never wavered. "And she did things for him, too—mending, baking, stuff like that. Mandy once said Betsy treated Steve like an adopted grandson, and he acted like one to her."

"Would he have a key to her house?" Cody asked.

Callahan nodded slowly, speculation morphing into a tiny smile, and his gaze turned back to Keira. "Betsy went to Palm Springs last month to visit her daughter. If she left a key with anyone…"

"I'll bet you anything you want to name, the key he gave you is to her house." Keira's excitement was barely contained now, and she turned to Cody. "And unless whoever killed him figured it out, which I doubt, I'll bet we'll find his real computer there, too." There was an expression on her face he was beginning to recognize—and it didn't have anything to do with love. She stared up at him, and for an instant it was as if they were alone in the room—no Callahan, no McKinnon—just the two of them, and Keira's excitement over solving the puzzle.

McKinnon broke into their fierce concentration on each other. "If we're going to check it out, Keira," he said. "I need my pants. Do you mind?"

She tore her gaze away from Cody and turned toward her partner. She smiled teasingly, picked up his jeans, and tossed them to him. "No, I don't mind," she said. "Go right ahead."

When McKinnon made as if to maneuver his lanky frame out of the lower bunk to dress, Cody grasped Keira's arm and hustled her toward the door, trying but

failing miserably to suppress the sudden surge of possessiveness.

"Coffee," he said, thinking quickly. "I can go without
breakfast, but not without coffee." He figured Keira had
no intention of staying there, but no way was he going to
let her watch another man get dressed—especially not
one as handsome as McKinnon.

Callahan stepped aside to let them exit. As Cody
passed him he caught the wicked gleam in the other
man's eyes; he knew Callahan could read his thoughts
and was enjoying his discomfort. A memory from another place and time flashed through his mind, and Cody
realized Callahan was probably remembering the same
thing—the two of them watching Mandy sleep six years
ago, their hostility toward each other barely contained.

Keira was already halfway down the hall toward the
kitchen, and far enough away so she wouldn't hear him.
"Don't push it," he muttered to Callahan, his eyes nar-
rowing.

"Wouldn't think of it," Callahan said smoothly. "Coffee's in the cabinet right above the coffeemaker."

A half hour later all four of them were in Callahan's
four-by-four, heading down the unpaved driveway. Dawn
was breaking, painting the eastern sky cloud layers baby-
bunting pink and blue, but sunrise was still more than
twenty minutes away when they pulled on to the highway leading to Black Rock.

Callahan had only driven a minute before Cody said
quietly, "We've got company."

"Yeah," Callahan growled. "I see them, too. They
were waiting for us." He slowed down slightly, and the
car behind them slowed also. Then he pressed down on

the accelerator, picking up speed quickly, and the car behind them did the same, maintaining the same distance.

"Open tail," Cody said. "They want us to know they're back there. Fibbies."

"Who else would utilize an open tail?" Callahan asked rhetorically.

"Yeah. I wouldn't put it past the FBI to leave a crew on watch. Especially since Holmes knows the agency is involved. He doesn't trust us." Cody glanced over at Callahan. "For protection, you think? Or out of suspicion?"

"Protection." Callahan laughed under his breath. "Otherwise, why the open tail?"

"What are you going to do?"

"I can't shake them...not out here in the middle of nowhere—there just aren't enough roads to turn on. But we don't want them following us to Betsy's house either."

Cody thought for a moment. "Where's the truck McKinnon was driving?"

"Back at the house, parked out of sight behind it. Why?" Callahan darted a glance toward Cody. "You thinking what I'm thinking?"

Cody laughed a little. "Probably." *We always were on the same wavelength,* he told himself. *That's never changed, not in all these years.*

He thought a moment. "Keep driving into town. Cruise around a little, like you're showing us the lay of the land—they'll suspect something if we don't. Swing around the rim road, pick up the highway on the other side, and head back to your place. Then you and McKinnon can drive out again heading in the other direction to draw them off the scent, while Keira and I take the truck to Betsy's house."

When Callahan opened his mouth—to protest, Cody was sure—he added, "It's the best chance we've got to search without company, and Keira knows what she's looking for. Besides—" he slanted a sideways look at the other man "—technically you need a search warrant. I don't."

"Agency rules?" Callahan asked, a dangerous edge to his voice.

"Latitude," Cody answered lightly. "If I were looking for evidence against Betsy I'd still need a warrant. But that's not the case." He saw Callahan's hands tighten on the steering wheel. "The world has changed," he said softly in response to what the other man was thinking.

"I know. But I don't have to like it. Makes me glad I'm a small town sheriff now. Most of the time, anyway. There's something to be said for breaking up bar fights and arresting drunk drivers."

"Ah, the good old days," Cody said, agreeing with him.

"You ever miss it?" Callahan asked him. "You ever wish—" He stopped abruptly, as if he suddenly remembered the real reason Cody had left Black Rock.

All at once Cody realized Keira and McKinnon could hear their conversation. They had been quiet this whole time, but that didn't mean they weren't listening. "Yeah," he said honestly. "I miss it sometimes. Denver's different from Black Rock—nothing against Denver, but living in a small town, where you know everyone and everyone knows you, has its advantages. But there's also a certain satisfaction working for the agency that I never got from being the sheriff here. It's a trade-off."

The sun was almost up when Callahan reached the center of town and circled slowly, weaving in and out of the town's few side streets. When they passed the sheriff's office, Cody was hit by a sense of nostalgia. He'd spent a lot of years as Black Rock's sheriff. But then he glanced at the passenger side mirror. "They're still back there," he told Callahan quietly.

McKinnon spoke up. "They just want us to know they're around. And that they're not going away." Then he chuckled. "It'll be fun leading them on a wild-goose chase," he told Cody, "while you and Keira accomplish our mission."

Cody and Keira waited in the truck behind the house after Callahan and McKinnon had left. "Give me five minutes before you pull out," Callahan had told them. "But don't wait any longer than that. You don't want to give them a chance to call up another team to tail the two of you, just in case they notice you're not with us."

Cody glanced at the clock on the dashboard, then put the truck into gear and slowly drove down the winding driveway toward the highway. Both he and Keira had their eyes peeled, but no vehicle appeared behind them or in front of them. Ten minutes later Cody turned into the driveway of Betsy Duggan's house and drove all the way around the back so the truck couldn't be seen from the road. "Stay here," he told Keira, hopping out of the truck and making his way cautiously around the side of the house, peering out.

Nothing. No cars, no people, nothing. He waited a couple of minutes, but still nothing, so he headed back to the truck. Keira was waiting beside it, shielded behind the passenger door. Her hand was tucked inside her jacket, and Cody knew she'd been ready to draw her weapon if necessary. He signaled to her that he was going to try the key on the back door. She followed him, but backwards, eyes on the alert for any sign of the FBI or anyone else.

Cody slid the key into the back door's lock and turned.

"Bingo!" he whispered. He smiled triumphantly at Keira, and the returning smile on her face said, "I knew it!"

They slipped inside, Cody taking the lead. Keira stopped to lock the door behind them, and they made their way through the kitchen into the living room. Cody had no intention of turning on the lights—that would be a dead giveaway to anyone who knew Betsy was out of town—but after a minute their eyes adjusted, and they were able to see clearly in early morning gloom.

The living room furniture was old-fashioned but neat and tidy, with only a fine layer of dust showing that the owner had been absent for some weeks. In one corner of the room stood a large desk Cody remembered had belonged to Roland's father. Roland had rarely used it, but it still had pride of place in the room. And on the desk stood a computer and monitor.

That's it," Keira said, walking quickly toward the corner.

"How can you be sure?"

Her gaze encompassed the computer. "This isn't something you can buy just anywhere," she said. "It's top of the line." She bent over and glanced behind the computer setup. "It's plugged in, but there's no DSL or anything connecting it to an ISP," she added, referring to an internet service provider. "No one would have this computer without internet access. It's *got* to be Tressler's."

She sat down at the keyboard, turned the computer on, and was immediately confronted by the need for a user password. As Cody watched, she typed *C-e-n-t-a-u-r,* but that didn't work. Then she tried *C-e-n-t-e-r,* but no luck there, either. She tried again, this time all lowercase, but again nothing. She made a face of frustration. "One of them *has* to be the password. Remember what Callahan said about Tressler's last word? But even if one of them *is* the password, it could be any combination of caps and lowercase," she told him. "Damn! I could sit here all day, but without a starting point…"

Something niggled at the back of Cody's brain. Something Keira had just said; something about a starting point. "Wait," he said, closing his eyes to concentrate, and Keira fell silent. Starting point. Starting point…

With Tressler dead we don't even have a starting point…. He'd said that to Callahan. Now his mind was doing free association. Starting point. Tressler. *Veni, vidi, vici…*

He could hear Keira saying, *The reference to Julius Caesar could mean anything—the Ides of March, Marc Antony, the Roman Legions, crossing the Rubicon. Even the month of July or William Shakespeare…. Did he say anything else?*

Then as if Callahan were standing right next to him, he could hear the deep voice saying, *One other word at the very end, but I couldn't really understand him…. It sounded something like* center *or* centaur, *but I can't swear to it.*

Roman Legions. Center. "That's it!" Excitement building, he leaned down over Keira's shoulders and typed *C-e-n-t-u-r-i-o-n*. Pennington's code name for him.

"And we're *in!*" Keira exulted as the screen opened into a standard computer desktop. She looked up at Cody, admiration glowing in her face. She turned back to the computer screen, running the mouse pointer over the icons scattered across the desktop. Cody recognized links to the names of many of the most popular online video games, but Keira kept going. Then the mouse pointer stopped abruptly at a link near the bottom right of the screen.

Veni, Vidi, Vici.

"It's an online video game," Cody whispered, stunned.

"I know," Keira said, but so low he had to strain to hear her. "It came to me in my dream last night."

He frowned. "But you never said that this morning...."

Keira kept her head down, staring at the computer screen. "I might have been wrong," she said in an undertone. "I didn't want..." She drew a sharp breath. "Actually, when I was researching a link between the Praetor Corporation and that phrase two weeks ago, I came across a few references to an online video game by that name," she confessed, as if she'd failed him somehow. "I just didn't make the connection until last night."

Cody reached down and turned her face so she had to look at him. "Don't," he said. "We're a team. Don't hold back when you have an idea just because you might be wrong. Hell, I'm wrong half the time myself," he said, exaggerating to make his point.

She hesitated, then said, "You're right. I should have trusted that you and Callahan wouldn't hold it against me if my theory proved wrong."

Cody realized Keira hadn't included McKinnon in that statement, and another surge of jealousy rose in him. Apparently she trusted her partner more than she trusted him...and that bothered him. A lot. *A hell of a lot more than just a lot,* he acknowledged, trying to squelch his unreasonable jealousy of McKinnon. In some ways Keira still didn't trust him, but there wasn't a damn thing he could do about it...not here...not now.

Chapter 19

They drove in silence to Callahan's house with Tressler's computer stowed in the back of the truck, the tonneau cover safely concealing it from curious eyes. Cody wondered what Keira was thinking but couldn't bring himself to ask—he was still coming to terms with the wound she'd dealt him without realizing it. Keira's lack of unquestioning belief sliced into Cody's psyche in a way he hadn't thought possible. "Trust me," he'd told her that first night, and she'd answered, "I will."

She trusted him with her body. Every step of the way in their one night together she had demonstrated her implicit faith that he would cherish the gift of her body in a way she had done with no other man.

She trusted him with her heart. That incandescent moment when she had cradled his face with her hands and whispered, "I love you, Cody," would warm him until the day he died.

But she didn't trust him the way he yearned for her to do—with every fiber of her being. McKinnon was more important to her than Cody was where her work was concerned. And her work was her life. *Trust me in that, too,* he wanted to plead, but he knew faith and reliance couldn't be won that way—not with words. They had to be given freely; they had to come from the soul. And in her soul she didn't trust him completely…not yet.

Just before the driveway leading to Callahan's house, Cody noticed another car parked down a little way on the side of the road. It wasn't the same one that had followed the four of them earlier, but it was too far away for him to make out the license plate or see if there was anyone in the car.

"No sense wondering," he told Keira as he kept driving past the driveway. He pulled over on the other side of the road and rolled down his window. After a few seconds the window of the other car also rolled down, and Cody recognized FBI Agent Jeff Holmes in the driver's seat.

"Good morning," Cody said with a grin only partially concealed. "You're up early."

He could see the tightening jaw on the other man's face. "So are you," Holmes replied eventually. "So is Callahan."

"Yeah. Things to do, you know." He debated with himself for a minute, then said provocatively, "If you wanted to know what we were up to, you could have asked." *Not that we would have told you,* he added silently, *but…*

"Right, Walker."

Cody rolled up his window, chuckled to himself, and executed a U-turn.

For the first time Keira spoke. "Whatever happened to interagency cooperation?"

He glanced at her. "Right. And I suppose you're going to tell him about the agency's secret data link into the FBI's computers in Washington?"

She laughed softly at the dryly teasing note in his voice. "Well, no, I wasn't going to go that far. But I wouldn't deliberately provoke rivalry, either. We *are* on the same side, after all. And he has his job to do, just as we have ours."

"I know." A tinge of contrition crept into his voice. "But they resent the hell out of us. And they don't trust us, not where the job is concerned. They never have." He took a deep breath. "Just like you don't trust me."

She cast him a look of shock. "I trust you," she whispered.

"Not completely," he told her. "In some ways you do, but…"

She didn't answer, and Cody knew she was thinking… really thinking about what he'd said, trying to decide if it was true. That was one of the wonderful things about her—she didn't automatically leap to her own defense. And she could admit her own failings. Not everyone could do that.

Cody pulled the truck up in back of Callahan's house, turned off the ignition, and waited. And waited. He watched her profile, saw the delicate color come into her cheeks as she realized he was watching her. She glanced away, staring out the window at the back porch, but he knew she wasn't really seeing it any more than he was.

After a couple of minutes, Keira turned, and her eyes met his. "What do you want from me?" she asked in a low tone.

"Everything." Her eyes widened, and her face took on a startled expression. He smiled faintly, then reached over and brushed the backs of his fingers against her cheek. "Heart, mind, body and soul. I'm thirty-seven, Keira," he confessed. "I've waited too long to settle for anything less. I can't…I *won't*."

"Do you know what you're asking?"

He was gambling everything on one roll of the dice. "I want you—you know that. But I want all of you. I want to go to sleep at night with you in my arms, and I want to wake up the same way. But that's not enough. Not for me…not for us. I also need to know that you trust me… in every way there is. Not just with your body. Not just with your heart."

"You're asking the impossible."

"I know." His voice was husky. "But it's all or nothing."

"I can't…it's not that easy…I…"

Cody unbuckled his seat belt and took the keys out of the ignition. "I'm not asking you to decide right this second," he said. "But I thought you should know how I feel." He opened the truck door and changed the subject. "Come on, let's get that computer inside and hook it up to the internet, see what else we can find out."

She caught his arm, and he turned back. "Wait, Cody. I…"

His heart melted at the confusion on her face. He knew he'd sprung this on her with little or no warning, and maybe it wasn't fair. Some people might say they barely knew each other, and maybe Keira was thinking that, too. But he knew everything important there was to know about her. And he hoped…prayed, really, that she would realize she already knew everything important there was to know about him, too.

He leaned toward her, hesitating just a little, then brushed his lips against hers in a kiss unlike any other he'd ever given her. He fought back the possessive passion that surged through his body unexpectedly at the touch of her lips. The alpha male side of him—the side he'd only recently acknowledged after all these years— wanted to deepen the kiss, to swamp her senses, to sway her with sensual promises. But instinctively he knew that wasn't what she needed right now. She needed to know she was safe with him. In every way. And only when she knew it was safe to trust him would she do so.

Trust. It was such a little word, but it meant everything.

His lips moved slowly, kissing her eyes closed. She caught her breath when he tucked a curl behind her ear, and his lips tugged at her earlobe. One hand clenched his arm, and Cody struggled not to pull her into his embrace. "Heart, mind, body and soul," he whispered. "That's all I want."

He didn't wait for a response, just drew away from her and exited the truck quickly before he could change his mind and tell her that whatever she wanted to give him was enough. It wasn't. It might be enough for today, for a week, for a month. But not for a lifetime. And that's what he wanted. A lifetime. His…and hers.

He went around the back and unlocked the tonneau cover. Keira was still sitting where he'd left her in the cab of the truck, and he smiled ruefully. He'd obviously taken her by surprise, and he'd given her a lot to think about. *I just hope she won't need to think too long.*

He grabbed the computer, hefted it under one arm, and strode purposefully toward the back porch, taking the stairs two at a time. He unlocked the door with the key Callahan had given him, and went inside. He came out a minute later for the computer monitor, and froze as soon as he pushed the door open. Keira was standing at the back of the truck, but she wasn't alone. A bearded stranger stood beside her, a gun pointed at her head.

"Stop right there," the man told Cody, moving quickly to shield himself behind Keira, wrapping his left arm around her throat for more control. "I know you're armed. Take the gun out real slow, and place it on the floor."

"Cody, no—" Keira gasped before the stranger's hand closed around her mouth.

Cody did exactly as he was bid. As if she'd screamed the words at him, the expression in her eyes told him not to, told him to keep his Glock and dash back inside the house where he'd be safe. And though his eyes answered, *Not a chance, sweetheart. I'm not leaving you out here alone,* a disconnected part of his brain registered that she was putting him first as he'd long dreamed. That she would rather die herself than risk him. *Can't think about that now,* he warned himself as he thrust the thought aside.

"Step down, away from the gun," the man ordered him, and again Cody obeyed. Time slowed to a crawl as his mind processed with incredible speed the data it had to work with, the same way it had when Keira had been dragged into the shack the first night he'd seen her. He knew instantly he had only one chance to rescue both of them, just as he'd known it then. It was a risk, but he'd taken bigger risks in his life before. This time, though, he wasn't just risking his own life.

Then from nowhere a certainty settled over him, and he knew...*knew*...Keira would tell him to take the risk. He knew that her mind was working feverishly, too, weighing each option just as he was. And he knew they were on the same wavelength.

Patience, he told her silently. *Patience.* If he could get the man to shift the gun into his left hand, and point it in his direction instead of at Keira's head... At the bottom of the porch steps Cody stopped. "She's armed, too," he said calmly. "Shoulder holster under her left arm."

She knows, he told himself when Keira's eyes didn't accuse him of betrayal, just stared unwaveringly at him.

But not by the flicker of an eyelash did he acknowledge that anything was coming.

A look of suspicion passed over the man's face, and he hesitated, his eyes darting left and right as if he feared some kind of trap. *Come on, you son of a bitch,* Cody thought, easing imperceptibly forward on his toes. *Come on.*

The seconds ticked away. Then the man's left hand slid away from Keira's mouth, across her breast, and under her arm. Cody could see the expression on the man's face change the instant he felt the lump beneath Keira's arm, could see the fear change to triumph, and then to frustration when he realized the angle of the holster containing Keira's gun wouldn't allow him to remove it with his left hand...not from behind Keira. *Exactly* as Cody had already known.

"Damn!" the man muttered. He backed away from Cody, dragging Keira with him, obviously wanting the safety of distance between them before attempting anything more. The man came to an abrupt stop thirty feet away and stared at Cody for a breathless minute. But Cody's passive stance must have convinced the stranger he was no threat, not without a gun. Slowly, his eyes never leaving Cody's face, the man shifted his own gun to his left hand, pointing it threateningly toward Cody. His right arm came around Keira, stretching awkwardly for the gun beneath her left arm.

"Now!" Cody shouted, and as if they'd rehearsed it in advance Keira jabbed her left elbow behind her, tearing herself away from the man's grasp and swinging around behind him, her right hand reaching for her Glock.

Cody hit the ground in a controlled roll, simultaneously reaching for the knife in his boot. The stranger fired, but with the gun in his left hand the shot went wide. Before he could shift the gun back into his right hand, a flash of silver was winging its way through the air faster than the eye could follow, thudding into the brachial plexus region of the man's left shoulder—precisely where Cody had been aiming.

The bearded stranger staggered back, the gun dropping helplessly from his suddenly nerveless left hand as he fell to his knees, his right hand scrabbling futilely at the blade embedded in his body. Then he pitched forward.

Her own gun drawn, Keira scooped up the stranger's gun, then whirled to confront him. But Cody was there before her. Only then did Cody allow his rage to sweep aside every other consideration. He ruthlessly flipped the man over on to his back and put a knee on his chest, then dragged the knife out and held the blade to the man's throat. Adrenaline pulsed through his body. A savage desire to slit the throat of the scum who had dared to hold a gun to Keira's head swept through him, and he fought it until his muscles screamed.

Keira put a hand on his arm. "No," she said breathlessly.

"You okay?" he asked her roughly without taking his eyes off the bearded face below him. The man was still breathing, but now that the blade had been withdrawn, blood seeped slowly high up on his left shoulder, staining the long-sleeved flannel shirt he wore. And his breath rasped in his throat. "Don't even think of moving," Cody told him in a voice like death.

"I'm fine," Keira said. As if she knew the impulse he was fighting, she said, "Don't, Cody. I'm fine." She didn't say anything more, just holstered her own weapon and moved quickly toward the porch to retrieve Cody's

Glock. She held it out to him with her left hand, her right hand still holding the stranger's gun.

Dare to move, Cody told the man in his mind as he changed the hand holding the knife to allow him to holster his gun with his right hand. *Come on, you son of a bitch,* he urged silently. *Give me a reason.* But the man didn't even twitch a muscle.

"We need an ambulance," Keira said after a minute, reaching for her cell phone. "We don't want him to die."

Yes, we do, Cody thought, but he didn't voice it because in the rational part of his brain he knew she was right. They needed this guy alive—able to answer questions—more than the short-lived satisfaction his death would give Cody. But that didn't mean it was easy. Not by a long shot.

Cody's jaw clenched. *It's my fault,* he told himself ruthlessly. *I should have expected something like this. I should have been on my guard.* He'd let himself be distracted for those few minutes when he was talking to Keira, and she had almost paid the price of his carelessness.

How did he get here? Cody wondered. He couldn't have driven up after they had—no way the man could have gotten past the FBI agents at the base of the driveway, and besides, he or Keira would have heard a vehicle drive up and been alerted to his presence. *He must have come through the woods before we arrived and was waiting his chance. That's the only possibility.*

Keira was talking into her cell phone, giving precise directions to the emergency operator, when Cody heard the sound of gravel crunching beneath tires. He glanced up fleetingly and saw Callahan's four-by-four whispering to a stop in front of the truck, before he returned his attention to the stranger.

Guns drawn, Callahan and McKinnon were suddenly there beside him. "What the hell happened?" Callahan growled.

"Ambulance is on its way," Keira told them. "But it will take a while—we should see what we can do to stop the bleeding in the meantime."

"I've got a first-aid kit in the house," Callahan told her, heading for the back door. He returned in a minute. "Let him go, Walker," he said in a deep voice that expressed understanding of the complex emotions driving Cody as well as concern for the wounded man. "I've got to see how badly he's hurt."

Cody drew a ragged breath. "He'll live." He abruptly pulled the blade away from the man's throat. "I didn't hit anything vital." *But he might never use that arm again.* The thought bothered him not at all. Cody looked down, saw the stranger's blood on his knife, and wiped it off on the man's shirt before yielding his place to Callahan. "Watch him, McKinnon," he said softly. "He had a gun to Keira's head five minutes ago."

McKinnon's eyes changed from questioning concern to cold anger that came close to mirroring Cody's own feelings. "That was his first mistake." His SIG SAUER pointed at the man's head. "Maybe he'll make another one." The threat...and the wish...were unmistakable.

Callahan was already unbuttoning the man's shirt and pulling it open to reveal an ugly gash that still bled sluggishly. He whistled tunelessly between his teeth. "I think you're right," he told Cody. "It's nasty, but it doesn't look life-threatening."

Cody bent and slid his knife into the sheath in his boot, then reached beneath the stranger, looking for identification. He found a wallet in a back pocket and, after a little difficulty, managed to extract it without interrupting Callahan's work.

"Ted Danvers," he read from the driver's license, along with a Buffalo address. "Either one mean anything to you?" he asked Callahan, who already had a pressure bandage in place.

"No." Callahan applied another strip of tape.

Cody rifled through the other items in the wallet: a couple of credit cards in the same name and some gas receipts. And almost four thousand dollars in cash—mostly large bills. Cody went through each bill carefully, making sure there wasn't a piece of paper hidden between the bills. There wasn't, but he noticed a couple of the hundreds had reddish-brown stains. *Blood?*

An idea occurred to him, and he moved toward Keira, who still held Danvers's gun. A detached corner of his brain noted the way she held herself so straight and unyielding after what she'd just gone through. Any other woman would be shaking. But not his Keira. He was so damned proud of her, his heart came near to bursting from his chest.

He held out his hand for the gun, but she must have known what was in his mind, because as she handed it to him she said softly, "It's a .357."

Just as softly, he said, "There are bloodstains on some of the money in his wallet."

"You think…?"

"It's possible. We need to get the gun and the wallet to the lab as soon as we can."

He went to the back of the truck, searched for and found evidence bags. He had just finished sealing each item up and marking the bags with his initials and the date when he stopped short, a realization sweeping over him.

His gaze moved to Keira, standing with her back to him. *Maybe you don't know it yet, sweetheart,* he told her in his mind. *But you trust me, all the way down to the soles of your feet. You knew I had a plan...and you trusted me to execute it with your help.* Heart, mind, body and soul. She trusted him...the way he needed her to.

He headed toward her, intent on only one thing. Keira's gaze traveled from the stranger's face to Cody's as he approached her, and she asked in a level tone, "Do you think we should carry him into the house?"

"No!" the man on the ground gasped before he could stop himself.

Cody froze, then turned and stared down at Danvers in sudden comprehension. Before he could say anything, Callahan put his forearm across the man's throat...and pressed. "That's my home, you bastard," he said in a deadly voice. "If there's something you want to tell me, you've got ten seconds to speak. Otherwise, we'll tie you up, carry you inside and leave you there...alone."

Cody remembered the firebombs that had almost taken the lives of Mandy and Callahan six years ago, the firebombs that had destroyed Mandy's house, this very house that Callahan had rebuilt himself for Mandy and their children. If Cody and Keira hadn't returned when they had, if they hadn't accidentally prevented this man's escape, Keira would have been inside...

Rage, burning hot and icy cold, flooded his body again, the same way it had when he'd seen Danvers with a gun to Keira's head. "Don't wait," he told Callahan, matching his deadly tone. "Just do it."

Callahan nodded and said, "There's a rope in the back of my four-by-four, Walker." Cody took two steps.

"No!" the man croaked from fear and the pressure

across his throat, but managed to add, "Bomb! Beneath the house."

Cody heard Keira's quickly indrawn breath. Callahan rose, and stood looking down at the man, a cold and deadly expression on his face that Cody understood and agreed with completely. Before Callahan could do or say anything, Cody jerked the man to his feet in one powerful motion. "In that case, you're going to crawl under there and pull it out."

Terrified, his left arm hanging almost useless, Danvers looked from Cody to Callahan to McKinnon. All three faces wore the same implacable expression. The man swallowed hard, then glanced at Keira.

"I'll get the rope," she told Cody, heading for the four-by-four.

"No!" The hoarse cry stopped Keira in her tracks, but she didn't turn around. "I'll do it," Danvers said. "Just let me go," he told Cody desperately. "There's not much time left."

Cody drew his Glock. No way in hell was this man getting away...no matter what he had to do. "Don't even think about running."

Chapter 20

Three hours later they still didn't have any answers. The ambulance had arrived shortly after the bomb had been removed from beneath Callahan's house by Danvers and disarmed by McKinnon. Cody had been surprised at first.

"No big deal," McKinnon had said, shrugging it off. "Piece of shit bomb like this is nothing compared to some I dealt with in Afghanistan."

The siren sound of the ambulance had split the silence then, and Callahan had hurried around the side of the house, directing the ambulance toward the back. And the ambulance had been followed by two sedans of FBI agents.

The FBI had stepped in, Agent Holmes asserting jurisdiction over the attempted bombing, leaving Cody, Keira and McKinnon little choice but to back off…for now. The questions Cody had been burning to ask Danvers would have to wait. The FBI had taken official custody as well, taking over guard duties of the suspect on his way to the hospital in Sheridan, and one car of FBI agents had silently followed the ambulance.

Cody and Keira had been hard-pressed to avoid being taken in for questioning themselves, and Cody suspected Agent Holmes would have loved to do just that on whatever pretext he could find if Callahan hadn't been there in his official capacity as Black Rock's sheriff. While the FBI could stretch a point in trying to tie the latest bombing attempt to the killings on the East Coast, Cody's attack on Danvers was clearly in Callahan's jurisdiction. And it was also clearly a case of self-defense.

That didn't mean the FBI had just let it go. Agent Holmes had insisted on being present as Callahan extensively and thoroughly questioned Cody and Keira separately. But their stories matched almost exactly, and nothing could shake them. So eventually the FBI had no choice but to leave, taking the disarmed bomb with them as evidence.

But Callahan had been adamant about not letting them take the stranger's gun or wallet, which was evidence in the assault on Keira and Cody. And neither Cody nor Keira had mentioned the computer sitting on the kitchen table inside Callahan's house. Callahan, after one meaningful glance from Cody, had refused to take the interrogation indoors. Callahan waited until Agent Holmes finally drove away, then asked Cody, "You want to tell me what really happened?"

Cody shook his head. "We already told you. Everything happened exactly as Keira and I described."

"What did you leave out?"

Cody turned and headed toward the back of the truck. "Nothing," he said over his shoulder. "Except Danvers's gun is a .357, it looks like there are bloodstains on the money in his wallet, and, oh, yeah, we found Tressler's computer at Betsy Duggan's house."

"I'll be damned." Callahan followed him.

Cody hefted the computer monitor in his arms. "Want to grab those evidence bags and close that for me?" he asked Callahan, and waited until he did so.

A short distance away Keira stood in earnest conversation with McKinnon, probably telling her partner the same things he was telling Callahan, and at first sight of them, Cody stiffened. It wasn't an embrace, but the other man's arm was around Keira's shoulders, and Cody struggled with the fierce possessiveness he couldn't prevent. He didn't want McKinnon…he didn't want *any* man touching Keira.

Then he remembered, and the possessiveness fell away, replaced by a secret exultation that raced through his blood. Keira trusted him the way he'd yearned just that morning for her to trust him—with every fiber of her being.

He didn't need to feel threatened by her relationships with other men. Not anymore. She belonged to him in a way she would never belong to another man, and it didn't have a damn thing to do with coercion on his part. It didn't have a damn thing to do with *making* her his. She belonged to him in the only way that truly meant anything—she'd *given* herself to him, freely, honestly. Heart, mind, body and soul, she was his—and he would cherish the gift as well as the giver for the rest of his life.

His eyes met Callahan's knowing ones, and he wondered just how much of his thoughts he'd revealed in the past few seconds. "Might as well tell the whole thing once," he told Callahan lightly before calling Keira and McKinnon over.

They set up Tressler's computer and hooked up the internet connection as Cody and Keira together told the story of what they'd discovered at Betsy Duggan's house. When the computer was turned on and ready to go, Cody pressed Keira into the chair. "You drive."

"I've got a theory," she said as her fingers typed in

the password, and they waited for the desktop to come up. "But…"

"Let's hear it."

She glanced up at him. "I could be wrong."

"So?"

The respect in his eyes warmed her, and she smiled at him. *Cody was right this morning,* she acknowledged. They were a team, just as she and Trace were a team. *As a team* they were stronger than either one alone, and there was truth in the old adage that two heads were better than one.

She double-clicked on the *Veni, Vidi, Vici* icon on the desktop, and the game opened. It defaulted to a username account, STRESSLER. "If he was smart, he'd have different passwords," she said. "But most people aren't that smart. They have one password they use for just about everything because it's easy to remember." Holding her breath, she again typed the password *C-e-n-t-u-r-i-o-n.*

Just that easily they had accessed Tressler's persona in the video game.

"This might take some time," she explained. "If this were a real video game, I might have to access level by level, but I don't think… There!" she said suddenly. She clicked on a series of shortcuts that looked incomprehensible to the men standing behind her until she reached a flashing bar that said "Password Protected Area!"

She turned toward Callahan. "Didn't you say Tressler accidentally came across that elimination list?"

"Yeah. But he wouldn't tell me anything about how he found it or who had it."

"I don't think it was a person. I think this is it. Tressler was probably like a lot of guys who're hooked on these online games—like a lot of hackers, too—he couldn't stand not being able to get into a password-protected area. So when he came across it, he tried to guess the password. And once he did…"

She turned to look at Cody standing on her other side. "I think Tressler just happened to have the same password for his personal use that was set up to unlock this area of *Veni, Vidi, Vici*."

"Look," she said, scrolling the mouse until it pointed to the copyright notice at the bottom of the page. The word *Copyright* was followed by the copyright symbol, a year, the letters *NWM, Inc.* and *All rights reserved.*

"NWM," she said. "New World Militia? I think this video game is one of their recruitment tools. I also think it's how they communicate with certain operatives within the organization." She clicked on the flashing bar, then her fingers moved to the keyboard and quickly typed *C-e-n-t-u-r-i-o-n*.

The browser window went blank. At first nothing happened, but after a few seconds the browser window came to life again, and when it did, a list suddenly appeared. Six names, each one indicating a link. Every name on the list known to the four people whose eyes were glued to the computer monitor. And one date, the Thursday before, followed by the letters *RIP*.

"Requiescat in pace," Keira whispered to herself. "Rest in peace."

All three men swore under their breath.

Keira double-clicked on the first name on the list, and a new browser window opened. Pictures of Callahan over the years lined up across the screen, from his official rookie photo with the NYPD to a recent unposed one of him in his Black Rock sheriff's uniform. His home address was also there, along with pertinent facts, including his weapon of choice, as well as the names of Mandy and their three children.

Callahan growled when he read the last part, but Keira ignored him and quickly saved the web page, then converted it into a pdf file for insurance. She returned to the original browser window and clicked on the second name on the list, already knowing what she'd find. But that didn't stop her heart skipping a beat when pictures of Cody appeared in the new browser window.

"So, that's why I was being followed," Cody murmured under his breath, stating what they had all been thinking.

His voice jumbled around inside her, and it was all Keira could do to save that web page and convert it also. She started to click on the third name, but then as suddenly as if someone had pulled the plug, the browser window went blank, and it stayed blank no matter how she tried to refresh it. Keira opened a new browser window and tried double-clicking on the *Veni, Vidi, Vici* icon on the desktop, but to no avail. They couldn't access the video game's website.

"Could be the internet connection," she muttered to herself. She double-clicked on the link to another online video game, and that one came up immediately, as did the next one she tried. She attempted to access *Veni, Vidi, Vici* again, both via the link and by typing in the web address, but nothing.

Keira suddenly felt cold. "Someone blocked our IP address."

"What's that?" Callahan asked.

McKinnon answered. "Internet protocol address. It's how data is sent from one computer to another over the internet, and uniquely identifies a specific computer. Kind of like the computer's fingerprint."

She glanced up at Cody. "I'm sorry. I shouldn't have tried to access the password-protected area."

"It's okay," he reassured her. "There are four of us to testify to what we saw, and you managed to save two of the web pages."

"Yes, but…now someone knows we used Tressler's account to access the site. Maybe even the people who killed him." Her eyes held regret as well as concern. "They know he's dead, so they know it can't be him. They have to know we're on their trail now."

Cody didn't say anything at first. Then he looked at Callahan. "I shouldn't have let the FBI take custody of Danvers. I should have insisted on questioning him when we had him."

"It's not too late." Callahan glanced at his watch. "We can be in Sheridan in less than an hour."

"Yeah, but I should have followed up right away. How did he get here? Earlier I was theorizing he came through the woods because there was no car, but he didn't walk here from Buffalo. He either left his car somewhere, in which case we should be able to find it, or he had an accomplice who is long gone by now."

Callahan thought for a moment. "How big would you say Danvers is?"

"Five-nine, five-ten at the most, a hundred sixty, maybe a hundred seventy pounds. Why?"

Callahan smiled coldly. "Steve Tressler was a big teddy bear of a guy—six-two, easily two hundred pounds. No way Danvers could have roughed him up on his own. *If* Danvers is the one who shot him, he wasn't alone. He had help."

"Let's make sure," Cody said. "Want to take a ride?"

"You read my mind." Callahan dug his hand into his pocket for keys.

Cody turned to Keira and McKinnon. "While we check it out, why don't you see if you can uncover anything on Ted Danvers? And while you're at it, call the agency, bring Baker Street up to speed, set things in motion." He knew he didn't need to be more specific.

Keira started digging even before Cody and Callahan left. She heard Trace on the phone with D'Arcy, but she wasn't really listening. She dragged her laptop out of the spare bedroom, hooked it up to the internet connection and accessed the agency's secure website via its virtual private network.

She blocked Trace's voice out as she concentrated on her assignment—learn everything she could about Ted Danvers before Cody returned. "It's too bad I can't access the FBI's files from here," she muttered to herself, but she didn't waste any time bemoaning that fact.

Fifteen minutes later she realized Trace was standing next to her, looking over her shoulder. She glanced up and saw he had two plates in his hands, one with a single sandwich and the other with two. He tried to hand her the single sandwich plate. "Eat," he said.

Her fingers kept flying over the keyboard, and her eyes returned to the monitor. "Not hungry."

He put the plate down on the keyboard, forcing her to stop. "You always say that," he said. "But we didn't have breakfast, and one cup of coffee won't cut it." He wolfed down half a sandwich in two bites, and Keira grinned up at him before taking a bite of her sandwich.

"Mmm, ham and cheese," she mumbled, realizing suddenly that she *was* hungry after all. "Thanks."

"What are partners for?" Trace said as he sat on the sofa. They ate in silence for a minute, then Trace said, "So, are you going to tell me? Or leave me to guess?"

"Tell you what?" She gave him an innocent look she knew didn't fool him.

"Walker was the one who rescued you before, right?"

Keira thought about it, then realized there was no reason not to tell him, and nodded.

A muscle twitched in Trace's jaw, but all he said was, "I'm glad he was there. I would have hated losing the best partner I ever had."

Keira felt a lump in her throat and a prickling at the back of her eyes. She waited until both subsided before saying, "I've only had one partner, so saying you're the best partner I ever had doesn't say much." She blinked rapidly as the prickling at the back of her eyes returned. "But I hope you know how I feel about you—I couldn't have had a better partner...or teacher. I owe you a lot, more than I can ever tell you."

"Thanks." He polished off the last of his sandwiches, then took her empty plate with his into the kitchen. He came back with a couple of freshly washed apples and handed one to her. "So, are you in love with him?"

"What?" she gasped.

Trace's teeth bit into his apple with a crunching sound. "You heard me," he said. "So, are you in love with Walker?"

Keira looked at her apple, then at Trace. "Yes," she said in a breath of a whisper.

"Well that's good, since the poor guy is hopelessly in love with you."

"How do you know that?"

Trace chuckled. "I've got eyes in my head. I don't need any special training to see it, either. He tries to hide it, just as you do, but..."

"Does everyone know?" she asked in dismay.

"Callahan knows, if that's who you mean. And Baker Street. I've known Nick D'Arcy a long time, and I'm sure he knows. But if you're worried about office gossip, forget it. Only people who know the two of you, who have seen you together, would ever figure it out." He finished the apple, then contemplated the apple core and asked casually, "So, are you sleeping with him?"

"Trace!" Keira felt her face flushing, and knew she'd betrayed herself.

He smiled wryly, and his eyes met hers. "Yeah, it's none of my business. I know that. But knowing you, if you *are* sleeping with him, you're worried I might think badly of you if I found out. I just want you to know I don't, that's all."

"I never thought you—that is, I *did* think you might— but I don't want—oh, God..." She was hopelessly lost in a morass of half sentences, none of which she knew how to end. Trace's eyes held understanding and a glint of humor. "Oh, damn you," she said without heat.

Chapter 21

When Cody walked into Callahan's house, the first thing he noticed was that Keira was studiously avoiding her partner, and his internal radar started buzzing. It wasn't anything either of them said, just a strange vibe, and he wondered what the hell had happened.

But before he could ask Keira about it, Callahan hollered from the kitchen. "I'm starved. Let's eat while we have the chance."

Keira followed him back into the kitchen, and while the two men ate, she told them what she'd found on Ted Danvers. "Two felony convictions, and a long history of petty crimes dating back to his teens," she said, reading from her cryptic notes. "And his name is on the NOANC donor list for the past five years."

"Suspicious," Cody said between bites, "but not proof of anything."

"No, but those two felony convictions give us leverage under the 'three-strike' law. If he goes down for attempted murder, it's the same as if he succeeded in killing one of us—a life sentence. We might be able to get him to talk for a reduced sentence."

"What else have you got?" Callahan asked.

"An extended cab pickup truck registered in his

name." She gave the make, model and year. "Did you find one on the road anywhere?"

"No," Cody answered.

"I didn't think you would." There was that repressed excitement again, as if she could hardly wait to tell them what else she'd uncovered. "Ted Danvers has two brothers, Brad and Joe, both younger. Same address. Also NOANC donors. And get this—Brad is an explosives expert—four years in the army, dishonorable discharge. He works for a construction company now."

Callahan swore. "Ideal recruit for the New World Militia."

"That's what I thought. Trace had the agency contact the Buffalo police, to see if they could track down either brother."

Cody asked, "And?"

Her smile lit up her eyes. "Unaccounted for. Both of them."

Callahan put down his half-eaten sandwich and picked up the phone. "Do you have the license plate number?" She nodded and held her notebook in front of him as he dialed a number. "Jerry? It's me. I need an APB on a vehicle, license plate…" He read the number for the all points bulletin off Keira's notebook, along with the make, model, year and the owner's name. "Ted Danvers is in FBI custody, but right now he's in the hospital in Sheridan."

He listened for a minute, then said, "Yeah. That's right. And I also want a BOLO for two men," he added, using the police acronym for be on the lookout. "Brad Danvers and Joe Danvers, both of Buffalo." He mouthed the word, "address," at Keira. She flipped back in her notebook and held it up so he could repeat it into the phone. "Got that? Good. Let me know the minute we get a hit on the truck or either man. Thanks."

He hung up and looked at Cody, who nodded and said, "You want to be the good cop or the bad cop?"

Callahan chuckled and picked up his sandwich again. "I'm always the good cop, even when I play the bad one."

Michael Vishenko's home phone rang. "Yes?" he said when he picked it up.

"We have a slight problem," the voice at the other end said.

"I see. Thank you for calling." He hung up, a muscle in his jaw twitching. He reached into a desk drawer, pulled out a cell phone, and stared at it. *Another failure.* How was that possible? His targets were mortal. How hard could it be to kill them?

Fools, he thought as he waited the requisite five minutes, his anger growing with each minute that passed. *I'm surrounded by fools.*

After five minutes he dialed a number. "What is the problem this time?" he asked when the call was answered.

"We need authorization to proceed with something other than the original approach."

Vishenko knew the voice was referring to his carefully constructed plan—agonizing death by fire for all his targets. Without that, Vishenko would not receive the full measure of his revenge. "No!" he shouted into the phone. "The original plan *must* be followed."

There was silence at the other end. "There is a problem with that."

"What problem?"

"A secondary failure. And a custody issue."

Vishenko translated the code phrases. Secondary failure—he'd already surmised as much. But custody issue was more serious. It meant one of his tools had been arrested.

"And what is your solution?" he asked.

"If we could deviate from the plan...it could also resolve the custody issue."

"Then, do it," he snapped. He barely disconnected the phone before adding viciously, "Just kill them. Any way you can."

It was late when they arrived at the hospital in Sheridan, but the sun was still up. Cody left Keira guarding Callahan's four-by-four and McKinnon guarding the front door of the hospital, while he and Callahan went up to Ted Danvers's room to question him. At first the FBI agent stationed outside Danvers' room refused to let them enter, but Callahan eventually convinced him they had legitimate business with the suspect.

Once inside they were confronted by another FBI agent. This one was even tougher to convince. Before he would let them interrogate Danvers, he called his superior, Agent Jeff Holmes, for permission, which was grudgingly given.

All told, it was almost thirty minutes before they were allowed to ask their first question...for all the good it did them. Ted Danvers might as well have been a sphinx. He answered none of their questions, just lay there secure in his rights against self-incrimination, his eyes glaring at both interrogators equally.

Finally Cody told Callahan, "Forget it. We're wasting our time here." He started for the door. "Maybe we'll have better luck with Brad or Joe."

"They won't—" Danvers was startled into saying before he caught himself.

"They won't what?" Callahan asked softly. "Talk?"

"Get the hell out of here," Danvers grated. "I know my rights. I don't have to talk to you. I want a lawyer." Then he shut his eyes.

The FBI agent sitting next to the bed made a facial expression as if to say, "What did you expect?" as they left the room.

Cody and Callahan rode down in the elevator. Cody glanced at the older man and said, "At least we know we're on the right track."

"Yeah," Callahan responded dryly. "But we're a long way from making a case."

They exited the elevator and walked to the front door, where McKinnon waited for them. The three men had no sooner stepped outside when FBI Agent Holmes appeared.

"Sorry," Callahan said, meaning it. "We didn't mean to drag you out here. We just needed to ask a few questions."

Holmes' jaw clamped tight for a moment. "It's *my* case," he said finally.

"Mine, too," Cody said quietly.

Holmes bristled. "Look, Walker—"

"No, you look." Cody was fed up with the FBI's attitude toward the agency. "Didn't they tell you it was *my* truck that was rigged to explode the other night, same as Callahan's?" His voice held an edge of anger. "I'm just as much a target as Callahan here, and if it wasn't for the agency, the FBI wouldn't know a damn thing about it, wouldn't know there's a link between those two dead prosecutors and the attempts on us." He took a step forward. "I'm sorry if you think I'm treading on your toes, but—"

McKinnon stepped between them. "Dial it back,

Walker," he said firmly. He glanced over his shoulder at
Agent Holmes. "You, too. I know the FBI doesn't like
the agency, but we *are* on the same side. Aren't we?" he
added pointedly.

Both men looked at each other, hostility slowly fading.

Cody glanced at Callahan, silently asking a question.
Callahan said, "It's your call." He smiled faintly. "It's
a hell of a situation if you can't trust the FBI…at least
partway."

Cody looked at Agent Holmes again. "We could pool
our resources." He heard the grudging note in his voice,
and deliberately toned it down. "We've got a couple of
leads we're willing to share, if the FBI will do the same."
He held out his hand. "Truce?"

Agent Holmes stared at the hand, then at Cody's face.
"Sounds like a good plan to me," he said finally, shaking Cody's hand. "What do you say we go back in here
and talk about it?"

"Works for me."

Callahan said, "I'll get Keira." He turned and headed
for his four-by-four.

Keira watched Callahan coming her way, wondering
what was going on. She'd witnessed the confrontation
between Cody and FBI Agent Holmes, had seen Trace
step between them, and then had seen the two men shaking hands. *Maybe they finally realized we're all on the
same side,* she thought, smiling.

The sun hadn't set completely, but shadows fell across
the parking lot in long, angular lines. Callahan was halfway there before she saw him signaling her to join them.
Keira waved in acknowledgement and began jogging toward the hospital entrance, and Callahan turned back.
Just then a truck slowly pulled into the parking lot on

Keira's left. She turned in its direction automatically...
and *knew*...

Everything happened in the space of three seconds.
The truck accelerated, and Keira raced forward, her
hand already on her Glock. "Callahan!" she shouted as
she drew her weapon, reaching him just as the truck's
passenger-side window rolled smoothly down, and the
barrel of a rifle appeared in the open window. "Federal
agents! Freeze!" she called out, stepping in front of Callahan and drawing a bead on the man in the window. She
squeezed the trigger.

Cody turned sharply when he heard Keira call out
Callahan's name. Saw Callahan reach for his .45...too
late. Reached for his own gun and started running...also
too late. Simultaneous gunshots rang out, and Keira was
spun around like a rag doll.

"No!" Cody shouted. Callahan was already firing, and
the truck swerved. Then Cody was firing at the truck,
too, obliterating the windshield as the truck headed
straight for him. He darted out of the way at the last
minute, still firing until his Glock locked open on an
empty clip. The truck veered, then crashed head on into
a light pole.

McKinnon and Holmes were racing toward the truck,
weapons drawn, and Cody knew they didn't need him.
He turned and saw Keira sprawled on the ground in a
pool of blood, Callahan kneeling beside her. An instant
later he was there, too.

On autopilot, his hands worked feverishly alongside
Callahan's. The bullet had entered through the unprotected armhole of Keira's bulletproof vest, he realized,
and had ripped through the right side of her chest. Suddenly McKinnon was there, and Cody ordered, "Get an
emergency team here now!" He didn't even look up to

see if McKinnon had obeyed. Since Callahan already had pressure on the entrance wound, Cody felt around with his right hand until he found the exit wound in the back and applied pressure there while his other hand reached for a pulse.

Her skin was cool and clammy to the touch, and her pupils were dilated; Cody knew she was already going into shock from loss of blood. But she kept whispering something, the same thing again and again even as her body shivered. Cody bent over her and heard, "Spec… sev…"

He knew then what she was trying to say.

Chapter 22

The waiting was the worst, Cody thought as he leaned against the wall in the antiseptic hallway outside the intensive care unit. He'd been in this same hospital himself six years ago, fighting for his life just as Keira was now. But he'd been in and out of consciousness, and the struggle to breathe then was nothing compared to what he was going through now.

If Keira didn't make it—*No!* his heart insisted. He wasn't going to think that way. Keira *couldn't* die.

Cody looked up and saw Callahan walking down the long hallway toward him, rolling down his sleeve over the cotton ball taped to the crook of his left arm, and he knew the other man had just donated blood.

Blood. There'd been so much blood on Keira, all of it hers. It didn't seem possible for a human being to lose so much blood and still be alive. If he lived to be a hundred he'd never forget the sight of Keira bleeding out with every beat of her heart. His hands had been covered with her blood as he frantically tried to stem the tide; thanking God wordlessly both he and Callahan had paramedic training that just might save her life. Thanking God, too, that they were in the parking lot of the hospital, and help was almost immediately forthcoming. But there had been so much blood on his hands that when they'd arrived in the emergency room one of the nurses there had been sure Cody was injured, too.

"No word yet?" Callahan asked in his deep voice.

Cody swallowed hard, fighting to keep his emotions under control. "No," he answered roughly. "Not yet."

Callahan leaned one shoulder against the wall next to Cody. After a long pause, he said softly, "She took a bullet meant for me."

I know, Cody wanted to say, but he didn't trust himself to say the words out loud, not when part of him was hating Callahan for being there—well and whole—while Keira... *All she ever wanted was respect,* he reminded himself as another little piece of his heart shredded. Well, she'd earned that respect, and then some, even if it meant...

"No one's ever done that for me," Callahan continued. "Not even Mandy. That's not how I wanted it to go down, not the way I—"

Cody's harsh laugh cut him off. "Special rule seven," he said bitterly. "That's all she said. She was already in shock, but...special rule seven."

Callahan asked quietly, "What's that?"

"The agency's special rule seven—protect civilians at all costs." Cody's voice grated on the words and nearly broke at the end, knowing the cost in this case might be Keira's life. "That means—"

"I know what it means," Callahan said. "I just never thought of myself as a civilian who needed protection. I was always on the other side, the one doing the protecting."

Cody shook his head. "Not to Keira. Anyone who doesn't work for the agency is a civilian." He thought about it for a moment. "And even if that weren't the case, she had another reason for walking into that bullet."

"What's that?"

"She promised Mandy she wouldn't let anything happen to you."

Callahan frowned. "When—"

"That morning at my cabin, before McKinnon took your family away. Mandy asked me first. I told her I'd do my best." His face contracted, the memory painful. "Mandy said that wasn't good enough. So she asked Keira, and Keira promised."

"Guts *and* brains," Callahan replied, respect and admiration evident. "She's one hell of an agent."

If only Keira survives to hear those words, Cody told himself. More than anything he wanted that for her, wanted her to *know.* He turned toward the door to the intensive care unit and stared, as if he could make someone appear there and tell him Keira was going to be okay by sheer force of will. He sensed rather than heard Callahan's departure. But Callahan returned within a few minutes, saying, "Here, drink this."

A cup of hot, black coffee was thrust in front of him. Cody didn't want it. But he knew Callahan was just stubborn enough to stand there forever until Cody took the cup.

He gagged a little as he drank the hot liquid. It wasn't very good. Wherever Callahan had obtained it, the coffeepot had probably been sitting for a while, and the consistency and taste reflected it. But it was hot. And he was so cold inside. So cold. That hard, cold knot inside him reminded him that he had failed to protect Keira. That was the bottom line. She was his woman, and he hadn't gotten there in time to save her.

His thoughts turned inward, every detail of every memory of Keira running through his mind; from the moment he'd first seen her, terrified but refusing to surrender, to the moment he'd kissed her and realized the deep core of passion she hid from the world, until the moment they'd wheeled her away in the emergency room, fragile, broken and bleeding.

He had never seen her cry.

That didn't mean she was cold, emotionless; he knew she cared passionately. It just meant she was tough. Tough enough to stand side by side with him against a world that contained too much evil; tough enough to see that evil, to fight against it and not let it destroy her soul; tough enough to walk in front of a bullet meant for someone else because to her that was her job—protecting others.

That's why he loved her.

Cody breathed deeply as he finally acknowledged the truth, the answer to questions he hadn't even known he had. He'd subconsciously fought calling it love, because the only other time he'd loved a woman it had ended in disaster. But he loved Keira. And just as he remembered every moment he'd spent with her, every word she'd ever said to him was imprinted in his heart, especially those two words, "I will."

"Trust me," he'd told her that first night, and she'd responded promptly, "I will." But now he desperately wanted to tell her other things, things he might never have the chance to say.

Love me.

Need me.

Marry me.

And he wanted to hear the same two words from her in reply—*I will.*

He couldn't fathom a world without Keira. He glanced up and caught Callahan watching him, compassion looking out of place on that hard, cold face. But Cody knew that if any man could comprehend the enormity of what he stood to lose, Callahan could, because that's how he felt about Mandy.

Mandy. Cody spared a moment to think about her, contrasting what he'd felt for her then to what he felt for Keira now. There was no comparison. Losing Mandy to Callahan all those years ago had torn out his heart. But he had survived. Losing Keira would tear out his soul. He would never recover.

"So where's McKinnon?" Callahan asked, breaking into his thoughts, almost as if he knew what Cody was thinking and wanted to distract him.

"Picking up the pieces," Cody replied. He laughed humorlessly. "At least that's what I figure he's doing—implementing the agency's special rule eight—when all else fails, pick up the pieces."

"You mean make them disappear?" That was a side of Callahan that was after Cody's own heart—he called a spade a spade, and didn't resort to euphemisms.

"Yeah. That's exactly what it means."

"I don't like it." Long before Callahan had become the sheriff of Black Rock, long before he'd gone undercover with the New World Militia, he'd been a New York City cop—a good one.

"I don't either," Cody admitted.

"So, what are you going to do about it?" There was a challenge in Callahan's voice.

"Not a hell of a lot I *can* do about it."

"If that's the case, seems to me the agency isn't much better than the organizations we're after," Callahan said slowly. "No one should be above the law—not the New World Militia, not NOANC, not Michael Vishenko. And not the agency."

"So, what are you suggesting?"

Callahan told him, in clipped sentences, and Cody

considered it. "It would almost certainly mean the end of my career with the agency," he said finally. "But—"

Just then the double doors swung open, and a tired-looking man in blue hospital scrubs walked out. Cody's breathing grew ragged, and his heartbeat kicked into overdrive.

"Are you waiting to hear about Keira Jones?" the surgeon asked. Cody and Callahan were the only ones around, so he had to know...

Cody took a step toward him. "Yes?"

"She's stable. That's about all I can tell you at this point. We got her heart started again...." At Cody's quickly indrawn breath he explained, "It's a condition called hypovolemic shock—she lost a lot of blood, and the drop in blood pressure caused her heart to stop beating. But we got it going again, we've replaced the blood volume she lost, and her blood pressure is up—these are all good things.

"The bullet was a through and through, so it didn't bounce around inside doing more damage, and we didn't have to extract it. One lung collapsed, but that's okay now, too. Our biggest concern at this point is the loss of blood, and whether we were in time to prevent irreversible organ failure. I'm afraid all we can do now is wait and see."

She's alive, a little voice whispered in Cody's head. *She's alive!* "Is she conscious? Can I see her?"

"You can see her, subject to certain conditions, but she's not conscious. We've medically induced a coma to help her body deal with the trauma. She won't be coming out of that for some time."

"What conditions?"

"We try to keep the ICU—the intensive care unit—as sterile as possible, to minimize the risk of infection to the patient. But we don't exclude a patient's loved ones—even though she's in a coma, she might be able to hear you. We can't quantify how much that matters in cases like this, but…" The surgeon made a face of frustration. "It *does* help. I've seen it myself."

"I need to see her," Cody said simply.

The surgeon nodded. "One of the ICU nurses will tell you what you need to do."

Ten minutes later, scrubbed and clothed in blue surgical garb, Cody walked into the dimly lit room where Keira lay. A nurse was there in attendance, checking readouts and doing things to various pieces of equipment, some of which Cody vague remembered from his own hospital stay. But he ignored her.

He walked to the bed and gazed down at Keira with love welling inside him. She looked so small and fragile lying there; readout wires attached everywhere, a saline drip connected via a clear plastic tube to her arm, a breathing tube in place. Her chest rose and fell, the movement slow and measured. But she was alive.

They'd washed all the blood away, and she was deathly pale, which made the sprinkling of freckles on her nose and cheeks stand out. Her red-gold curls were subdued beneath a paper cap, and her expressive brown eyes were closed, but she was still his darling. And she was alive.

He started to take her hand but caught himself and asked the ICU nurse, "Can I touch her?"

"So long as you don't interfere with anything connected to her," the nurse reassured him in an undertone. "And don't touch any bandages."

His left hand enfolded Keira's left hand, the only part of her he dared touch as he stood by her bedside. There were so many things he wanted to say, all the things he'd thought of while he'd been waiting to hear if she'd survived—*love me, need me, marry me.* All the things to which he desperately wanted to hear her say, "I will" in response—but the presence of the nurse inhibited him.

Instead he squeezed Keira's hand and said, "I'm here." She didn't respond, but he hadn't expected her to. The fingers of his right hand brushed gently against her cheek. She never stirred, but her skin was warm to the touch. That meant she was alive.

He glanced at her right chest and shoulder swathed in bandages, and relived in slow motion the moment that would haunt him forever. Keira stepping in front of Callahan, firing her weapon. His own anguished cry of rage and denial. The bullet slamming into Keira, spinning her around and knocking her to the ground. Callahan firing his Smith & Wesson. And he, emptying his Glock's thirty-three-round clip with deadly intent and even deadlier accuracy.

The veneer of civilization had vanished in that instant; he had wanted nothing more than to obliterate the men who had shot his woman. It was primitive, visceral. It was nothing like when he'd helped kill Pennington, the only other time he'd ever taken a human life. He'd known as he fired tonight he was too late to protect Keira; but he could avenge her. And he did.

Now as he stood watching each breath Keira drew he accepted that he was only human after all. His conscience troubled him, but there wasn't a damn thing he could do about it. *Deal with it,* he told his conscience, remembering another time and another place, and Callahan telling him the same thing. *Deal with it.*

Not every man would understand what had driven him tonight, but Callahan would. Cody drew a small measure of comfort from that knowledge. He felt a kinship with the other man, almost as if they were brothers. Maybe, in a sense, they were. They both knew what it was like to love a woman to the edge of death…and beyond. And each of them had been willing to kill or die to keep his woman safe. The only difference was Callahan had saved Mandy every time. Cody had saved Keira twice, but…

Don't let her die, he prayed. *Not now.*

"Stay with me," he whispered, his hand tightening around Keira's, and in his heart he heard the echo of her words from that very first night, "I will."

Other words crowded his throat as he realized he'd never said he loved her. Even when he'd told her he wanted all of her, even when he'd told her that he needed her trust in every way there was, somehow he'd never been able to get the words out. Each time he'd started to admit it to her and to himself, he'd drawn back.

You were afraid.

He closed his eyes for a moment. Yes, he'd been afraid. He'd made love to her, and the beauty of that one night and her priceless gift to him he would take to his grave. He'd told her she was his woman, and he'd meant it, then and now. He'd even told her he wanted nothing less than her heart, mind, body and soul. But he'd never said…

"I love you, Keira," he whispered, squeezing her hand.

Had she known what was in his heart? When she'd told him, "I love you, Cody," had she known even then he loved her, too? God, he hoped so. Somehow it seemed important that deep inside her she knew how much he loved and needed her. That she remembered it in the recesses of her soul, so that wherever she was, wherever she went, she carried that knowledge with her.

And that the knowledge would bring her back to him.

"Stay with me," he whispered again. He bent down

and brushed her cheek with his lips, and when he straightened he had to blink several times to clear his vision.

He was still there twenty-four hours later. He'd dozed fitfully in the chair beside her bed, but he refused to leave or even to relinquish the left hand lying so still and white against the sheet for more than a couple of minutes. When his own arm turned numb, he switched positions and switched arms, but he refused to break the connection.

It was almost as if he could somehow transmit his own breath, his own blood, his own strength into her body by holding her and never letting go. "Stay with me," he whispered time and again. And throughout the endless night and the following day she did, her quiet breathing reassuring him that she was still alive.

He was still there when they came the next morning to tell him she would live.

Chapter 23

Cody stood in D'Arcy's office. "I can't go along with it," he said steadfastly. "It's not right. You know it and I know it. I'll do whatever I have to do to stop you from applying special rule eight in this case. Even if means the end of my career here."

One corner of D'Arcy's mouth lifted up in a half smile. He shook his head. "Don't worry, Walker. I had no intention of applying special rule eight. It won't be easy, but this case is going to trial."

Cody sighed with relief as a huge weight lifted off his shoulders. Not that his job was safe, but that he hadn't been wrong about D'Arcy after all.

But D'Arcy wasn't finished. He said softly, "And it's not the end of your career with the agency. Just the end of being a special agent."

Cody's brows drew together, puzzled. "I don't follow you."

"You can't be a special agent if you're sitting behind this desk."

Stunned, Cody said, "What?"

"I've been waiting years for someone with enough courage and conviction to buck me on special rule eight…and the guts and determination to make it stick. I knew when the agency first crafted it that special rule eight was too broad, too vague. But I trusted myself to know when and how to apply it…and when not to. I just needed to find someone else I could trust knew it, too." Now both corners of D'Arcy's mouth lifted in the beginning of a real smile. "I thought all along it might be you."

"You're leaving the agency?"

D'Arcy chuckled. "Hardly. But the head of the agency in Washington wants to retire next year. He's been pressuring me to become his deputy, preparatory to taking over the whole organization when he retires. I just couldn't do it until I found a replacement for me here."

Cody still couldn't believe it. "Me? Become you?"

D'Arcy threw back his head and let out a belly laugh. "No, Walker," he said when he finally stopped laughing. "That would be a mistake on both our parts. You can't be me, and you shouldn't even try. But you *can* make the job you. That's all I did when I started. That's all anyone *can* do." He paused for a minute. "So, what do you think? Are you willing to give it a shot?"

Cody took a quick turn around the room. He'd come in here thinking his career with the agency was over, and now…unexpectedly…he was being offered the opportunity of a lifetime, a chance to head up the Denver branch of the agency. The one who had the final authority, but also the crushing responsibility.

Could he do it? And even if he *could,* did he *want* to do it?

"The agency needs people like you to run it," D'Arcy stated, as if he sensed Cody's dilemma. "There aren't many absolutely incorruptible people, but you're one of them."

Cody smiled faintly as he remembered when he'd said the same thing to himself…about D'Arcy. If D'Arcy believed he could do it, how could he turn it down?

Then he remembered Keira and frowned. No. If he were in charge of the Denver branch, it would be impossible for her to work here, and he couldn't do that to her. She loved both her job and him. If he asked her to choose, she'd be torn, but he knew she would choose him. He just couldn't ask that of her. Not now. Not ever.

It was a tough decision, but...

"If you're thinking about Special Agent Jones," D'Arcy said, reading the play of expressions over Cody's face, "I have an idea about that."

"How did you know I—" Cody began.

"It's my business to know everything," D'Arcy said, his grin lighting his face. "Didn't you know? Why do you think they call me Baker Street behind my back?" He waited for that to sink in before adding, "And soon it will be your business to know everything, too."

Cody shook his head firmly. "I can't ask Keira to give up her career with the agency. And even if I could, she's too damned good at what she does. The agency needs people like her, too."

D'Arcy nodded. "With her skills at research and analysis, that's just what I was thinking. But there's a way around that. What if she worked directly for me—" He held up one hand as Cody started to interrupt. "Just hear me out, Walker. What if she worked directly for me, but on detached status...here in Denver?"

Cody's heart thudded suddenly, as he realized it just might work. "Permanently?"

"As permanent as I can make it."

He considered the offer from every angle and couldn't see a flaw. "She'll have to agree first," he said, already knowing in his heart what her answer would be. *We can have it all,* he thought suddenly, wanting nothing more than to see Keira's expression when he told her, and his smile lit up his face.

"Then it's a done deal." D'Arcy held out his hand, and Cody shook it. "Welcome to your new job."

The door to Keira's hospital room swung open, and she turned her head toward it eagerly, hoping against hope that this time it was Cody. He hadn't been near her for three days, and she missed him so much it was like a physical ache...worse than the one in her chest because there was nothing the nurses could give her to alleviate the pain in her heart. A tall blonde walked through the door, and the eager light in Keira's eyes faded. *Mandy Callahan.*

The last time Keira had seen Mandy she'd been wearing a sling containing her dark-haired baby daughter, with her two blond sons at her side. Now she was alone, and even more stunningly beautiful than Keira remembered. "Hi," she said, knowing without being told why the other woman was here. But she didn't want thanks for doing her job. She just wanted...

"Ryan's been like a bear with a sore head," Mandy said out of the blue. "He's mad at me for asking you to protect him, and he's mad at you for doing it." She laughed a little but with a touch of hysterical relief thrown in, and Keira couldn't help but smile.

"Cody told me once that your husband was a tad old-school. *I* said he's a dinosaur."

Mandy moved toward the bed. "You're right, he *is* a dinosaur. But he's *my* dinosaur." A glitter of silver sparkled in her eyes, and she blinked several times to hold back the tears. "And I...I just had to thank you for saving his life."

Keira started to shrug, but the stabbing pain in her

chest radiated to her right shoulder, stopping her. "It was my job," she said quietly.

Mandy surveyed her for a moment. "No, you don't want gratitude, do you? Not mine, not Ryan's. All you want is respect." At Keira's sharply indrawn breath, Mandy added, "For what it's worth, you have it. After Ryan told me what happened, he said, 'In my whole life no one's ever taken a bullet for me.' It shocked him, I think. Not just that someone would do it, and not just that a woman would. But that *you* would."

Something in Mandy's voice told Keira everything she needed to know about her. "You would have done it, too," she said. "You would have taken that bullet for him."

Mandy nodded slowly. "And he knows it. But I love him. You don't. That's the difference between us. I would do it for Ryan and my children in a heartbeat. But I don't know if I could have done what you did for someone I didn't love. I don't think I could. But Ryan could. Cody, too. They're protectors...just like you."

Keira couldn't help the way her pulse kicked up a notch at the mention of Cody's name, but the respect in Mandy's eyes warmed her to the core. "Thanks," she said gruffly.

Mandy edged backward toward the door. "That's all I really came to say. I didn't want to intrude, but I just had to—"

The door to Keira's room opened again, and Cody walked in. Keira didn't say anything, but she didn't have to—she knew everything she was feeling was written on her face.

"Time's up," he told Mandy, but he smiled to soften the order.

Mandy smiled in return, then leaned up and brushed a kiss against his cheek. "Thanks for letting me go first," she said. She cast one more glowing smile in Keira's direction, then went out quickly.

Cody stood with his back to the door, watching the warm color come and go in Keira's face, loving it. Loving everything about her. She looked a thousand times better than the last time he'd seen her, still in intensive care, but safely out of danger.

"Miss me?" he asked as lightly as he could, his heart racing at the terrible memories he would never be able to blot out. Not completely. He crossed the room to the left side of the bed before she realized he'd even moved. Then he was cupping her face in his hands, turning it up to his for an endless kiss. When his lips finally left hers, all he could manage was a husky, "Yeah. You missed me. Almost as much as I missed you."

"Where were you? I—" She chopped off the rest of her sentence, as if she didn't want to betray to him just how abandoned she'd felt, even though he knew she'd had visitors—the twenty-four hour guard on her door had kept a detailed list. Her mom had been there every day—she'd flown up from Denver as soon as she'd heard the news—and a few close friends, including some ex-marine buddies, had driven up to see her. And all four of her brothers had called several times to check up on her. Cody had kept a close enough tab on Keira to know about every visitor, every caller.

But he knew it wasn't enough. Not for an agent. He'd been in a hospital bed just like this one for more days than he cared to remember while the world moved on without him, and the not knowing had driven him crazy. "We still had things to wrap up," he told her. "I couldn't just leave it to Callahan, McKinnon and Holmes to pick up all the pieces by themselves, especially after Danvers finally talked."

"Oh," she said. "I wondered. But there wasn't anyone I could ask."

"After the night you were shot, after his brothers were killed, I think Danvers was more afraid of us than he was of Vishenko. He gave us enough to go on. And it turns out the FBI had a little something up their sleeves, too, where Vishenko was concerned." He smiled ruefully. "You were right about that. We *are* on the same side. Once Holmes and I had a heart-to-heart talk…we were able to put a lot of things together."

He drew her left hand to his lips and kissed it. "Where was I? Oh, yeah. We arrested Vishenko yesterday, along with New York's junior senator and a half dozen others. And that's just the start. Vishenko's not talking—surprise, surprise—but the senator sang like a canary. Guess being a former FBI agent, he knew when to cut his losses and cut a deal."

She searched his face. "So it's all over?"

"I wish. The agency and the FBI have put together a task force. As soon as you're well enough, you'll be on it—Holmes was damned impressed with what you'd uncovered, and he pretty much insisted." He laughed softly, shaking his head. "He's a little suspicious about how you came across certain FBI documents, but I'm sure you'll manage to gloss that over."

Keira laughed a little at that, too. "I'll think of something," she said.

Cody's expression turned serious again as he toyed with her fingers. "Part of me would like to ask you never to do this to me again, but—"

"You can't," she interrupted, trying to pull her hand away from his. "You can't ask me to—"

"I'm not," he told her, firmly retaining her hand and letting his respect and pride shine through his eyes. And his concern. "I'm not asking you to be less than you are." One corner of his mouth twitched into a half smile. "But I wouldn't be human if I didn't want to protect you from everything. Don't ask *me* to be less than the man I am."

"Oh." Color rose in her cheeks, and Cody was satisfied they understood each other.

"We've got a long road ahead of us building our case," he said, as if the conversation had never detoured into their personal lives. "And there are more arrests in the works. We still don't know who was following me, or who set the bombs on the East Coast or in Denver. Danvers couldn't tell us. But he and his brothers are the ones who rigged Callahan's SUV, and they're the ones who killed Tressler, on orders of the man who was their go-between with Vishenko—he's one of the ones we arrested yesterday. If we can get him to roll on Vishenko…we'll have to see about that. And the trials could take years, so I'm not holding my breath."

"But you're safe now? You, Callahan, Trace and D'Arcy?"

A muscle twitched in his cheek. "Safe is a relative term. Without Vishenko bankrolling things…yeah, we're safer. But I won't lie to you—we'll never be *safe* as long as we live. There's always the chance that…" He left it at that, knowing he didn't have to fill in the details. "How's the injury?" he asked, changing the subject as he leaned against the side of the hospital bed.

"It's there," she said dryly. "You should know—you went through it yourself."

Cody chuckled. "Yeah, but the body doesn't remember the pain—just the *idea* of the pain. And thank God for that. Otherwise, no woman would ever have a second child."

Their eyes met. Cody caught his breath at the sudden yearning in Keira's face, and he had the answer to the question he'd wanted to ask her the night they'd made love. She wanted his child…his *children*…with an intensity that equaled his.

"It's a risk," he warned her, touching her cheek with fingers that trembled slightly. "Callahan calls them hostages to fortune."

"But Mandy doesn't," Keira told him firmly. "She took that risk for the man she loves. And I will, too."

Cody's heart contracted in love and pain. "Are you sure, Keira?" he asked. "I'm willing to risk it if you are, but I couldn't bear it if someday in the future…if something happened and you blamed me…and stopped loving me…"

She shook her head, and her left hand reached for his right one. "Life is a risk. Love is a risk. We just have to trust in ourselves and each other that we will do everything in our power to keep our children safe."

Cody swallowed the lump in his throat, remembering all the things he'd told himself he would say to her…if only she survived. *Love me. Need me. Marry me.*

He didn't need to say those things now, because he already knew her answer. Her welcoming kiss had told him that much. But he *had* to ask, "Will you do that, Keira? Will you trust me enough to have my children?"

She looked at him with that solemn expression he knew so well, then smiled her slow smile. It was like a Wyoming sunrise coming up to meet the day—soft, warm, unique. And full of promise. "I will."

Epilogue

Cody sat on the porch steps of his cabin near Granite Peak, waiting for the sunrise. He loved the early morning in the mountains, always had. There was something fresh and clean and untouched about it, the morning air crisp and cool even in the middle of summer, and he needed memories like these to carry him through the hectic days of his life in Denver.

The task force set up between the agency and the FBI had borne fruit. As he'd learned long ago, Keira was a tigress when she was working a case. And just as McKinnon had once said, research and analysis were her forte. She'd been relentless in uncovering Vishenko's insidious web *and* documenting everything. There was no such thing as an airtight case, but they had compiled enough evidence for conviction of every major player in Vishenko's organization, and quite a few of the minor ones.

The trials they would have to testify at were still months away. Delay after delay had been won by the defense teams, but the prosecution's day in court was coming, and Cody could hardly wait. Not that they would ever truly be safe…just safer, once the convictions started piling up.

The creak of the front door opening behind him was followed by the faint whisper of footsteps, and a steaming mug of black coffee was set down beside him. Cody ignored the coffee, instead turning and reaching for Keira and drawing her down to sit between his legs. Only then did he pick up the cup and drink deeply, making an appreciative sound.

"Morning," he said, putting the cup down and cradling Keira back against his body, breathing in the scent of her that never failed to arouse him—plain soap and water and warm woman. Very warm woman.

"Good morning," she answered, cuddling back against him. He thought about turning her in his arms for a coffee-flavored kiss, but decided to wait for the sunrise—postponement of pleasure always made it sweeter in the end. Especially where Keira was concerned.

He slid his hands up her arms to rest on her shoulders, then gently kneaded the muscles on her right side until she sighed with contentment. "Thanks," she breathed.

"Aching again?"

"Just a little. How did you know?"

"Been there, done that. Mornings are the worst. It *will* get better. Trust me, I know."

"I know," she said quietly. "And I do."

Eleven months had passed since Keira had left her hospital bed. Ten and a half months since they had married in a private ceremony with her right arm still in a sling to keep her right side immobile while the healing process continued. But neither of them had wanted to wait.

Cody glanced down at the plain gold wedding band on Keira's left hand, smaller than the one on his hand but identical in every other way. He remembered the moment he'd slid the ring on her finger, pledging his life to her and accepting the gift of her life in return. Two words were engraved inside both rings—*I Will*.

As Cody had known she would, Keira had accepted the job working for D'Arcy and the assignment to the Vishenko/NOANC/New World Militia task force. It had meant giving up McKinnon as her partner, and although it had made her sad at first, she had done it willingly... for his sake. If she regretted it, she'd never said a word to him. For the past nine months Cody had been running the Denver branch of the agency, most of that time without having to rely on advice from Baker Street. D'Arcy had been right—Cody couldn't be him, but he *had* finally succeeded in making the job his.

Nine months, Cody thought, his hands tightening imperceptibly on Keira's shoulders. *Long enough to have a baby.*

The sun peeked over the horizon to the east, and they watched in silence as the sky changed from indigo-blue to rosy pink with streaks of gold. Cody slid his hands beneath Keira's arms and around her swelling waistline where his child lay nestled, safe and warm.

He closed his eyes against the emotions that swamped him, wishing he could put into words what she meant to him, what this child meant to him. But all he could do was hold her...and breathe.

"Are we heading back right after lunch?" she asked presently.

Cody's eyes opened. "That's the plan."

"Good. I have an early meeting tomorrow morning with the task force."

"Yeah, I've got a full day tomorrow myself, starting with a budget conference call and ending with an 'all hands' staff meeting. And the rest of the week only gets worse." His hands were still caressing her, still making concentric circles that soothed both of them.

"We both need a good night's sleep." She made a small snorting sound. "At least as much of a good night's sleep as the baby will let us get. Sorry about that."

"Hey, did you ever hear me complain? So I'm a light sleeper. So what? We're in this together, remember? What's mine is yours, and vice versa."

She laughed wryly at that. "I don't think baby-induced insomnia was covered in our marriage vows."

"Sure it was. 'For better, for worse,' remember? That pretty much covers the gamut. If tossing and turning and losing a little sleep is the worst thing you can throw at me, sweetheart, I'm home free." His eyes drifted closed again as he savored her nearness.

"Do you ever wish…?" Keira began, then stopped.

"Wish what?"

"That we'd let them tell us if it was a boy or a girl?"

Cody's eyes flicked open, and he stroked his fingers back and forth, feeling the life growing there—strong, vibrant. Like Keira.

"No," he said. "I'm glad we didn't. Not knowing now will make it all the sweeter…later."

She chuckled softly, and her curls tickled his chin. "Not much longer to wait."

"I know. But I can be a patient man." He brushed the backs of his hands gently against the outside curves of her breasts, telling her without words exactly what he meant. "Very patient. Now that I have everything I ever wanted."

"A woman who can make a good cup of coffee?" she teased.

"Yeah." He picked up his coffee mug and sipped. The

coffee had cooled, but it was still good. "Not just a good cup of coffee," he said in a husky voice, trying to match her teasing tone. "A *damn* good cup of coffee."

Keira turned in Cody's arms so that her cheek snuggled trustingly against his shoulder, and time stood still.

* * * * *

REQUEST YOUR FREE BOOKS!
2 FREE NOVELS PLUS 2 FREE GIFTS!

⬢ HARLEQUIN®

ROMANTIC suspense

Sparked by danger, fueled by passion

SPECIAL EXCERPT FROM

(H) HARLEQUIN®

ROMANTIC suspense

With his town under quarantine and an escaped killer
on the loose, Sheriff Flint Colton must protect the one
woman who can testify against the murderer, but getting
close to Nina could just prove his undoing.

Read on for a sneak peek of

HER COLTON LAWMAN

by *New York Times* bestselling author
Carla Cassidy, coming November 2014 from
Harlequin® Romantic Suspense.

Pink panties.

Hot pink panties.

Flint closed the door to his master bedroom and began to
change out of his uniform.

He'd gone into the store on high alert, hovering near
Nina and watching to make sure that nobody else got close
to her.

What he hadn't realized was that shopping with a woman
could be such an intimate experience. He'd been fine as
she'd grabbed several T-shirts and sweatshirts, some jogging
pants and a nightshirt.

His close presence next to her felt a little more intrusive as
she shopped for toiletries. Peach-scented shampoo joined a
bottle of peach and vanilla scented body cream. It was then
that things began to get a little wonky in his head.

He imagined her slathering that lotion up and down her

shapely legs and rubbing it over her slender shoulders. He imagined the two of them showering together, the scent of peaches filling the steamy air as he washed the length of her glorious hair and then stroked a sponge all over her body.

He'd finally managed to snap himself back into professional mode when she'd headed to the intimates section. He was okay when she grabbed a white bra and threw it into the shopping basket. He even remained calm and cool when the bra was followed by a package of underpants.

It was when she tossed that single pair of hot pink panties in the cart that his head once again went a little wonky. Pink panties and peach lotion, those things had been all he'd been able to think about.

He sat on the edge of his bed to get every inappropriate vision and thought he'd had of Nina over the past couple of hours out of his head.

She was the witness to a vicious crime and a victim of arson. She was here to be in his protective custody, not to be an object of his sexual fantasies. Speaking of protective custody, he pulled himself off the bed, grabbed his gun and went in search of his houseguest.

Don't miss
HER COLTON LAWMAN
by *New York Times* bestselling author
Carla Cassidy, coming November 2014 from

⬡ **HARLEQUIN**®

ROMANTIC suspense

HARLEQUIN®

ROMANTIC suspense

Heart-racing romance, high-stakes suspense!

TEXAS STAKEOUT

by *New York Times* bestselling author
Virna DePaul

A killer in waiting. A brother in hiding.
Could they be the same person?

Dylan Rooney is out of his element. A U.S. marshal and
city-wrangler at heart, he must adopt a new cover—and a
new client—in the heart of Texas. The assignment: protect
Rachel Kincaid...a widow with a young son who realizes her
struggles are just beginning when her ranch hand is killed.
Posing as the new ranch hand, Dylan quickly learns that
catching a killer may not be so simple—especially when
Rachel's fugitive brother is the prime suspect. And the
woman he's vowed to protect is the same woman he's
falling in love with.

Available **NOVEMBER 2014**
Wherever books and ebooks are sold.

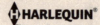

ROMANTIC suspense

Heart-racing romance, high-stakes suspense!

DESIGNATED TARGET
by **Karen Anders**

A NCIS agent must protect a brainy scientist who criminals are after—for her mind.

NCIS special agent Vincent Fitzgerald's mission: to find missing naval scientist Dr. Skylar Baang. The brilliant American-Filipino beauty has been kidnapped for her brain and research on top secret projects. But even as Vin rescues her from a dangerous group, he knows they'll be back.

A long-ago promise has kept Skylar committed to her work—love is a distraction she's never allowed herself. Now in the protective custody of a complicated NCIS agent who surprises her at every turn, Skylar wants to stop thinking and start *feeling*. But as the thugs come after her, she'll need everything she is—and smart, sexy Vin—to stay alive.

Available **NOVEMBER 2014**
Wherever books and ebooks are sold.

HRS78961

Love the Harlequin book you just read?

Your opinion matters.

Review this book on your favorite book site, review site, blog or your own social media properties and share your opinion with other readers!